Rodney slipped through the iron gate before I opened it and rambled ahead. The stranger's grave was on Duke and Desmond's land on the other side of the churchyard, beyond the grove of lilac trees, now tightly budded in the shade of the conifers. Here's where Helen would have pondered her life and decided she'd waited too long. Life was for the living—not for the waiting.

Uncharacteristically, Rodney raced back to me and mewed.

My breath came more quickly. "What, baby?" Rodney scampering ahead, I crossed the cemetery. Lassie had nothing on him. "Wait up."

Rodney stopped to peer around a headstone at me then trotted to the fence separating the churchyard from Duke and Desmond's property. I froze. I knew exactly where Rodney was headed. Dread weighed on me. I plunged ahead, but at a much slower pace.

When I arrived at the old cedar tree at the churchyard's back fence, I closed my eyes and leaned against the heady scent of its bark. Rodney rubbed against my calf, and I reluctantly opened my eyes.

I saw exactly what I'd feared . . .

Books by Angela M. Sanders

BAIT AND WITCH

SEVEN-YEAR WITCH

WITCH AND FAMOUS

WITCH UPON A STAR

GONE WITH THE WITCH

Published by Kensington Publishing Corp.

GONE WITH THE WITCH

Angela M. Sanders

Kensington Publishing Corp.
www.kensingtonbooks.com

For my favorite nonfictional witch,
Pomegranate Doyle.

CHAPTER 1

"Poor devil." Duke gazed into the open grave. In a nod to custom, he wore black. Black jeans with a crease, a black Western shirt, and black work boots. A raindrop slipped off his Brylcreemed hair.

"Whoever he was," added Desmond, also in black work clothes.

I tilted my umbrella against the drizzle shifting in the breeze. The spring afternoon thickened with foreboding, and I couldn't help but feel we were being watched. A crow landed nearby and shook rain from its wings.

Duke's shovel crunched clay-burdened soil, scooping and showering each load into the open pit. We weren't in the cemetery, which we glimpsed in the churchyard through the wooden fence. Furthermore, the grave held no casket. In fact, it didn't contain a body at all, just a pile of splintered planks topped with a toilet seat.

This was the funeral for an outhouse. When Duke and Desmond had cleared their new property a month earlier, they'd been surprised to discover a decrepit outhouse under a thicket of blackberry bushes. Their surprise deepened when they found long-decayed human remains inside. The bones were now the state's responsibility and rested in an evidence locker at the county seat. However, they'd been found on Duke and Desmond's property, and Duke and Desmond liked to do things right. They'd insisted on a proper burial, even without the body.

When I worked for the Library of Congress, before I'd come into my magic, interring an outhouse would have earned someone a bed in a mental institution. Here in Wilfred, Oregon, it felt somehow right. Respectful, even.

Besides Duke and Desmond, Lindy Everhardt and her grown son and daughter stood at the head of the grave. Mrs. Everhardt had sold the property to Duke and Desmond earlier in the year. She'd owned it for decades, presumably including when the "poor devil" had met his fate. As a librarian, the nearest thing Wilfred had to clergy, I was here to deliver the eulogy.

"Rest in peace, Reginald Doe," Desmond said. He'd declared that the stranger deserved something more distinguished than "John." Duke had agreed, pointing out that in this case "John" was a little too on the nose.

A layer of mud now covered the demolished outhouse. Duke's tractor would finish the job later. We raised our heads in acknowledgement of a job well done, and Lindy Everhardt, leaning on her walker, tossed a branch of lilacs into the grave.

Duke rubbed his palms together to warm them. "So that's that. What do you say we repair to the café for a slice of pie? My treat."

The crow cawed from the churchyard fence. It stared right at me.

The warm bustle of Darla's Café was a welcome change from Duke and Desmond's damp, cold yard. Even after the lunch rush, half of its tables were full of Wilfredians dawdling over coffee and steaming the windows with speculation about the upcoming summer's berry harvest and the vendors in Patty's new antiques mall.

"I still can't figure out who those bones belong to," Lindy Everhardt said. She stood back, purse clutched against her belly, as Duke and Desmond moved two tables together to accommodate the crowd. "To think of them, rotting away on our land all those years."

"We used to play right next to them," Kaydee said, an eye on her phone. She'd carved out an hour for the burial from her schedule as a nurse at the hospital and mom of tweens, and I didn't expect she'd stay long.

Duke took a seat and launched into the story he'd been telling around town all month. "I had a funny feeling about that hill the whole time. Didn't I say so, Desmond?"

Desmond nodded.

"I says to Desi, are you sure we should bulldoze

that mound? Does the new garage really need to go there, all the way at the back of the property?"

"I told him, 'Why not? Give us a little separation from work.' "

"So I took a run at it with the Caterpillar and hit a structure. I got out to see what it was."

"An outhouse," Desmond supplied, as if we didn't know. "Complete with a half-moon cut out above the door. We'd thought that mound was just an extension of the root cellar behind it."

"There, sticking up in the planks, was a leg bone." He paused for effect. "And it wasn't the only one. Two hours later, we had a complete skeleton. Who could it be?"

Wilfredians had thoroughly pondered this question since. When the bones were found, the state troopers' office ran through a database of missing persons and came up dry. At Mrs. Garlington's urging, they even tested the bones' DNA. Her husband had disappeared nearly fifty years earlier. However, the comparison of the DNA to that of her son showed no relation.

"I see it like this." Duke leaned back in his chair, raising its front legs precipitously. "Some fellow was wandering through town—"

"On foot?" Desmond asked. For such a taciturn man, he'd fit into Wilfred remarkably quickly. His friendship with Duke had really opened him up.

Lindy Everhardt nodded. Even now, at eighty-plus years, her profile was crisp and jaw strong. She must have been a looker in her day. "We never found a car. It's not like we ever used the outhouse, either."

"The stranger may have had a reason to travel

below the radar." Desmond looked at us with meaning. No one talked about it, but it was common knowledge Desmond had done a stretch in prison, making him a superior source of knowledge in certain areas.

"As I was saying," Duke continued, "He was wandering through town and found he had to take a leak. Providence provided an outhouse."

"Then what?" Lindy's son asked. Travis was a big man with a trim reddish beard and hands that looked made for physical labor. He was a baker in Gaston, the town next door, and supplied the café with the bread that went into its sandwiches and French toast. "Someone popped up from the toilet seat and stabbed him?"

"We don't know if he was stabbed," Kaydee pointed out.

"No one knows how he died," I said.

The bones were old—the medical examiner had told us that much—but since they didn't match any missing persons report, the state police had shelved the remains and promised to investigate "later." In the meantime, it would be up to Wilfred's vigorous grapevine to reconstruct the story.

Kaydee slipped her phone into her bag. "Mom and I are going to have to miss the pie. Julia needs to be at cheerleading practice by three." She helped Lindy rise. For health reasons, Lindy Everhardt had recently moved in with her daughter, thus freeing up her longtime home for Duke and Desmond. The sale had been friendly, and they'd even exchanged recipes and dahlia tubers.

As Darla arrived to take our orders, I felt a tap on my shoulder. It was Orson, the bartender on the café's tavern side. "Josie, can I talk to you a moment?"

This was interesting. Up until now, the only personal conversations I'd had with Orson were about keeping beer out of the library's kitchen, one of the town's unofficial meeting places. He drew me to the open doorway connecting the diner to the tavern.

"What is it?" I asked.

He nodded toward the tavern. "It's Helen." Mrs. Garlington. "I don't know what to do about her. She goes on and on about her husband, and she's drinking me out of our sherry. I've never seen her so upset. Could you talk to her?"

As Wilfred's librarian, my duties apparently included addressing the full gamut of problems, not just writing eulogies for bulldozed outhouses. I glanced back at the table I'd just left, now deep in speculation about the bones as Darla distributed plates of pie. They'd never miss me. "Take me to her."

Helen Garlington sat at the bar, murky brown dregs in the small glass in front of her. Her lavender-tinted hair was disheveled from its usually pristine bouffant, and her eyes red and watery. This was not the Mrs. Garlington I knew who sipped tea, played rousing Bach cantatas on the library's organ, and wrote poetry to commemorate the town's doings.

I took the stool next to hers. The bar was dark after the café's cheerful light, and instead of coffee and BLTs, it smelled vaguely of stale beer and pine cleanser. "Mrs. Garlington?" Above her, the TV droned a basketball game.

She shifted her glazed focus to me but didn't reply.

I laid a hand on the sleeve of her cardigan. "Mrs. Garlington, are you all right?"

She lifted her empty glass and unsteadily returned it to the bar. "Martin."

Of course. Helen Garlington was grieving—perhaps the only genuinely sad Wilfredian that afternoon. However, she wasn't mourning the dead stranger, she mourned her long-vanished spouse.

"I'm so sorry," I said. "You must feel awful. To have thought maybe it was your husband they'd found, then to be disappointed." I'd only been dating Sam a few months, but the idea of losing him was a pitchfork to my heart. How must she feel? Martin Garlington's disappearance had been hard enough, but she'd lionized him in the decades since. I searched my mind for something to comfort her. "Could I bring you a pad and pen? Maybe you'd like to write a sonnet about it?"

Pity in her eyes, she smiled at my efforts. "No, honey. I'm all right. This is something I have to endure alone. You go back and join the others." Her gaze slipped from me to the television above my head as she pushed her glass across the bar. "Orson, another sherry, if you please."

"We're all out, Helen. There's a bottle in the kitchen, but Darla keeps it for the chicken liver special. Maybe you'd like to switch to something else? I could make you a pot of tea."

"Is there anything I can do for you?" If I were at the library, the books would murmur suggestions for soothing reads. Here, the bartender's reference guide under the counter whispered something about a pink lady cocktail. I ignored it. Without books to fuel my magic, all I could do was make a mental note to set aside some BBC historical dramas for her.

Mrs. Garlington sighed in reply, but that was all.

If she didn't want to talk, I wouldn't force her. I shrugged at Orson, who was pretending to wipe down the other end of the bar.

"Mrs. Garlington, I'm going back to the café. Please let me know if you change your mind." Sympathy coursed through my body. Before I could tamp it down, it erupted into a flash of energy. This happened sometimes, and I was still learning to control it. Strong emotion could spark an electrical surge, usually flickering lights. This time, the television above me abruptly changed channels. I froze, but no one seemed to notice the electrical freak-out.

Half-listening, Mrs. Garlington nodded and lifted the empty sherry glass to her lips. I rose and she grabbed my sleeve. She gasped and pointed at the television. "Look!"

The channel had changed to a game show. The screen showed two men, both at lecterns reading *Tick Tock Cash* in moving lights. Each lectern was equipped with a gigantic lever mimicking that of a slot machine and labeled *Wham Bam Pow* in flashing letters. The man on the left, an older gent with glasses and wavy white hair, pulled his lever. Confetti rained from the ceiling.

"Yes?" I said. What could she want with this?

Mrs. Garlington's features, slack only seconds ago, tightened to attention. "That's him!" Eyes wide, she inhaled sharply. "That's my Martin!"

CHAPTER 2

"It was the craziest thing," I told Sam that night. "One minute she was crying into her sherry, and the next she was jumping around the tavern shouting, 'Martin! He's alive!'"

Sam leaned forward on the couch. "Was it him?"

Sam was still in his sheriff's uniform, but he'd left his boots and belt in the kitchen and unfastened the top few buttons of his shirt. Before we dated, we'd spent a few evenings a week talking through his cases. Now it was nearly daily, and Sam often made dinner. Tonight, homemade minestrone soup warmed on the stove and *Rigoletto* played in the background, with Joan Sutherland as Gilda. I knew this because the liner notes whispered an ongoing commentary only my ears could hear. Sam's son Nicky occupied himself with a toy fire truck. Nicky was slow to talk, except for his favorite word, "no." At fourteen months old he was a champ at working his way around the house in a drunk man's swagger, so Sam had placed baby gates at the room's entrances. My black cat Rodney, his tail switching, watched from under the coffee table.

"His nameplate said 'Bruno Gates.' I pointed that out to Mrs. Garlington, but she wouldn't hear me. She kept saying, 'You think I don't know my own husband?'" I remembered the undiluted happiness in her eyes, and my heart fell. "She'd had a few to drink. The body Duke and Desmond found—it really messed her up when she discovered it wasn't Martin's. Darla took her home. I bet she'll feel awful in the morning." I shook my head. "Down-market sherry's got to deliver a wicked hangover."

Sam listened with a blank face but intensity in his gaze. His lips turned down to a vague frown. My heart warmed. Sam frowned when he was happy, a habit that confused others but thrilled me. Of course, everything Sam did now—a mere four months into our relationship—thrilled me.

"It's been a while since her husband left, hasn't it?" I asked.

"At least forty years. Maybe fifty." He rose and offered a hand to pull me up next to him.

I took the opportunity to lean into him and breathe his skin's salty scent before following him to the kitchen. How did I get so lucky?

He stirred the soup and I placed bowls on one end of the long kitchen table. "You don't remember Martin Garlington, then. Did the police investigate his disappearance?"

"I don't know. It would have been up to Helen

to file a missing person's report." He turned from the stove and frowned. Happy. "You want to know what happened to Martin, don't you?"

"Aren't you curious?" Wouldn't anyone be? People don't transform into vapor and blow away.

"It's a very cold case, but if you'd like, after dinner we can look through my parents' photo albums. Maybe we'll find a few pictures of him."

An hour later, we sat on the couch with an album and two shoeboxes of photos on the coffee table. Nicky sat surrounded by wooden blocks on the rug. He clumsily built stacks and demolished them with squeals of "No!"

I pulled the photo album nearer. "Why haven't you shown me these sooner?"

Sam looked at me in astonishment. "You're interested?"

"Of course I am." At the library, I'd seen a few photographs of Wilfred in its heyday, when the timber mill was busy night and day and the main drag boasted a soda fountain, drugstore, and general grocery. Today, the former post office housed a grocery store, and besides Darla's Café and her sister Patty's This-N-That across the street, Wilfred was quiet. Some of the old mill workers still lived here, but boarded-up houses dotted its streets. However, the new retreat center was on track to change all that. Already the town was stirring to life again, with talk of bed-and-breakfasts and new shops.

"Wilfred had a movie theater." I pointed to a photo of a neon sign reading *Empress* in green letters. "Isn't that the storefront two down from Patty's?" Without a marquee and movie posters, the building might have once been anything from a shoe repair to a butcher's shop.

"Closed sometime in the 1970s. Mack Jubell—Orson's dad—owned it. Old-timers still complain they have to drive all the way to Forest Grove for a movie."

I turned the page. More than getting to know Wilfred's history, I wanted to see Sam as a baby. Right away, I was rewarded with a photo of a toddler with his hand on a German shepherd's back. It wasn't the baby's features that assured me this was Sam, but his riveting gaze.

"That's you," I said. Rodney hopped into my lap and popped his head over the pages.

"Me and Rover." At my raised eyebrows, he added, "My parents weren't very imaginative."

"And a black cat." Rodney's double sat on the broad railing encircling Big House's front porch, where the photo had been taken. Rodney's origins were mysterious. According to locals, he'd appeared at the library a few days before I arrived. There was no way the cat in the photo could be him—or could it?

"Aunt Marilyn's cat. She loved black cats."

I flipped the page. My interest in Martin Garlington faded as I scanned photos. Sam moved to the cushion next to mine and sneezed at Rodney. He was allergic cats, but tolerated Rodney since he had essentially saved Sam's life—with magical assistance from me, although Sam didn't know it—after I'd first taken the job as Wilfred's librarian.

Sam studied the pages, too. "We look like a normal family, don't we?"

I glanced at him in surprise. "Sure. Mom, Dad, you, family dog. Why?"

He rested a finger on a photo of him and his father. Sam was just a kid—maybe in first grade—and his smile showed a gap in his front teeth. The family stood in front of the old Wilfred mill, steam billowing from its chimneys. Men worked in the background and one had stopped, staring. He didn't look friendly.

Sam tapped the bystander. "We weren't popular."

"Your dad was the boss. It's a longtime custom to rag on the boss. You couldn't help it that the mill shut down."

Sam's expression told me he wasn't convinced. I knew he'd always felt like an outsider. Although he'd never talked about it, I had a hunch that returning to Wilfred was an attempt to achieve the normal life that had always eluded him. The town had eventually welcomed him back, and Nicky had made it all the easier. Seeing Sam's vulnerability despite his wicked intelligence melted what remained of my already-in-a-puddle heart.

He craved a regular life. I didn't want to know how he'd react if he knew he was dating a witch.

I looped my arm in his and turned the page. "Who's that?" Sam's father posed with a couple that could have been on the cover of a magazine for healthy living. The broad-shouldered man draped his arm around the shoulder of his doe-eyed wife. She wore a peasant blouse and embroidered jeans, and her chestnut brown hair was braided and wrapped around her head.

"The Holloways. Frank and Lindy. They were the Holloways then, that is, before Lindy remarried. My parents used to talk about them. I bet this photo was taken at Timber Days. See the booths in the background?"

Even in a photograph, I could feel the beauty of a Wilfred summer—cool mornings, pine-scented afternoons, and sky as blue as delphinium petals.

"What happened to Frank Holloway?"

"Don't know. He was gone long before I was born."

I pointed at a figure in the background. "Isn't that Mrs. Garlington?"

"It is. And her husband. Look."

Mrs. Garlington couldn't have been much older than I was now—in her late twenties. She wore the same slightly bouffant hair that she did today, but instead of a lavender rinse, it shone blond. She gazed with love at a gawky-looking man in glasses. He was tall, like the man in the game show, and had a similarly thick mop of hair. Printed on the photo's white border was *Kodak* and *1974*.

"That had to be just before he disappeared," Sam said.

"Mrs. Garlington looks the same, except younger," I noted. "I think I've even seen her in that blouse." Grief must have frozen her in time. These days, women in their seventies traveled the world and showed up on best-dressed lists. She seemed unable to move on. "I feel awful for Helen, believing some stranger on TV was her husband. Sam, you should have seen her. She always has such dignity, but this afternoon . . ."

Sam smoothed my hair away from my forehead and kissed it. I relaxed into him. "Maybe this will bring closure," he said. "Maybe it's what she's needed all along."

Nicky grabbed a shoebox and, chirping with joy, dumped its contents on the rug. Rodney jumped off my lap to sniff at the photos.

"I'd better take him to bed." Sam scooped up his son and patted his diapered rear end.

"I'll clean up," I said, already kneeling near the coffee table.

As Sam moved around upstairs—the water went on, then off, and the mattress in Nicky's crib creaked—I laid my hands on the photos. Books spoke to me. The energy their authors and readers had funneled into stories sent information directly to my brain. I'd never tried reading photographs.

A bare tingle rose to my palms. Could the photos tell me anything? "Photos," I whispered, "where is Martin Garlington?"

Dates and names whooshed through my mind, as well as fragments of sentences. "Sam's first haircut," a woman's voice said. Sam's mother? "Timber Days 1968." "Darla's Café grand opening." "Lyndon's roses."

All I got from the photos were words, not information. Tonight, Helen Garlington and I were in the same boat, adrift, with Martin Garlington somewhere ashore. Alive or dead, we didn't know.

CHAPTER 3

A mournful cross between a wail and a honk shattered my morning calm. It emanated from across the library's atrium, hung in the morning air a few interminable moments, then plunged down the scale before groaning to a stop.

"For crissakes, keep it down!" came Roz's voice from the conservatory, where she worked on her latest manuscript. Roz was the assistant librarian and a romance author. She'd come in early today.

I set down the coffee mug I'd been filling in the tiny kitchen of my apartment on the library's third floor and leaned over the railing to gaze into the library's atrium. Wilfred's library was in the Victorian mansion built by Sam's great-great-grandfather, a timber baron and Wilfred's founder. Books filled the mansion's former bedrooms, and an organ had been somehow crammed into the second-floor dressing room, now the music room—the same music room that sounded like it housed a suffering walrus. Even the full-length portrait of Marilyn Wilfred, the library's founder, seemed to grimace.

"What do you think, Rodney?" I glanced down at my cat, who'd abandoned his food dish to stare toward the music room with me. He trotted to the service staircase connecting my apartment with the rest of the library, and I followed.

The library wasn't due to open for another two hours, but Mrs. Garlington had permission to give organ lessons a few times a week before patrons arrived. Normally, she was a strict instructor, and wayward students were forced to repeat scales until they could turn out a reasonable facsimile of "Red River Valley," one of her training tunes. If anything proved she wasn't in her right mind, this was it.

I arrived at the music room's doorway, Rodney at my heels. "Mrs. Garlington?"

She slumped on the bow-backed chair next to the organ bench. She turned her head toward me and blinked red-veined eyes. Her usually tidy hair was a mess, and her peony pink lipstick covered a phantom set of lips just to the right of her own.

"Hi, Josie," said Hazel, a bright-eyed middle schooler who dreamed of playing the organ at Roller Derby games. From her muscular build and lackluster musical talent, my guess was she'd be better in the rink than at the organ.

"Are you okay?" I asked Mrs. Garlington.

She rolled her head back to the organ and rubbed the space between her eyes.

Hazel smiled cheerfully. "She went on a bender last night. She's hungover. Right, Mrs. G?" Hazel turned to the keyboard and launched into the opening notes of her song, eliciting fresh shouts from Roz.

"Hazel, let's cut your lesson short today," I said. "Ask your mom to pick you up at the café, and tell Darla to put an order of waffles on my tab."

Hazel leapt up from the organ, and, still smiling—that girl was nothing if not good-natured—skipped down the stairs. The front door shut a moment later.

"Mrs. Garlington? Come with me to the kitchen. I'll make you a strong cup of tea. Would you like a couple of aspirin, too?"

My arm around her shoulder, we worked our way around the hall overlooking the atrium to the main staircase at the library's rear. I settled her at the long oak table in the house's old kitchen and put on the electric kettle. I'd never seen her so distraught. She winced when I turned on the overhead light. Mornings came late this time of year, and orange light was just filtering through the fir trees between the library and the river.

"Martin," she said. "It was him. I know it was."

I sat next to her. "You're not yourself right now."

She fixed me with her gaze. "You don't believe me, do you?"

"It was on a television screen." Not to mention the copious quantity of sherry you'd consumed, I wanted to add. "Maybe the stranger's burial brought back old grief."

"I know Martin. Did you see how he rested his left hand on the podium and tapped his index finger? My Martin did that. And the wave of hair over his ear? Martin." Her voice picked up force. "It was Martin, I tell you."

The kettle clicked off. I rose to pour water into a teapot. "His nameplate said Bruno Gates."

She shook her head. "Obviously a pseudonym."

"Your husband's been gone a long time," I added.

"You think I don't know that?"

"Why? Why would he leave Wilfred and change his name?" And then flaunt himself on a game show for all the world to see?

"That's not the issue here. The issue is that I saw Martin on television yesterday. He's alive." Her strength faltered and she shrank into her chair. "Derwin deserves to meet his father."

My heart broke for her. I could only guess how terrible she felt, believing she'd seen the man she still loved but who'd walked away from her. She was courageous—and possibly delusional. "I understand."

"Will you help me, Josie? Will you help me track him down?"

As a librarian, I'd certainly responded to odder requests for information, from what to feed beetle larvae to translating ancient Armenian letters to ridding carpets of rust stains. Surely finding Bruno Gates and gently confronting Mrs. Garlington with his real identity would be no problem. It was a small request.

"All right," I said. "I'll do it."

CHAPTER 4

Tick Tock Cash's PR department was active, and news about the game show saturated the internet. It took mere seconds to find a profile of Bruno Gates. According to social media, Bruno Gates was an undertaker in Pacific Grove, California with a love of puzzles. He was a longtime fan of *Tick Tock Cash*, "thrilled and delighted" to take part in the show, and ladies should note he was single.

Searching for funeral homes and Bruno's name brought me to a facility advertised with swaying palm trees and gold script reading *Eternal Respite*.

I dialed and a young woman answered with a chipper, "Good morning! Eternal Respite, meticulous care for your loved one."

"May I please speak with Bruno Gates?"

She hesitated. Perhaps the legions of *Tick Tock*

Cash fans had already stormed the phone lines. "May I tell him who's calling?"

"It's Josie Way." Realizing my name would mean nothing to him, I added, "From Wilfred, Oregon. Make sure you mention that." If he really were Martin Garlington, it would mean something to him.

She put me on hold, and for a few minutes I listened to a medley of Beach Boys tunes interspersed with ads urging "Before the Grim Reaper knocks on your door, be sure to knock on ours."

The receptionist returned just as I was learning about pastel caskets. "He's unavailable."

"May I leave my number?"

"That won't be necessary." The receptionist hung up.

Bruno Gates had chosen not to take the call. I shouldn't be surprised. Mrs. Garlington's judgment had been muddled by grief and sherry. She'd wanted to see her husband, so when a man who vaguely resembled him had appeared on TV, she'd immediately grasped at him as Martin. Meanwhile, Bruno Gates knew nothing about Wilfred and apparently had no intention of finding out.

I stared out the window and pondered my next move. Book titles trundled through my mind like railroad cars. *Magical Thinking, The Delusion, Understanding Your Grief.* I'd promised to help Mrs. Garlington and I'd done what I could. I could suggest she see her doctor. A course of therapy and antidepressants might be what she needed. Then another title settled in my brain, a classic by C. S. Lewis: *Miracles.*

Maybe I'd give it one more try. Longtime Wilfredians might know what really happened to Martin Garlington and hadn't wanted to tell Helen. If the truth was out there, she deserved to know it. I could gently break the news and she could move on.

A few hours later, Roz's work on her latest romance—a sequel to *The Whippoorwill Cries Love* titled *The Chickadee Chirps Passion*—was finished for the day, and Roz clocked in to work. Leaving the library under her command, I walked down the hill to downtown Wilfred—if the few blocks merited the lofty designation of "downtown."

Patty was at the nexus of Wilfred's active grapevine. If Wilfredians had a hunch about Martin Garlington's disappearance, she'd know. Patty's This-N-That stood on Wilfred's main street, flanked by boarded-up storefronts. Pickup trucks and family wagons crowded the café's parking lot across the street. I'd bet every table was full of Wilfredians digging into fluffy pancakes, world-class omelets, and Darla's signature shrimp and grits.

The This-N-That was in the middle of a transition from a single store to an antiques mall. Before now, Patty had filled the store's windows with whatever obsessions had gripped her: candles one month, birdcages another, and ribbon and scissors yet another month. The prior summer, vintage kitchen appliances had crowded the front yard, a few of them powered by extension cords running into the store, turning the yard into a community grill.

Patty still loved variety, but she'd tired of scouring the county for inventory. Converting her boutique into an antiques mall solved that problem. Better, it freed her to pursue another of her enthusiasms: fitness. Passive fitness, that is. As in watching fitness videos, talking about physical training, and preaching the benefits of protein shakes—which, in her case, usually included ice cream.

This was my excuse for visiting. Patty's order of a paleo diet book had come in and I'd decided to deliver it in person.

Despite the cool spring air, when I arrived, the This-N-That's door was off its hinges and leaned against the front window. "Patty?" I shouted into the building's dim depths. The counter at the store's rear still stood, but the rest of the boutique had been stripped to the studs. A bare light bulb lit a stack of two-by-fours, and blue tarps covered the floor. The smell of old wood and fresh dirt permeated the air.

"Over here." Patty sat on a wooden crate near the wall. She wore a sweatshirt reading *Built for Speed.* "I'm visualizing. Have a seat."

I pulled up a Victorian footstool with an embroidered seat. It was out of character in the construction site. "Very nice."

"Buffy brought it down," Patty said, referring to her granddaughter, who with her brother Thor was always scheming to turn a buck. "She tried to sell it to Duke, but I put a stop to it. Honestly, those kids."

I handed the cookbook to Patty and settled on the stool. "What's going on with the door?"

"Duke's automating it. We're making the shop

handicapped accessible for one of the new vendors." She smiled. "A seller of rare books."

My heart leapt. Rare books! I wondered what they'd have to tell me.

"Thought you'd like that," Patty said. "Although why he decided to set up shop here beats me. He couldn't get many walk-in customers."

"Who else will be here?" I visualized a stall lined with old books, their vanilla-scented pages humming with stories.

"Two others so far. You know Gidget?"

I nodded. Gidget was a native Wilfredian. She checked out all the new craft books at the library and made occasional visits to Lalena's trailer for psychic readings.

"She'll be selling her jewelry. Plus, we have someone new. A textile vendor. Sells vintage sheets, curtains, tablecloths—things like that."

That tantalized me, too. Since my magic had been unleashed, my senses had deepened, and the thought of decades-old linen dishcloths under my fingers was alluring. But I hadn't come here to talk thread counts.

"Have you seen Mrs. Garlington lately?" I asked. "I'm worried about her."

"I hear she's convinced Martin is doing game shows these days," Patty said. "Saw him on *Tick Tock Cash* and hit the sherry hard."

The grapevine had been busy. "This morning she asked me to help her find him. She's positive the game show contestant is her husband. I tracked him down to his workplace, but he won't take my call. I really doubt he's Martin Garlington."

"You and the rest of us. Poor Helen."

I adjusted myself on the footstool. It might have been a good size for Buffy, but it was small for my grown-up hind end. "I was hoping you could tell me a little bit about him. Do people know what really happened to him?"

Patty set her mug near the wall and leaned back on an ancient wall stud with fresh wiring running through it. "Come to the town history repository, have you?"

"You always seem to know the scuttlebutt," I said. "You don't mind, do you? I'm a librarian. We go for the most reliable sources first."

The flattery had its effect. "I was in my teens when Martin disappeared. Early 1970s. I guess I took him for granted."

"What was he like?"

"Thin, timid, surprisingly thick hair. Tendency to become obsessive. A mortician, if I remember right."

A mortician. Like Bruno Gates. His looks might have changed over the years, but the man I'd glimpsed on the game show was also thin, and he had a thick head of white hair. I leaned forward. "What else? Were there any theories about what happened to him?"

"Can't say. As far as I can tell, no one really knows. He and Helen seemed madly in love. We were all stumped when he took off. First Frank Holloway, then Martin—"

"Stop there. Lindy's first husband also disappeared?"

"He was put away," Patty amended. "Prison. Frank was charming, but get a few drinks in him and he was downright mean. I can't tell you how many fights he got into behind the tavern." She shook her head as if remembering one especially nasty incident.

"He was sent to prison for picking fights, then."

"Nope, robbery," Patty said. "He robbed the Empress and got away with a full weekend of receipts. Mack Jubell turned him in. In the end, I think Lindy was glad. It wasn't the first time Frank had been involved with theft, and he wasn't a good husband." Patty's gaze focused somewhere near the opposite wall, and she shook her head. "Once I saw her with a heck of a shiner. I asked my mother about it, and she gave me a lecture about dating only men who respected me."

I filed this information away. "Let's get back to Martin. You say he was obsessive. Was he fixed on anything in particular when he vanished?"

"You'd have to ask Helen. For a while, he was really into spontaneous combustion." At my puzzled expression, she added, "It was a fad at one time. Everyone was talking about cases where people burst into flames. You don't hear much about that anymore. I wonder why that is?"

"What else?" I prompted. If Patty got going on spontaneous combustion, she could talk until lunchtime. Unless someone had discovered an unexpected pile of ash near the Garlington residence the time Martin disappeared, I wasn't interested.

"Butterflies. I remember him wandering the hillside with his net. He'd stop anyone who'd listen and wrangle them into a discussion of the monarch butterfly's migration patterns. Helen used to brag that he'd never kill them, he just drew them in colored pencil."

"Patty." A comfortably built older woman with chic eyeglasses picked her way through the shop floor's debris. "I wanted to take some measurements for my space, if you don't mind." She tipped her head to examine me over her glasses and smiled.

This wasn't Gidget or the rare books man, so she must be the new textiles dealer. Something about her felt familiar to me, and I couldn't help but like her right away. I rose and proffered a hand. "I'm Josie Way."

She shifted a leather tote bag to her other arm and shook my hand. "Babe Hamilton. I'll be setting up shop here."

"You sell textiles," I said.

"Indeed, I do, and I recognize that tone of voice." She smiled. "Are you a fabric nerd? I have a line on half a dozen vintage French métis sheets, some with gorgeous embroidery."

It was as if she'd read my mind. I loved my cozy quilts, but lately I'd been dreaming of a long top sheet to fold back over the blankets as I'd seen in books about old country houses in Europe. I wasn't ready to go all lace-edged bed pillows—Rodney would love nothing better than to sharpen his claws on them—but a handwoven sheet? Yes, please.

"I look forward to some shopping once you're set up." I turned to Patty. "I'd better get back to the library."

"Josie is Wilfred's librarian," Patty told Babe

Hamilton. Then, to me, "Thanks for the cook-book."

"Thanks for the intel."

If Patty said no one knew what had happened to Martin Garlington, then the reason for his disappearance was truly a mystery and not just kept secret from Helen. At least I wouldn't have to break that news to her. Telling her that Bruno Gates had refused to take my call was bad enough.

CHAPTER 5

I climbed the hill toward the library, counting on work to distract me from the unpleasant task ahead. Maybe Darla would agree to put off the tavern's sherry reorder for a few months while Helen's grief subsided.

Instead of entering through the side door to the library's kitchen, I took the front door for the glorious experience patrons had. If it wasn't for the brass plaque engraved *Wilfred Library* on the porch, visitors could be excused for thinking they'd wandered into a gothic novel. The library was a Victorian Italianate classic, with a squared central tower over the mansion's front half and three stories of moldings, French doors, bay windows, and chimneys. On one side spread the woods of Oregon's Coastal Range, and on the other side, just over the Kirby River, lay the town.

At the sound of steps crunching on gravel, I

turned to see Darla's husband Montgomery coming toward the library. He passed the caretaker's cottage, where Lyndon lived, separated from the mansion by a lawn and a few ancient oaks. Beyond the cottage stood Big House—Sam's home, built by his great-grandfather. At night, I could open my sitting room window and hear strains of Sam's beloved operas drift across the garden.

"Good morning, Josie. I thought you'd be inside, not hanging out on the porch." Montgomery caught up with me, and he opened the library's heavy wooden door, letting us into the tiled, oak-paneled foyer. He stepped in front of me to open the foyer door with its stained glass windows and let me pass into the atrium.

"Your history of Chinese philosophy is in," I told him. As the energy from the library's thousands of volumes seeped into my body, a title slipped into my head: *Bali for Lovers.* Could Montgomery and Darla be planning a belated honeymoon? It wasn't my business to say, but maybe I could hint. "Is there anything else I can recommend for you?"

"Since you mentioned it, we've been thinking of taking a vacation. Somewhere warm."

Bingo. Montgomery was from Alabama and hadn't yet adjusted to the Pacific Northwest's damp cold. Witness this morning, when he was bundled up in a parka and stocking cap, even though most Wilfredians considered April semitropical and fended off the chill with hoodies and light jackets.

"Have you considered an exotic destination, say"—I wrinkled my brow as if pondering—"Bali? If so, I have just the book for you." I jotted down the title and handed it to him.

I crossed the atrium on my way to my office and stopped a moment to smile hello to the portrait over the door of Marilyn Wilfred, the library's founder. As always, title suggestions flowed through my mind like cars on an interstate highway. *First Aid for Bunions*, whispered a booklet as I passed a farmer examining DVDs. *Oliver Twist*, said a British voice when I glanced toward the prep cook from Darla's looking for something to read on his day off. *101 Dog Treats to Make at Home* said a book as I waved at Mona, on a rare break from tending foster animals.

"How are things this morning?" I asked Roz, who was refilling her coffee mug in the kitchen.

"Same as always. One of the Loeffler children destroyed *Bunny Goes A Bowlin'*, and two members of the knitting club got in a fight about the TV show *Real Housewives of Sacramento*." She flipped open a fan and batted at a hot flash. Dark circles ornamented her heat-reddened cheeks.

"You were here early this morning," I said. "Is everything all right?"

"I haven't been getting much sleep, that's all."

"Where have you been staying, anyway?" Since she and Lyndon had returned from their honeymoon a few months earlier, they split their time between Lyndon's cottage and Roz's trailer in the Magnolia Rolling Estates.

She let rip a sigh that might have blown out the windows. "I don't want to talk about it."

So, that was it. They hadn't figured out where to land together. "You're sure?"

"Positive."

I lifted an eyebrow, giving her another moment to unburden herself, but she didn't take it.

Instead, she stuck the closed fan into her rear pocket and pushed a book toward me. "I found this propped on the table in the atrium. I wonder who left it?"

I hefted the fat red volume and flipped it over to see its cover. *The Complete Original Illustrated Sherlock Holmes*, it read, "with all 356 original illustrations by Sidney Paget." It was a message from the books. About what? "I'll drop it on the cart to reshelve. I need to spend an hour in my office on a book order, but I'll be out in time for your lunch."

After leaving the book in circulation, I went to my office in the house's old pantry, tucked under the main staircase at the atrium's rear, keeping it cozy. Casement windows looked out to the cottonwoods along the Kirby and down the embankment to Wilfred proper. Rodney was already curled in the armchair.

"Rodney," I said to the cat, a bundle of warm black fur. "Make room for me. We have work to do. Just because Bruno Gates won't talk to me doesn't mean I can't learn more about him."

I pulled out my desk drawer for a pen but withdrew my hand before reaching in. There on top of the usual mess of paperclips and pens rested a fat red book: *The Complete Original Illustrated Sherlock Holmes*, the volume I'd just left across the library.

I'd barely had time to register the book's reappearance when the phone buzzed from circulation. "Josie," Roz said. "You have a call." Before she forwarded it, I heard her yell something about not bringing dogs into the library, because Rodney didn't like it. In the background, a hound bayed.

"Hello?" I said when the call buzzed through. "This is Josie Way. May I help you?"

"Bruno Gates. I understand you called for me?"

I clutched the phone nearer. "Mr. Gates. I didn't leave my number."

"It's on caller ID. You wanted to speak with me."

Bruno Gates's voice was gentle, hesitant. I wondered that he had the moxie to appear on a game show. I was certain he'd told the receptionist to blow me off.

"Yes. Thank you for returning my call. Does the name Martin Garlington mean anything to you?"

He started to speak, stopped, and began again. "Never heard of him. Why? Is he a recently deceased loved one? If so, I'd be happy to refer you to our finance department. I believe we're running the Elysian fields special for spring."

My disappointment surprised me. I didn't realize how much I'd been hoping Mrs. Garlington had been right and she'd rediscovered her long-lost husband on a TV show after all. Talk about magical thinking.

"No," I said. "It's silly."

"It's clearly important, or you wouldn't have called," Bruno Gates said.

"Crazy, really. You see, a woman in our community—"

"In Oregon, I believe from your area code?"

"Yes. Wilfred, Oregon. A neighbor saw you on

Tick Tock Cash and was sure you were her husband."
A lengthy pause greeted my words. "Hello?"

"I'm here. That's quite a claim."

"He vanished almost fifty years ago. We all figured he'd died."

"Her husband was Martin Gattlingford?"

"Garlington. Right." Rodney slinked from the armchair to my lap and snuggled against me, purring. Sometimes I wondered if when I talked on the phone he thought I was talking to him, since no one else was around.

At the other end of the line was silence but for soft breathing. "She must have really loved him."

"Still does, as far as I can tell."

"I understand your neighbor's grief at losing her spouse. Tell you what. You say you're in Oregon?"

I sat straighter, interrupting Rodney's purrs. "Western Oregon. Not far from Portland."

"I have business in Seattle in a few weeks. How about if I stop by and meet your neighbor, this Mrs.—"

"Garlington," I supplied.

"Maybe it will put her mind to rest to see me and know for certain I'm not her husband."

Something in his response put me on alert. "This is awfully generous of you."

"Not really," he replied. "You're not far off my path. I won a little money on the game show, and I'm looking for a place to retire. Oregon is on the list. Besides that, in my business, I've come to appreciate the value of closure. Anywhere nearby to stay the night?"

Meeting Bruno Gates would bring Helen face-to-face with reality. While it might sting for a few days, it would help release her fantasies of reuniting with her husband. Sometimes a serious ill required strong medicine, and meeting Bruno Gates might provide a jolting but necessary dose.

"Do you have a pen handy?" I asked.

CHAPTER 6

No sooner had I hung up the heavy desk phone then I picked up my cell phone to call Helen Garlington. I pictured her in a flowered house-dress, steeping Darjeeling in a Blue Willow teapot and humming a Bach cantata. Reality turned out to be something different. "Hello?" she croaked. She was still working through her hangover.

"Sorry to disturb you," I said. "I wanted you to know that I found Bruno Gates. He's coming to Wilfred a week from Thursday."

On the other side of the phone line, something dropped with a thud. I hoped it wasn't Mrs. Garlington. "A week from Thursday? For real? Oh, Josie."

As I listened, I pushed open my office's case-ment window. The day looked to be warming and the sweet smell of the river wafted in. A crow lit on the low branch of an oak tree and edged sideways.

Another crow landed next to him. Both stared in my direction.

"Josie?" Mrs. Garlington said.

"Sorry. I was distracted."

"He's coming Thursday. I have so much to do." Now her voice was stronger. I had the feeling Orson's sherry reserves would cease to be drained. "I have to freshen up the house, tell Derwin—did you know Martin has never even met him?—and get my hair done."

"This could be the chance for a makeover," I said. "Trixie might have a great idea or two for you."

"Oh, no. Martin knows me like this. I couldn't change it, at least, not now." The joy in her voice washed through the phone lines. "I'll never be able to thank you enough. But I have to go. I have so much to do!" she repeated.

"Remember," I said quickly, before she could hang up, "He was firm that he wasn't your husband."

"That's what he says, but I know what I saw. Maybe all those years ago he had amnesia and wandered off. When he sees me, it will come together for him. I've waited so long for this."

I tapped *end* and laid down the phone. Rodney leapt to the desk and tucked his head under my fingers. I obligingly scratched between his ears. "What do you think, Rodney? Have I made a mistake by getting involved?"

What would I do if Sam were to disappear as Martin Garlington had? I winced to think of it. Already I couldn't imagine my future without him. Would I wear the same hairstyle for fifty years in the belief we'd someday be reunited? There was a lot I'd do for him, even now. What I was less sure about was what he'd do for me. For instance, would he accept that I was a witch?

Rodney, staring at the crows, growled low in his throat. One of the crows set off, his beak hard and yellow, his black feet sharp with talons. I closed the window.

Tuesday nights, Lalena came to the library for dinner and a bath in the mansion's claw-foot bathtub. She used to show up sporadically, a basket of soap and towels in one hand and her dog Sailor's leash in the other, complaining about the cramped tub in her little pink trailer at the Magnolia Rolling Estates. Eventually, I'd convinced her to schedule bath time outside business hours, and I'd even managed to limit it to Tuesdays.

Since then, I'd come to look forward to Lalena's bath night—even now, when I giddily spent most evenings at Sam's. I kept a box of chardonnay in the refrigerator for her, and we often made a dinner of treats her clients had brought her, along with whatever leftovers I had. Meanwhile Sailor and Rodney chased each other through the library, shooting in and out of the cat door at the top of the service stairs.

Tonight, Lalena settled across from me in my apartment's kitchen and dived into Mrs. Garlington's situation right away. "Patty says you're trying to track down the man Mrs. Garlington saw on TV."

"I found him." I unpacked deviled eggs from

her basket. A thank-you note from one of her clients was still taped to the top.

"Theresa," she said, pointing to the note. "In thanks for helping me patch things up with her mother. They're a little heavy on the pickle relish. The eggs, that is."

"Theresa's mother died over Christmas, didn't she?"

"They had a dozen unresolved arguments when she passed. I had to do some serious channeling to clear them up."

Lalena made her living as a psychic. For her, "psychic" had more to do with theater than supernatural skills. She specialized in palm and tarot readings, but she'd been known to chat with a dead loved one and occasionally read an aura. She had no idea a bona fide witch sat across the table from her, and if I told her, she'd laugh and inform me that witches weren't real.

She turned to the refrigerator behind her to fill her wineglass. My kitchen was small enough that she didn't have to leave her seat. "I feel awful telling you this, but I hope Bruno Gates ends up not to be Martin Garlington."

"Why would you say that?" I asked, after downing a deviled egg. Lalena was right about the relish. "You know how hung up Helen is on Martin."

"Because for the past five years she's hired me to communicate with him almost weekly. If he showed up in the flesh, my credibility is in the toilet. I just don't know how to spin that."

I couldn't help but laugh. "Oh boy."

"It's not just money, it's professional standing."

"Don't worry. Mrs. Garlington was way in her cups. It could have been Santa Claus on the screen, and she'd have sworn it was her husband." I paused, deviled egg midair. "Although Martin Garlington was an undertaker, and so is Bruno Gates. What are the odds of that?"

"You don't think Helen was right?"

I shrugged. "Bruno Gates insists he has no idea what she's talking about. If he truly wanted to hide his identity, he'd hardly agree to come to Wilfred, would he?"

Sailor barked from the atrium. He and Rodney were no doubt racing circles through the ground floor. A joyful yip followed.

Lalena grew thoughtful. "People come to me with concerns about everything from would-be lovers to health scares to worries about paying the mortgage. Getting all the secrets straight isn't easy."

Secrets. Thinking of Sam and the huge secret I withheld from him, I asked, "What's it like? To keep secrets like you do with your clients?"

"You mean the secrets they tell me?"

"What you don't tell them. That you're basically their therapist, not predicting their future or talking with their dead relatives or whatever."

She cocked her head. "Why do you ask? Are you keeping any secrets?"

Psychic or not, Lalena was a good reader of human nature. I put some cheer into my smile. "As if. I'm an open book. So to speak." Even from two floors up, I heard the humor section snicker. My smile dimmed. Lalena was right, of course. No one outside my immediate family knew I was a witch. That hadn't bothered me until I met Sam. All Sam wanted was to be normal—and I was far from it.

She leaned back. "I suppose you are pretty obvious. When you fell for Sam, everyone knew. Except Sam, that is."

Warmth suffused me. My brilliant, clueless Sam.

Her expression became serious again. "But, secrets. I guess I figure I do more good by hiding some information than revealing it. I mean, is it so bad if I look at someone's palm and tell them they're capable of creating wonderful music when all I see is a callus from playing the guitar? I give people a new way to see themselves. Most of the time, that's all they want—hope and the courage to believe in themselves."

"What about Mrs. Garlington, for instance? What do you tell her?"

This apparently called for a refill from the wine box. When she returned to me, she said, "I tell her Martin is watching over her—what you'd expect. The tricky part is when she wants Martin's advice."

"Advice?"

"She'll ask if she should get a new roof, for instance. Those questions are easy. I tell her Martin advises her to consult with Duke."

Solid. "What are the harder questions?"

"Lately she's asked a lot about death. What it's like on the other side." She toyed with the stem of her wineglass. "I tell her the afterlife is full of beautiful music."

I laughed. "Hers will be. I'm sure of it." Despite my laughter, I still felt uneasy that Sam didn't know about my magic. But it was so early between us. Would there ever be a right time? My thoughts raced ahead to a wedding, children. What if I gave birth to a witch? It could happen.

Lalena examined me. "Something is bothering you, isn't it?" When I didn't respond, she added, "Is it about Sam? We can talk about it. Not as psychic-client. As friends."

The urge to unburden myself swelled to bursting. Would there ever be a right time? "I don't know . . ."

"It's all right, Josie. I'm listening."

"There is something I need to tell Sam, but I'm afraid."

"Tell me." Lalena's focus rested on me, as if I were her only concern in the world. No wonder her clients loved her.

I shook my head. "It wouldn't be right to say anything without Sam knowing first." My throat thickened. "Will you pour me a glass of that wine?"

Lalena twisted to open the refrigerator. She tipped the box to dribble an inch into my empty water glass. "Here."

I downed its contents. "I'm afraid if I tell him, he'll leave me."

"You've got to be joking. What could be that bad?" She leaned forward and said in a conspiratorial tone, "Foreign spy? Secret baby? Oh, I know—you're already married."

Despite myself, I laughed. "I shouldn't have even brought it up."

"Are you sure? You may be blowing this issue way out of proportion. Sometimes a good chat is all a problem needs to disappear."

If only. "Really, forget I said anything." I shifted the subject to safer ground. "Let's talk about something else. Have you heard about the vendors in Patty's antiques mall?"

Lalena hesitated, then, seeing I wouldn't be unburdening myself this evening, nodded. "Gidget's selling her earrings, plus there's a lady stocking vintage fabric. But, best of all"—a smile widened over her face—"is the dreamy new guy."

"Dreamy, huh? I'd heard there was someone selling rare books."

"I saw him at the café. He's the brooding type, and it took a few minutes to get him to open up. He went for the palm reading routine, though." Her expressions softened as if she were remembering something especially worth savoring. "Then it turns out he specializes in parapsychology."

My neck felt cold, then hot. "As in talking to spirits?"

She nodded. "Among other topics. Phrenology, ESP, throwing bones, things like that. Maybe *dreamy* isn't the right word. He's kind of odd looking, really. Dark hair that could use a cut, clothes that don't fit well." Her gaze caught mine. "He has this strip of white hair in one eyebrow, just the width of a pinky finger. And a scar on the side of his face, like a pirate." She drained her wineglass. "I'm looking forward to getting to know him better."

I wasn't sure if I could say the same. My birthmark—the star-shaped mark on my shoulder that signified my unusually strong power—began to warm. What was I supposed to notice here? I slipped a finger under my collar to press it and noticed Rodney at my feet, looking up.

Lalena rose. "Time for my bath. It's getting late. I'll let myself out when I'm finished." She placed her dishes in the sink, then paused at the doorway. "If you ever want to talk about your secret, you know where to find me."

CHAPTER 7

The next week passed slowly, then quickly. Helen spent it readying herself for her husband's arrival—steam cleaning her carpets, getting a pedicure, and who knew what else. She'd persisted in calling Bruno Gates "Martin," and she'd talk about him to anyone who fell into her path. I even caught the PO Grocery closing five minutes early when the cashier saw her coming to avoid a prolonged conversation about destiny, true love, and happy endings. Her organ lessons bubbled with jubilant music. She was so convincing that townspeople who had written Martin Garlington off as dead now speculated he'd fallen victim to some sort of fugue state and had adopted a new identity. He was coming home at last.

I prayed Helen wouldn't be disappointed.

At last, it was the evening Bruno Gates was set to arrive. Helen was flushed with happiness and had just concluded a rousing performance on the organ of the first movement of Beethoven's Ninth Symphony—the *Ode to Joy*.

"Don't get your hopes up." I hadn't meant to say these words. I'd meant to be encouraging, positive, to let Mrs. Garlington have whatever experience she needed to have.

Mrs. Garlington snapped shut her compact mirror and dropped it into her handbag. Pearl pink lipstick flawlessly applied? Check. Hair bouffed and shellacked? Check. New blouse and pants—same style, however—pressed with a color-coordinated manicure? Check and check.

She laid a hand on my arm. "Honey, I know you mean well. Don't worry about me. Fate demanded Martin and I would eventually be reunited. I knew in here." She pressed a palm to her chest. "The time has come at last."

We stood in the library's atrium. The library was officially closed for the day and the sun had set, but I'd made circulation as cheerful as possible with lamps glowing here and there and armchairs dragged in from popular fiction.

Mrs. Garlington had agreed not to meet Bruno Gates in her home—who was to say he wasn't a predatory imposter?—although only reluctantly, and mostly because she meant to re-wallpaper the dining room before her husband saw it again. Meeting at the café was out of the question. All of Wilfred would have been in attendance. I pictured the knitting club in back-to-back booths with their knitting needles poised pointy side out in case Bruno Gates was up to no good. The library seemed the best option. My plan was to introduce them, then discreetly disappear into the conservatory.

My heart was prepared to break.

Someone knocked on the front door. The library used to have a doorbell with the full chimes of Big Ben, but after too many kids rang it during business hours, Lyndon disconnected it.

"Are you ready?" I asked Mrs. Garlington.

Breathless, she nodded. She'd posed herself next to the table in the atrium, one hand on the table's edge and the other artfully draped at her side. Lyndon had arranged branches of plum blossoms in a crystal vase, and she really did look as pretty as a picture.

I crossed the foyer and opened the library's heavy front door. Bruno Gates stood under the weak porch light looking as I'd remembered him from my brief glance on TV: thatch of white hair and thick-framed black glasses. He was shorter in real life than I'd recalled, but they always say that about people on the screen. He gave me an appraising glance, eyes lingering uncomfortably long on my chest, and winked.

Stiffly, I said, "Mr. Gates? Thank you for coming. Helen is inside." I led him to the atrium and, as agreed, retreated to the conservatory to wait. Rodney trotted after him. If they adjourned to circulation as planned and things went well, Mrs. Garlington would take her husband to her house for the dinner she'd readied of cold roast chicken and potato salad—Martin's favorites. She'd leave through the front door, and I'd hear her on her way out. Tomorrow, she'd introduce him to his son, Derwin, before Derwin started his postal route.

If Bruno Gates turned out not to be her husband, Helen would exit the kitchen door at the library's rear and leave me to usher him out the front.

While I waited, I paced the conservatory, pausing to look out the rain-spattered windows. The corner of a novel caught my eye from a side table. I lifted it. *Mistaken Identity*, a gift from the books. Not a good sign. What was happening between Bruno and Helen?

I didn't have to wait long to find out. Rodney trotted into the conservatory with Bruno Gates not far behind. He stood at the doorway, his coat in his hands.

"I didn't even have to break the news," he said. "She took one look at me, smiled, frowned, and made for the back door."

Despite that this was what I'd expected, I felt unaccountably sad. Fate had punished Mrs. Garlington, raising and dashing her hopes like a trailer in a tornado. She was strong—she had to be, raising a son without his father, getting by on dignity and organ lessons—but no one should have to endure this kind of heartbreak.

"I'm sorry," was all I could mutter.

"Don't be sorry, gorgeous. This frees me up for the evening. What do you say to a bite at the café I saw down the hill? I'm buying."

After I extricated myself from Bruno Gates and watched the taillights of his car recede up the driveway, I ran across the garden to Big House. Sam was waiting for me at the back door.

"I saw Mrs. Garlington leave," he said.

Behind him, in the doorway to the dining room, Patty stood, holding Nicky on her hip, flanked by her elementary school-aged grandchildren, Buffy and Thor. "No dice?" she said.

"Nope. It wasn't him." I was split between wanting to sink onto a kitchen chair and cry for Helen and reveling in the warmth and love of my own situation with Sam.

"Didn't think so, but Helen was so sure." Patty shook her head. "She had even me convinced."

Sam slipped his arm around me, and I leaned into him. "Patty said she'd watch Nicky tonight so we could go out."

Patty liked to keep "a hand in the baby game," as she put it, so she volunteered to babysit from time to time. Buffy and Thor required a fee for amusing Nicky, and two five-dollar bills rested on the counter for them.

"Maybe you want to go dancing and drink champagne," Buffy said. Tonight she wore a sparkly pink tutu and a matching headband.

"Or play pinball." Thor was obsessed with pinball machines, to the point of actually spending his hard-earned quarters on them. He unsuccessfully lobbied Darla, his great-aunt, to buy one for the tavern. Darla had pointed out he was too young to go into the tavern anyway.

Sam's wool shirt scratched my cheek as I leaned into him, but I didn't care. Spending an evening with him was the remedy I needed. I was too blue to go far, even if Buffy's fantasy of adult nights out was something we could find within a reasonable drive of Wilfred. "Do you want to stay in town?

Maybe get dinner at Darla's? Helen's situation has put me in a mood. The rain has eased up. We could go for a walk afterward."

A few minutes later, we were on our way down the hill to the café, hand in hand. The evening smelled of rain and fresh soil. Spring was coming, then the summer's heat, then autumn again. The cycles of life continued no matter what.

"I hope she didn't take it too hard," Sam said, his sympathy giving me yet another reason to love him.

"She left before I had the chance to talk to her." I squeezed his hand. "She'd been so sure it was Martin. I feel terrible. Maybe I should have seen this coming and refused to track him down."

"It's all right. You did your best."

As we walked, a crow seemed to follow us, flying from tree to tree, rustling on the wet boughs. Soon it was joined by two others. One cawed a warning to the others.

"Have you noticed the crows lately?" I asked. "I swear I see more of them than I ever have."

"Not particularly," Sam said. "But isn't it strange for them to be out at night? I thought crows couldn't see in the dark."

The café was about half full—full enough to flood the room with chatter and good smells, but empty enough that we'd be able to catch up about the day. We took a booth near the café's rear. From across the table, Sam took my hands in his, and all thoughts of crows and Mrs. Garlington melted away.

"There's Bruno Gates." Sam nodded toward a table across the room.

I turned to see Bruno ostentatiously examining the menu. We weren't the only customers checking him out.

"Was it hard?" Sam didn't need to elaborate. His hair had begun receding early, and although it was still rich brown and his body strong and straight, I could imagine what he might look like in old age. I hoped I'd be with him to see it.

I nodded. "She wanted Bruno Gates so badly to be her husband. I can't even say she was hopeful— she was more than that. Expectant. She told me she'd known they were destined to be together again." And that belief was crushed. I ran a palm up Sam's arm to feel the muscle and little dark hairs growing there. I was so lucky. Mrs. Garlington was not.

Darla was at the cash register, and our waitress was one of the seemingly endless supply of Tohler teenagers. We didn't need menus. I ordered the special, sight unseen. Whatever it was, it was sure to be good.

When the waitress left, I leaned forward. "Do you think it was another woman that lured Martin away?"

"Somehow, I doubt it. Helen doesn't seem the type to get involved with a player."

Unlike Bruno, I thought as I caught him eyeing the Tohler teenager's derriere. "It almost would have been better had the bones at Duke and Desmond's turned out to be Martin Garlington's. Helen would have had closure at last."

Sam reached across the table, placing his hands over mine. "You're kind to care so much. But this

is Helen's grief to work through. You can't do it
for her, as much as you'd like to."

"If we just had a hint. Maybe Martin was scared
away. Or had to run to avoid arrest." I looked at
the ice in my water glass as if it were a crystal ball.
"This might be a leap, but what about the bones in
the outhouse? Could he have had something to do
with that?"

"You think he murdered someone and skipped
town? You have quite an imagination." Sam gave
me a look with some of the same warmth I felt
coursing through my own body. He nodded toward a table out of my sight. Thanks to his FBI
training, out of habit he took the seat giving him
the best view of the room. "Bruno Gates. He's in
the corner booth talking with Mona, and from the
looks of it, attempting to get somewhere with her."
His gaze shifted. "All while keeping an eye on the
waitress's backside." He relaxed again into his seat.
"Kindly old mortician or not, Bruno Gates has an
eye for the ladies. And he's throwing money
around like confetti. I just saw him point at a table
and motion for the bill. A table of two women."

I remembered the head-to-toe assessment he'd
given me. "I'm glad Mrs. Garlington isn't here to
see this."

Our food arrived. Mine was jambalaya. Darla's
love of all things Southern, combined with the
best local ingredients, meant I would eat probably
the only jambalaya served with Dungeness crab
and a filé of last summer's Oregon-grown peppers.
Although Sam was a committed home cook with a
palate to match, he loved breakfast out, no matter

what the meal. His dinner was an omelet stuffed with the area's first crop of morel mushrooms.

Travis Everhardt came in to pick up a to-go order. He waved as he passed our table. "Dinner with Kaydee and Mom." His glanced strayed toward the table where Bruno Gates was attempting to make time with the waitress. He scowled and headed for the door.

"What was that about?" Sam asked.

"Travis and Derwin are friends. Old schoolmates. He probably feels for Helen Garlington."

Sam raised an eyebrow. "News travels fast."

A cool breeze hit my back as the door opened again. This time, silence fell over the dining room. I turned to see Helen Garlington frozen just inside the entrance, her eyes locked on Bruno Gates. Bruno, oblivious to the change in mood, was trying to snake his arm around Mona's back.

Helen's expression morphed from relaxed to horrified to painfully frigid. She swiveled and left. The door slammed closed just as Mona smacked Bruno Gates's hand.

"Oh, Sam," I said. "Should I get something to go for Helen?"

"She might need time to herself right now," Sam said gently.

He was right, although it broke my heart to think of her alone. "In the morning, then. I'll go see her in the morning."

CHAPTER 8

The next morning, armed with cinnamon rolls warm from the café's oven, I walked to Mrs. Garlington's house. Rodney scampered along with me, darting up to a tree, then lagging behind to sniff at something on the ground only he could see. A drizzle brought out the morning's freshness.

I was afraid I wouldn't find Mrs. Garlington quite as fresh. Shifting my fragrant bundle to my other arm, I mounted the steps to the porch and knocked on her screen door. Rodney waited at my feet.

Mrs. Garlington cracked open the door. "Hello?" She clearly hadn't slept much or dusted her face with the peachy powder she usually used. Yet she was smiling. I was encouraged.

"I wanted to check on you. See if you needed

anything." I showed her the cinnamon rolls. "For your sweet tooth."

"That's so kind, dear. Come in. I'll make tea."

Mrs. Garlington led me through the narrow track in her living room, between the baby grand piano, armchair, and fireplace. All the lights were on in the dining room. An open cardboard box sat on one end of the table, and photos covered the other.

"You've been looking at photos of Martin, haven't you?" I asked while Mrs. Garlington put on the kettle.

"Those days always seemed so recent. I thought I'd never forget them. But at some point last night, they fell away." She returned to the table and handed me a square photo. "Here we are playing miniature golf."

A much younger Helen Garlington wearing plaid pants and a cardigan—the blurry green and red of an old Polaroid—and the same lacquered hair stood with a man wearing glasses in front of a shed-sized windmill. His thick hair and thin body made his head appear overly large. Even given the changes decades could make on a man, it was clear that Bruno Gates was not Martin Garlington.

She returned to the kitchen to scoop tea into a teapot. "After I left the café last night, I took a long walk. I was out for hours. The café was closed on my last turn. I even stopped for a while at the churchyard and looked at the tombstones."

From my seat in the dining room, I could see only Mrs. Garlington's back, but the sounds of clinking teacups and pouring water reached me.

"Did it help?" When she'd first seen Bruno Gates on television, she'd spent hours wandering town, too. And drinking sherry. Neither seemed to have gotten her far.

Rodney's tail crossed my peripheral vision. He was wandering Mrs. Garlington's ground floor, patrolling for who knew what. The curtains next to me fluttered as he batted behind them.

"Sometime during the night, I had an epiphany." Teapot in hand, she turned to face me. "I've been dead, too."

"What do you mean?" I kept one eye on Rodney. He had that furtive how-can-I-make-trouble look.

"Honey, I've lived like a fly frozen in amber. Look at me. I haven't even changed my hairstyle since the early 1970s. When Cindy retired at the Beauty Palace, they had to train my new stylist with a pile of old *Ladies' Home Journal*s and instructions to watch *Father Knows Best.*"

Rodney chose this moment to rocket up the drapes, leaving a trail of pulled threads behind him.

I leapt to my feet. "Rodney! Get down from there."

He stared at me from the valance, awkwardly balancing himself. He glanced toward the dining room table, the shortest stop on the way down, but apparently decided against it due to the slick waves of photos. Instead, he eased himself down, shredding the curtain as he went, until I could grab him and march him out the front door.

"I'm so sorry," I said when I returned. "I'll replace your curtains right away."

Mrs. Garlington poured tea for us. "Don't think twice about it. I'm having the place redecorated. Things are going to change around here. As soon as the salon opens, I'm making an appointment for a new hairstyle." She waved toward the living room and, shocked, I saw that the photo of her husband she'd kept on the piano was turned face down. The red silk rose remained, but the votive candle had been snuffed.

"You're not being too hasty?" I said.

"Hasty?" She snorted. "After almost fifty years? No, I'm way behind." She pushed her teacup to the side. "There's no reason for me to keep my life exactly as it was when Martin left. After all, he certainly didn't keep his life the same. He walked out, leaving me with no way to get in touch with him. Sure, he sent money for a few years, but was he there when Derwin was born?"

I didn't need to reply.

"No," she continued. "He was off living an entirely new life while I halted mine to be ready for him when he returned." Her voice caught. "I was so sure he was coming back. I was so sure we had a special love. I was a fool."

"Not a fool. Hopeful. Your love—the love you felt—truly must have been special."

"Thank you, Josie, but I let hope overcome reason. All those years I was so sure he'd return. Positive." She shook her head, remembering. "I did a real number on myself."

"I'm sorry," I whispered.

Her voice picked up strength. "I'm not. All I know is that if I see Bruno Gates again, I will thank him for opening my eyes."

"Mrs. Garlington, I have a whole new respect for you." Her pain might have become anger. Instead, it transformed into courage. Courage for a new life.

"Did you know I've never been abroad? I'm looking into tickets to Prague for the International Organ Festival. Plus, Pastor Williams has been giving me the eye. I've seen him checking me out while I play at funerals he officiates. He's been frisky since his wife died. Who knows? I might take him up on his invitation to coffee." She played with her cinnamon roll, but it was clear she was too worked up to eat. "Later, I'll see Lalena about communicating with Martin's spirit to tell him I'm letting him go. He'll always be special to me, but it's well past time to move on."

"Mrs. Garlington, you—"

She held up a hand in *stop* position. "No more 'Mrs. Garlington.' That's so old-fashioned. It's Helen from now on."

"Thank you, Helen." She'd surprised me and yet, reflecting on it, not. Helen Garlington was a romantic, but also built of steel forged by love and loss. She had a lot to teach me.

An hour later, after talk of potential hairstyles and new drapes, I waved goodbye and started for the library. It would be opening soon and Roz would not stand for my being late. I braced myself for the barrage of suggestions the books would have for Helen Garlington—everything from fashion to travel to self-help.

Rodney had been waiting for me in the crab apple tree in Helen's yard. He ran ahead when I opened the gate and led me through Wilfred's early morning streets, woodsmoke rising from chimneys here and there, and the smell of bacon and coffee coming from others.

Here's where Helen wandered last night, I thought, probably looping up by the retreat center on the access road, through the trailer park, and around the east side of town. She said she'd passed through the churchyard. Maybe I would, too, and pay homage to Wilfred's dead and the changes they'd instigated in Helen Garlington's life.

Rodney slipped through the iron gate before I opened it and rambled ahead. The stranger's grave was on Duke and Desmond's land on the other side of the churchyard, beyond the grove of lilac trees, now tightly budded in the shade of the conifers. Here's where Helen would have pondered her life and decided she'd waited too long. Life was for the living—not for the waiting.

Uncharacteristically, Rodney raced back to me and mewed.

My breath came more quickly. "What, baby?" Rodney scampering ahead, I crossed the cemetery. Lassie had nothing on him. "Wait up."

Rodney stopped to peer around a headstone at me, then trotted to the fence separating the churchyard from Duke and Desmond's property. I froze. I knew exactly where Rodney was headed. Dread weighed on me. I plunged ahead, but at a much slower pace.

When I arrived at the old cedar tree at the churchyard's back fence, I closed my eyes and leaned against the heady scent of its bark. Rodney rubbed against my calf and I reluctantly opened my eyes. I saw exactly what I'd feared.

Stretched on the outhouse's grave, toupee askew, was Bruno Gates.

CHAPTER 9

Bruno Gates lay face up on the grave, his eyes half open. A fine layer of mist covered him, beading on his jacket and slickening his forehead. As I stood rooted in place, the toupee slid to the ground. I involuntarily jumped back.

I reached for my phone, but my fingers didn't want to cooperate. Finally, I managed to turn on the voice function and whisper "Sam." The phone dialed.

When he answered, I said, "Duke and Desmond's. It's Bruno Gates." My heart raced and breath came so fast I had to gasp before I could finish my thought. "He's dead. Where the old outhouse was."

I returned the phone to my bag and examined the body. To keep my footprints from contaminating evidence, I remained in the shelter of the cedar tree, but it was hard to see how staying put

would have made much difference. The mud
around Bruno Gates was thoroughly trampled. No
blood. No obvious murder weapon.

I lifted my head as words drifted through the
ether. Did Bruno have a paperback in his pocket?
No, it was one sentence. A note. A note written
with enough emotion to give energy to its message. It spoke to me as faint as a whisper. *Meet me
under the cedar in the churchyard at midnight.*

A chill gripped the base of my skull. Bruno
Gates had been lured to his death. Helen had told
me she'd been wandering Wilfred last night.
Could that have been a cover for her real motive,
to kill Bruno? I couldn't shake the image of the
pain and humiliation on her face as she'd stood in
the café's entrance last night. In a sudden rage,
she might have struck him with a branch or a rock.
I scanned the ground but saw nothing but churned
earth and fallen cedar boughs, with the faint rise
of the root cellar beyond the grave.

Another possibility was that someone believed
Bruno to be Martin Garlington and wanted him
dead before the sun rose. After all, something had
driven Martin from Wilfred all those years ago.

Sam arrived from the back of Duke and Desmond's property. He glanced at Bruno, then circled him to join Rodney and me under the cedar.
He clasped my hands. "The sheriff's office should
be here any minute. In the meantime, tell me what
happened."

I ran through the morning's activities, from visiting Helen Garlington to the detour though the
churchyard and ultimately to finding Bruno Gates's
body just beyond the fence. Reluctantly, I added,

"Helen said she took a long walk last night and she came through here, too." There was no way she'd killed Bruno Gates, but she might have seen something. Or was I wrong about that? Something had certainly transformed her overnight.

By Sam's nod, I knew he would remember everything I said, word for word. "Someone else was here, too," he said. "The grass doesn't show much, but there are footprints all around. Maybe a scuffle. The crime scene investigators will be able to tell us more."

"How did he die?"

Sam shook his head. "I don't want to turn him over until the others arrive, but I don't see anything obvious. We'll know more soon."

An SUV from the sheriff's office appeared at the far end of Duke and Desmond's property, lights flashing, but no siren. Sam went to join them while I stayed under the cedar's tightly knit branches. Rodney rubbed against my leg and looked at me, asking me to pick him up. This was unusual. Normally, he didn't like being restrained when he was outside. I snuggled him against my chest.

While Sam and a colleague inspected the body, another deputy interviewed me. Her badge read Deputy Rosello, and she was all business, from her tidy ponytail to the way she sharply cleared her throat.

I estimated the time I'd found Bruno Gates, as well as when I'd left the library and arrived at and departed from Helen Garlington's house. Rodney purred against my chest.

"And last night?"

I nodded at Sam. "Sam and I had dinner at the café."

Deputy Rosello dropped her hands and glanced at Sam, then back to me, a look of recognition coming over her face. "You're that Josie." The deputy applied herself once again to her notebook. "And after?"

"I hung out with Sam for a few hours, then returned home to my apartment on the library's top floor at about eleven." Surely, she wouldn't want more detail than that.

"Got it." She flipped shut her notebook without looking at me. "You can go now. We'll be in touch if we need you."

I took one last glance at Sam and the deputy surrounding Bruno Gates's body. They were extracting his wallet from his back pocket. Even from where I stood, it was clear the wallet was stuffed with cash. The death wasn't a robbery. A folded note came out with the wallet, the note that had spoken to me. The deputy unfolded it and pointed at something for Sam to see.

Sam turned and nodded at me. I waved and gestured up the hill toward the library. Roz would be furious I was late, but I had a very good excuse.

I'd been right. Roz met me at the library's kitchen entrance, batting her fan at her chest in anger. Sleepless nights were not helping her mood.

"You told me you'd be back before the library opened. I knew you'd be late. I just knew it. How am I supposed to get any writing done if you don't respect my work hours?"

"Bruno Gates is dead." I dropped Rodney, who ambled to his water dish, seemingly forgetting the morning's drama.

"It's all about you, isn't it? If I don't"—her fan hit the floor with a clatter—"What?"

"I'm sorry about the delay. On my way back from Helen's, I found Bruno Gates dead on Reginald-the-stranger's grave."

Roz felt behind her for a chair and sat. "Bruno Gates is dead."

I nodded. Meanwhile, the thought that Helen might be a murderer burned at the forefront of my brain.

"How?"

"I don't know. I didn't see a weapon. No blood, either."

"Strangled?" Roz guessed.

"He could have used a shave, but his neck looked fine. At least, what I could see of it."

Ruth Littlewood wandered into the library's kitchen, her bird-watching binoculars slung around her neck, as usual. "Don't you people ever work? I wanted to talk with you about changing up the birdseed in the feeders for warmer weather, and here you two are, shooting the breeze on the company's dime." She looked at us confidentially. "At least, I wanted to talk to you about the bird feeders in a minute. First, I have a particularly juicy nugget to impart."

Word had already gotten out about Bruno Gates. Astonishing. Wilfred's grapevine made fiber optics look like the pony express with three-legged horses.

Mrs. Littlewood beamed at us in triumph. "You won't believe it, but Helen Garlington is getting a new hairdo." When we didn't respond, she added, "How do you like them apples? I had it straight from Patty who got it from Darla who got it from the Beauty Palace when they called in their lunch order." She shook her head in amazement. "I guess all that sherry went to her head."

"Bruno Gates is dead," Roz said.

Mrs. Littlewood spun toward her. "Come again?"

"It's true," I added. "The sheriff's department is at Duke and Desmond's even as we speak."

Mrs. Littlewood's jaw dropped in shock. "The would-be Martin Garlington is dead." She snapped her mouth closed and zipped up her jacket. "I've got to get down to the café. See you two later."

To calm my spinning head, I headed for interior design, a quiet corner of the library upstairs. While I reshelved and dusted, the books might calm me with visions of drawing rooms in English manor houses and soothing chatter about waxed mahogany and collections of Clarice Cliff teapots. Roz could take care of patrons downstairs.

Someone was in the armchair in garden design on the other side of the room. I rounded the rows of shelves to see if the patron needed anything and was surprised to find Lyndon with a picture book of Gertrude Jekyll–designed gardens in his lap and a forlorn expression on his face.

"Lyndon," I said. "I thought you'd be in the garden. Weren't you talking about mulching the roses?"

"Yep." Lyndon wasn't much of a talker, but his eyes were expressive enough to communicate whole conversations, and this conversation wasn't upbeat.

Gardening was his passion, and I suspected he'd come to this corner of the library for the same reason I had: distraction.

I leaned against the shelf near him. A book on climbing plants whispered the glories of the Armand clematis growing through a climbing rose. I could practically smell a warm lawn and hear the buzzing of bees.

"What's wrong?" I asked him.

He stared resolutely forward. "It's Roz."

I waited for him to expand on this. It was hard to believe he'd given me the creeps when I first met him. At first glance, Lyndon might have been an Oregon-style extra for *The Munsters*. Once I got to know him, I realized his lanky build and solemn expression enveloped a softhearted vegan who loved babies and gardening. And for decades, he had adored Roz from afar while she'd harbored a secret love for him. Now they were married.

"I can't live in that trailer," he finally said.

I sat on the windowsill and faced him. Behind me, a gentle rain pattered on glass. "Too small for the both of you?"

"It's not that. I don't need a lot of space. After all, I've lived in the caretaker's cottage for years. No, it's the garden. There's no room at the Magnolia for growing things."

"You have all the land around the library to garden, if you want," I pointed out.

He looked at his hands. "That's what Roz says, too, and that's fine while I'm living in the caretaker's cottage. But it's no good if I'm way down at the trailer park. There are no trees to prune. No compost pile." He moved the book from his lap to the table. "Plus, Roz needs space to write. She was writing at the kitchen table last night, but I needed to repot a Cymbidium suave, and between the orchid bark and all that paper . . ."

The expression on his face told me all I needed to know. "Not easy."

"No. Roz says she already owns her home, and that we have to think of our future."

This might have been the most I'd ever heard Lyndon say at one time. "And your cottage is out, I suppose."

The cottage truly was too small for two people. No one except Lyndon—and now Roz—had been in it for years, and its contents were much speculated about. Roz refused to talk. Lyndon lived there, so it had to contain at least a bed, and a long one at that. It also had some sort of kitchen, since in warm weather he was often found under the apricot tree with a bowl of some fragrant grain and bean entrée. A chimney anchored one side of the cottage, so I factored in a fireplace. Beyond that was anyone's guess.

"Hmm," was his only response, and then, "Have you seen a lot of crows around recently? Ruth Littlewood says they're acting out of character."

"Don't change the subject. There's no question of buying a new place? Or maybe building something? Roz's latest novel has done well." *The Whippoorwill Cries Love* had leapt to the top of the bestseller lists and was even set to be released as a movie.

"She won't budge. Says financial security comes first, and the life of an author is too unpredictable to take on a mortgage."

"Maybe we should look at your salary," I said, searching for any solution. "When was the last time you had a raise?"

"I'm getting a fair wage, plus lifetime use of the cottage. I can't complain." He raised his eyes to mine. "Anyway, you're kind to care, but this isn't your problem."

It was my problem if Roz was going to be bearable to work with, I thought. A voice at the door interrupted us.

"Josie. There you are."

I turned to see a stranger—yet, not a stranger. Standing in the doorway was an older woman with a glossy pink mouth and a golden sheen to the new bob in her white hair. She wore a smart floral tunic and a long, beaded necklace over trim jeans. My eyes widened. Could it be?

"Morning, Helen," Lyndon said.

Helen Garlington had officially moved on. "Helen," I said once I'd recovered my voice. "You look terrific."

"Never mind that. What's this about Bruno Gates?"

If Helen were the killer, she was a good actress.

Like a grizzled spider, Lyndon unfolded himself from the armchair. "I'd best be getting back to work. Those roses won't mulch themselves. Thank you for the talk, Josie." He tipped an imaginary cap at Helen Garlington and disappeared through the doorway. The book he'd left behind sighed at his departure.

"Josie, I need your help," Helen said. "Come to the music room and we'll talk. I do my best thinking there."

It seemed my day would be spent as a librarian-therapist. I followed Helen to the music room down the hall and took a seat on the organ's bench. Helen moved some sheet music from a chair and settled herself in.

"I understand you found Bruno Gates expired on the outhouse's grave."

It was disorienting to sit with this new Helen Garlington. Her trip to the Beauty Palace had transformed her almost completely. Earrings swayed under her bob. She even seemed to have adopted a new matter-of-fact tone of voice.

To her curt nods, I filled her in on what I knew of Bruno Gates's fate. Watching Helen's sharp attention and her murmuring of "oh my" and "poor man," I became convinced she couldn't have killed him. No matter how disappointed she'd been to discover Bruno Gates wasn't her husband, and even though she admitted to wandering town last night, there was simply no way this kind-hearted woman could have murdered someone. The thing was, would the sheriff's department believe so?

"Helen, you know you'll be a suspect."

Her gaze was steady. "I expect they've already stopped by the house. Of course, I was at the Beauty Palace."

"Once they learn you were out last night . . ."

Helen reached for a notebook in her bag—this was new, too, I noted. I expected her to make notes for a tragic poem, but she had other plans.

"I'll list our assignments." She scrawled something in the notebook.

"Assignments? What do you mean?"

"None of this would have happened had I not lost my head and thought I saw Martin on TV," she said. "This fellow Bruno Gates would not have come to Wilfred and consequently would not have died. He'd still be tending corpses and flirting with the ladies. Besides that, locating the real killer is the best way to clear my name."

Apparently nothing had escaped her. "What does this have to do with me?"

She looked up in surprise. "You're going to help me find the murderer, aren't you?"

"Me?" I asked. "Why me?"

Helen looked at me as if I were a kindergartner and she were the teacher tasked with explaining how to tie my shoes. Her eyebrows, once a white that had blended with her skin, were now golden brown and added emphasis to her words. "You're the one sleeping with the sheriff."

Warmth spread over my face and I knew I'd probably turned the color of Helen's new pink manicure. Coupled with that, my birthmark tingled.

"It's not like you haven't done this before," she added. "You will help me, won't you?"

If it weren't for me and my accidental burst of magic flipping the television stations, Helen would have never seen Bruno Gates and mistaken him for her husband. More than that, Bruno Gates would still be alive. I reluctantly said, "We can talk about it."

"Excellent. We'll meet tomorrow at my place before the library opens, and you'll tell me what you've learned." She reached for her purse and picked up a fat red book instead. "What's this doing in the music room?"

It was *The Complete Original Illustrated Sherlock Holmes*. Again. "I'll put it back."

"Fine." With that, she smiled brightly, and sporting all of the old Mrs. Garlington's dignity with a new, youthful vibe, she nodded once and left.

CHAPTER 10

That night at Big House, Sam cracked open the kitchen window to let in a warm, moist breeze. He pulled me next to him so I could rest my head on his chest. As spring deepened, days grew longer. A dusky sunset settled in the distance. Mother Earth kept turning and time rolled on for its inhabitants.

Except Bruno Gates.

I returned to the chopping board where Sam had set me up with a knife and a pile of herbs. Rodney had jumped into the playpen with Nicky and curled up on his blanket for a nap. Meanwhile, Nicky carefully stacked wooden blocks around him, occasionally tossing off a "no" to no one in particular.

"Isn't this great?" Sam said. "To some people it might seem banal—two people cooking dinner together—but to me it feels right. There's nowhere

I'd rather be." His gaze worked on me like alchemy, transforming everyday cares into a powerful emotional rush.

"You've had domestic bliss before." I tried to put a laugh into my voice, but I was intent on his response.

He shook his head. "Life with Fiona was chaotic. This is what I always wanted. You, Nicky, and a rich, happy life where the little things are the most important. Could it get any better?"

Not to me it couldn't. I'd rather cook dinner with Sam than dine at the top of the Eiffel Tower with Cary Grant. Threatening my happy cloud was the fact that I only appeared normal.

When my two sisters and I were kids, we were fascinated by reruns of the television show *Bewitched*. We didn't know yet about the magic in our bloodline, but the show's star, the witch Samantha, pulled us like a magnet and one by one we'd drop whatever we were doing and land, riveted, in front of the television screen. In the series, Samantha's husband forbade her from using her magic. We'd all agreed Samantha was a chump for signing on to that.

No one could persuade me to cap my magic. No one—not even Sam, who I loved with a dizzying steadfastness. Besides, I wasn't sure I could stem my power even if I wanted to. For the moment, I let myself enjoy my feelings, but sooner or later the bill would come due. Sam would have to know about my abilities, and he would have to accept them. Or . . . I didn't want to think about the alternative.

I changed the subject. "Have you learned anything more about Bruno?" I worked to keep my tone neutral.

I hadn't fooled Sam. From the stove, where he turned on the burner under a pot of water, he gave me side-eye. "You aren't thinking of getting involved, are you?"

"Why should I?" I said lightly and focused on the chives.

"Because you had a hand in bringing him here. Because you care about Helen Garlington." He put a lid on the pot. "Because you can't help it."

"Ha-ha." I really tried to make it sound like I thought he was funny.

He drummed his fingers on the counter a moment. "Since you asked, yes, there has been a development. A big one, in fact."

I set down the knife and gave him my full attention. Either Sam was going to lay a joke on me, or he had something important to say. It had better not be the joke.

"Bruno Gates wasn't Bruno Gates at all. He was someone named Larry Sutton."

As in a cartoon, my mouth dropped open. "What?"

Sam shook his head. "I know. Not only was he not Martin Garlington, he wasn't even Bruno Gates."

"Are you sure?"

Sam turned to the stove. "His driver's license checks out, as does the registration in his car. We're following up from there."

I was too stunned to reply. Bruno Gates wasn't Bruno Gates?

"I'm serious about you stepping back, Josie." He dried his hands and tossed the dish towel aside. "If it turns out Larry Sutton was murdered, Helen will be at the top of the list of suspects. She's already admitted to being in the churchyard that night. From there it's two steps through the fence to where he died."

"I talked with her this afternoon. It's impossible. You don't really think—"

"I don't think anything. It's all about the evidence."

Last night Helen Garlington had seemed to break with her past at last. Something had motivated a hard turn, but I'd attributed it to her recent flare of mourning and the shock of meeting Bruno Gates. It was as if she had to scrape the last bits of grief from her emotional bucket, and she'd finally been ready to toss it aside and move on. Surely, murdering Bruno Gates-slash-Larry Sutton hadn't been the catalyst.

Then there was the question of how Bruno/Larry died. He wasn't obviously murdered, yet someone had drawn him to the gravesite. Suicide seemed unlikely, too, unless he'd taken an overdose. The medical examiner would test his blood for routine drugs. Still, a man so depressed that he'd poison himself and lie down to die on a stranger's grave wasn't generally known for hijinks and fanny-pinching mere hours before.

No, what seemed more likely was that someone killed Bruno/Larry, thinking he was Martin Garlington. Which led back to the original question of why Helen Garlington's husband left Wilfred in the first place. What reason would be so powerful as to drive Martin away and keep him there? Not only that, but to reawaken a killer who'd been sleeping for almost half a century?

"Any cause of death yet?" I asked.

"The medical examiner's working on it."

"What about that wad of cash in his pocket? And the note asking him to meet?" Shoot. I wasn't supposed to know about that.

Sam swiveled to face me head-on. "The cash, I get that. You saw his wallet. Maybe you even saw the note. But you couldn't have seen what it said. You didn't go through his pockets before we arrived, did you?" Sam smiled. Not happy.

"Of course not. I called you and backed off. Didn't you tell me about the note? Someone did." I hated lying to him. I needed to come clean. Just not tonight.

His relaxed. "Now you're going to ask me who Larry Sutton is."

"You bet I am, unless you tell me first." I could see a game show contestant giving a fake name to protect his identity. However, the funeral home in Pacific Grove knew Bruno Gates. Supposedly it was Bruno Gates I'd talked to last week. As I pondered this, I piled the chives next to the chopped basil and parsley and took a seat at the kitchen table.

In the playpen, Rodney had awakened and knocked over a wall of blocks. He leapt out, to Nicky's mournful "No."

"It's interesting, actually," Sam said.

"Yes?"

"I never would have guessed."

I stood and wrapped my arms around him.

Nice, long Sam, warm and smelling so good. "Stop torturing me."

He slipped fingers through my hair. "Why would I torture you?"

I forced myself to pull away. "Who is Larry Sutton?"

Sam laughed. "An undertaker. He worked with Bruno Gates. According to Bruno, Larry had begged him to let him come to Wilfred in his place. He thought it would be a hoot to look around, pacify an old woman."

Strange as it sounded, I could see that. Larry seemed like a practical joker. More than that, he'd been almost reckless last night. Then another thought came to mind.

Before I could express it, Sam said, "I know what you're thinking. You're wondering if Bruno Gates really is Martin Garlington, and he sent Larry so he wouldn't be found out."

"Exactly." Sam was a mind reader.

"The answer is no. Bruno Gates showed local police his ID and it checks out. Bruno Gates is an innocent game show contestant who, by total coincidence, appeared on TV at the same moment, seven hundred miles north, a grief-addled Helen Garlington looked up."

While Sam added pasta to the water, now boiling, I took it all in. Helen Garlington sees her presumed-dead husband on TV. She meets him and he turns out to be someone else. Then, he's found dead. Then another twist: that someone else is identified as yet a third person, another stranger.

Sure, it could be a series of unfortunate coincidences. Thing was, I didn't believe in coincidences.

* * *

That night, rain pattered gently on my bedroom windows. I lit a beeswax candle and set it in a saucer on my dresser. Rodney, purring, leapt to the bed to settle on the quilt. Tonight, I was drawn to pull a lesson. The urge often came over me when life thickened with trouble, and trouble had certainly descended on Wilfred.

Now I would listen to my grandmother's words.

It had been only a year and a half since I'd come into my magic. My grandmother had known I was a witch, and a powerful one at that, but my mother had coerced her into tying my magic with a spell—a spell that had shattered when I'd arrived in Wilfred. Somehow, she'd foreseen that I'd need guidance and that she would no longer be alive to provide it. So, over the years she'd written magic lessons for me, each sealed in an envelope and piled into a green chest. She'd also left me her grimoire, full of spells, potions, and rituals that thrilled and terrified me.

I pulled the chest from under the bed and dove my hands into the envelopes. Even though I'd pulled perhaps a dozen lessons since the chest had arrived, they seemed to repopulate by themselves. I let my fingers slip among the cool paper until one envelope felt hot and was drawn into my fingers. This was it. This was tonight's lesson.

"Ready, Rodney?" I sat on the bed and pulled the quilt over my lap. He instantly settled next to me, purring to rival a lawn mower. I clicked on the bedside lamp. Usually, a book or two I was meant to read would be casually stacked on my nightstand. Tonight its surface was bare. Tonight was all about the lesson.

I slipped a paper knife under the envelope's flap. As I unfolded the letter, my grandmother's voice materialized in my mind. I felt her love and smelled the dried herbs and settling jars of berry jam that often filled her kitchen.

> *Dear Josie,*
>
> *This evening I'm prompted to write to you about courage. Honey, you're a truth teller. Even now, it's apparent that injustice cuts you almost physically. You'll need courage to pursue this way of life.*
>
> *In short, courage is the ability to do something right despite the mental, emotional, or physical costs. However, courage, when it's warranted, helps you achieve something more important than whatever you risk.*
>
> *The opposite of courage is cowardice. Cowardice might masquerade as courage, but it is fear, pure and simple. Fear persuades us to believe what we want to believe, including that we are courageous. Does this sound confusing? Let me illustrate with a few examples.*
>
> *We'll start with something small. For years, Barb Glickman had pain in her hip. She ignored our pleas to visit the doctor. She said she needed to save the money for her son's education, and that the pain wasn't that bad, anyway. She bore her pain like courage. Truth is, she was afraid of the doctor. What she paraded as courage was the need to protect herself from her own fear. By the time she finally went, she needed a hip replacement, when,*

earlier, physical therapy might have saved her an operation.

Here's a more tragic example: I'm sure you remember Edwin Fletcher, the mechanic. After years of talking to him, trying to get him to curb his drinking, his wife planned to leave him. Edwin couldn't bear to face his own demons, and in a show of what he touted as courage—after all, how dare his wife leave him?—he burned down his own house so she'd gain nothing in their divorce. He didn't know she was inside. Edwin's fear had devolved to desperation, a desperation he masked as strength. Not a month later, he died with a bottle in his hand.

Courage is neither knee-jerk instinct nor the powerful reaction to fear. It's a considered response. It's the ability to overcome fear to do what is right, even if it feels like a dive off a cliff into the ocean when you've only ever paddled in the shallows.

Courage is built every day through learning and good intention. As you become wiser, you build courage's reserves. I can't give you answers, but I can provide questions that may help you find your own answers. When facing a situation where it seems there is no painless action, look at the alternatives and ask yourself, Who is hurt? What is it I fear? Can I live with the outcome? Take note that inaction is action. Courage engenders courage.

I don't know, dear Josie, what situation has brought you to this lesson, but chances are it's something that will have a long and deep effect on

*your life. Perhaps it seems you have no good
options. This may be true. But you likely have a
right option. I hope you will have the courage to
pursue it.*

*All my love,
Grandma*

I held the letter against my chest. Where did I
need courage now—or, where would I need it
soon? I didn't yet know what Helen's and my investigation into Larry Sutton's death would bring.
But there was one area of my life where fear bound
me, and that was with Sam. I was holding a huge
secret from him, and I was a coward.

CHAPTER 11

This time when I went to visit Helen Garlington, I left Rodney at home so he wouldn't destroy the curtains. I needn't have worried. Helen's curtains were gone and morning sun streamed through the windows. The smell of something warm and yeasty wafted from the dining room, where Derwin, Helen's son and Wilfred's postman, pushed a fork through a trail of maple syrup.

"Would you like a waffle?" Helen asked. She wore a zip-up floral housedress I'd seen her in before, but her new bob and soft lipstick brought it up to date.

"No, thanks," I said.

"I'd better be going." Derwin followed the words with a swallow of milk and pushed back from the table. He was in his full postal uniform, complete with a rain hat already pulled over his mop of hair.

Although I'd seen Derwin hundreds of times as he delivered mail, I didn't know him well. He was well into his forties, single, and took most of his meals with his mother. Something about his cluelessness appealed to the ladies, because word was he had no shortage of girlfriends on his mail route.

"Honey, your shirt is untucked on the side." Helen watched her son straighten his postal uniform. "That's better."

We waved him goodbye.

Before the mail van had even started up outside, Helen turned to me. "Did you get anything out of Sam?"

Helen 2.0's life apparently included a mass sorting of books and tchotchkes, leaving almost enough room to settle in the living room now, had we wanted. The music books stacked here and there murmured Gregorian chants. I knew how a dog felt, being able to hear things others never suspected.

"I did. You'll want to sit for this." I pulled out a chair and told her about Bruno Gates's real identity as Larry Sutton. "The sheriff's office up here got in touch with the Pacific Grove police, and they say Larry Sutton was one of Bruno Gates's coworkers."

Digesting this news, Helen took Derwin's place at the table. Even her movements seemed to have loosened since she had broken free of Martin. "Sam is sure? Maybe the real Bruno Gates is my Martin."

"They're satisfied. They checked ID."

"It's not impossible to fake a driver's license." At

my raised eyebrow, she shook her head. "I know. It's the habit of decades of hoping Martin would return, all the while fearing he never would. I couldn't help but believe my feelings were some kind of special knowledge. That Martin and I had a psychic bond. Ridiculous, isn't it?"

"Not ridiculous," I said. If only she knew about my magic. I'd learned the world was full of energy we sensed but dismissed. This energy was too often masked by fear, habit, and yes, hope.

"Bruno Gates is someone named Larry Sutton. When will this craziness end? I was so sure he was Martin . . ." Helen pulled her gaze from the window to me and said with resolution, "That's all in the past. I'm free now. Or, I will be once we figure out who killed poor Bruno or Larry or whatever his name is. I feel responsible. If I hadn't assumed he was Martin . . ."

"We're guessing that's why Larry Sutton was killed. We don't know it. We don't even know yet how he died."

"Why else would he have been killed? Something dire drove Martin from Wilfred and kept him away. Whatever it was hasn't lost its power. It's still a threat."

"Bruno-slash-Larry might have had his own enemies." Even as I said the words, I didn't believe them. Sure, Larry Sutton was a womanizer, but from what I'd seen, not all that successful at it, and it was hard to imagine a scorned woman flying to Oregon, hunting him down, and killing him through some as-of-now undetectable means. She could have knocked him off more conveniently at home.

"It's about Martin. I'm sure of it." Helen rose. "I have his journals. They might have some clues about why he left."

I sat up straighter. "Martin kept journals? Written by hand?"

"Yes." Helen raised an eyebrow at my obvious excitement. "They won't be particularly thrilling to the outsider. Mostly notes about his work. And butterflies."

Even after so many years, Martin's energy might linger. "Let's see them."

She went upstairs and returned with a small suitcase. From it she lifted four spiral notebooks. "You're welcome to read through them to see if I missed anything that hints at why he left."

The moment my fingers rested on the top notebook, I knew little of Martin was left in its pages. Most of what I felt was Helen. She'd clearly read these journals many times, and her grief was as palpable as Martin's tiny, precise handwriting.

"Could I take them home and look through them there? Maybe there's something you missed. Something small that could point us in some direction."

"You may. Keep them tidy, please. They're all Derwin has left of his father."

"I will." I chose my next words carefully. "Has the sheriff's office been in touch with you? About the night Larry Sutton died?"

"Of course." Helen shrugged.

"You're not—you're not concerned they'll take you in?"

"Why should I be? I didn't kill anyone. Now,

let's get down to business. Besides the journals, what can I tell you about Martin that will help solve this mystery?"

Helen's blithe lack of concern about her status as a murder suspect worried me, but since it didn't bother her, I didn't see any reason to stir the pot. "Tell me about the day he left. Was there anything unusual about it?"

"You mean other than the fact that the love of my life vanished for good? Not really." She sat back as if she'd told this story many times before. "It was August eighteenth, 1974, a Saturday. Martin went into work. They were shorthanded at the funeral home, and Esther Hinkle had to be laid out that afternoon. Martin never came home." Her gaze took a faraway look and she absently traced a paisley on her tablecloth with a freshly manicured finger.

"What did the others at the funeral home tell you?"

"That he'd prepared Mrs. Hinkle—apparently there was some dispute about a lip color, although I'm sure Martin chose something tasteful; he was good at that—and he left midday, saying he was coming home for lunch."

"He had his car?"

"A '68 Datsun. It was found parked on the street in Gaston with the keys still in the ignition. I drove that car another ten years."

"He hadn't taken anything with him?"

She shook her head. "I've been over this a thousand times. He kissed me goodbye that morning the same way he did every morning. No special look, no special words. Nothing. Except . . ."

"Except what?"

The morning sun now splashed over the breakfast table, drawing out the crinkles on the back of one of Helen's pink and white hands. "Except a call around noon. The phone rang, but when I answered, no one was there. I said 'hello' a few times and hung up. I was getting a tuna casserole ready for Martin's lunch, so I didn't think anything of it until later."

"When did you realize he was gone?"

Helen slumped in her chair. Her grief had left a stubborn residue. "I called the funeral home that afternoon, and they said he'd left a few hours earlier. This was all long before cell phones, you know." She looked up to be sure I could imagine a world before the internet. "I called everyone I could think of to see if they'd seen him. No one had. That night the sheriff found his car." Her eyes reddened. "The next week, I discovered I was pregnant with Derwin."

For all her seeming delicacy, Helen Garlington was strong. My respect for her rocketed. "I'm so sorry."

"It was a long time ago, honey."

The mantel clock ticked and birds chirped from the crab apple tree in the front yard. Helen rose to open the front door to let the cool spring air wash through the screen door.

"Tell me about Martin," I said. "What was he like?"

"Oh, honey." She returned to the table. "He wasn't every woman's idea of a dreamboat, but I loved him."

I knew how crazy love could be. Even the thought

of Sam's prematurely receding hairline sent tingles through me.

"He was tall with thick black hair. Like Derwin's. That was part of what tricked me into thinking the fellow from the game show was Martin. His hair would have been white by now."

Larry Sutton's white hair had been a toupee. I remembered how it slid off his scalp and lay by his head like a dozing ferret. "What was he like as a person?"

"Martin was a thinker. He loved being an undertaker because there was so much to study. He could get obsessive when he was digging into a subject. And he was an awful coward." The thought made her crack a smile.

Last night's magic lesson leapt to mind. "What do you mean?"

"He could think his way around anything, but if it meant confrontation, forget it. Martin didn't have the moxie." She grinned. "Why, as crazy as he was about me—there was no doubting it—I had to ask him to marry me. 'If you asked me to marry you, Martin,' I told him, 'I'd say yes.'" Her face fell. "I'd never choose that again. Don't marry a coward, Josie. It's the one lesson I instilled in Derwin. Be brave. Have the courage of your convictions."

"You think it was cowardice that kept Martin away?"

"Almost certainly. He sent money for a few years and it was helpful as I was building my music lesson clientele. I could never trace where it came from. It appeared in my bank account, and that's all I knew. Then the money stopped. I assumed he'd died. What else could I think?"

"How did you meet?"

As Helen's thoughts dipped into the past, she visibly relaxed. "We'd known each other our whole lives and I was always certain Martin was for me, but it took him a few years to recognize it. In high school, he was sweet on Lindy Everhardt. She was Lindy Renton then and a few years ahead of him. Didn't matter. All the boys were crazy about her."

"She's a beautiful woman," I said.

Helen nodded. "Lindy was out of Martin's league, but she encouraged him, let him bring her little presents."

"That didn't bother you?"

Helen lifted her gaze to mine. Her eyes were the pale blue of a winter sky. "No, dear. Why would it? She was an infatuation, an 'other.' I was Martin's soulmate. I knew he'd understand that eventually and I was right."

Martin Garlington had become legend in Wilfred, and I'd never stopped to consider that he was a real man and not simply another one of the town's many stories. He'd mattered. "You say he was obsessive. Was there anything that obsessed him around the time he disappeared?"

She waved her hand in a dismissive motion. "Sure, but nothing that might have become a threat. At that point, he loved butterflies. Could talk about them for hours." She nodded toward the box of journals. "You'll find drawings."

Patty had mentioned Martin Garlington's butterfly hunting outings. It was hard to link insects to murder, but perhaps it was Martin's wanderings that were important and not why he wandered. It was a thin lead, but it was all I had.

"Until the sheriff's office sorts things out, it would be better if you lie low. In the meantime, I'll see what I can find out about Larry Sutton's death."

"Thank you, Josie. I'm so grateful." Helen pushed the suitcase holding Martin's journals toward me. "Here are Martin's notes. Take them. Maybe you'll see something I missed."

CHAPTER 12

I set the suitcase with Martin's journals next to the circulation desk and hurried through the library, pulling curtains open and flipping on lights to ready it for opening. The book return box was empty except for the collection of *Miss Marple* DVDs Darla's husband Montgomery had checked out. Roz was already in the conservatory at work on her novel.

"Should we make a fire today?" I looked toward the tile stove. This morning, sun through the conservatory's green glass walls warmed the room enough that Rodney lay, belly up, in a splash of light near Roz's desk. His birthmark—a match to the one on my shoulder—showed where his belly fur was thin. He blinked lazily at me.

"With my hot flashes?" Roz replied without lifting her fingers from the keyboard. "No thank you."

I paused at the atrium's entrance. "I bet you'll

be glad when you and Lyndon find a home and you can have your own writing space there."

Her fingers froze. She swiveled toward me. "What did you say?" I started to reply, but she cut me off. "Have you been talking to Lyndon?"

I adored Roz, I really did, but sometimes her crankiness got on my nerves. "The question is, Have *you* been talking to Lyndon?"

"Lyndon's and my life is none of your business," she shouted after me.

My next stop was the kitchen. This time of day, Wilfredians generally eschewed the front door in favor of the kitchen entrance, where they could stop for a cup of coffee. Buffy and Thor were already here, Thor sitting at the table looking at a comic book and Buffy standing on a chair, scooping coffee into the coffeepot. My presence hadn't disturbed Thor, who quietly turned a page. The comic book murmured, *Adventures of King Arthur's Court*, with an accompanying soundtrack of whinnying horses and clanging swords. Thor's eye patch—purely ornamental, along with his cape—was flipped up.

"What are you doing on the chair?" I asked Buffy. "How come you two aren't in school?"

"Duh," Thor said without looking up. "It's Saturday."

"I'm helping with library chores," Buffy said. The glitter on her T-shirt's unicorn sparkled as she pushed the now-familiar red volume of *The Complete Original Illustrated Sherlock Holmes* toward me. "Somebody left this here. For a small fee, I might be able to return it, plus do other tasks. Say, brush Rodney?"

I had an idea. "Do you really want to earn some money? Say, big money—maybe as much as twenty dollars?" I paused for dramatic effect. "Each?"

This got their attention. Thor even dropped his comic book. "Speak, milady."

"Find somewhere for Roz and Lyndon to live together. Roz's trailer doesn't have a garden and Lyndon's cottage is too small. They need a home big enough for both of them, with a garden and a study. One that's affordable. Preferably, somewhere they can move right away."

"Roz has been grouchy lately," Thor said. "Grouchier than normal."

"Exactly. She and Lyndon need a home. You can help them find one. You'd be doing a public service."

Buffy shoved the coffee scoop back into the bag of grounds and scrambled down from the chair. "Board meeting," she told Thor.

Satisfied, I returned to circulation and spread out Martin's sketchbooks and journals. By lunchtime, between helping one patron collect information about raising guinea pigs and another complete her Brontë sisters reading, I knew Martin had indeed been a butterfly afficionado. In his sketchbook, he'd dated his outings with the butterfly net and listed the species he'd seen, along with drawings in colored pencil. The cold, wet months had scant entries, except for a moth caught at the screen door. As winter turned to spring, drawings filled the pages, including an Echo Azure butterfly with blue wings rimmed in white, a Western Tiger Swallowtail with its cello-shaped wings, and a vivid yellow Orange Sulphur. He almost made a butterfly convert out of me, too. I wondered what Sam would say to an afternoon of butterfly hunting when the weather turned warm.

From these pages, I determined that Martin was detail-oriented and had a good eye, but there was nothing to hint at why he'd left town. I turned to his journals. After five minutes of flipping through them, I had to admit Helen had been right. There was nothing here, either, to point to why Martin had left Wilfred. He'd kept copious notes on makeup colors for clients—he favored a taupe eyeshadow for gray-haired customers, I discovered— and experimented with drawings for hairstyles for the departed, with a special emphasis on framing the face—but hadn't noted much else.

I swiveled to return the notebooks to the suitcase and found Rodney napping in it. "Get up, lazybones. I need to put these away."

Rodney stretched, his back rising like a camel's, before blinking at me sleepily. Although he now stood—progress—he refused to budge.

"Get out, kitty," I told him, and he twisted in a circle in preparation to lie down again. "Don't say I didn't warn you." I tipped the case and Rodney with it, to the floor. A claw from a hind leg stuck in the lining, and when he yanked it free, I heard fabric rip. Unconcerned, Rodney moseyed toward the atrium, probably on his way to his food dish.

I swore under my breath. Helen Garlington had entrusted me with one of her few links with her husband, and now I had to tell her I'd wrecked it? Maybe I could repair the tear. I pulled the suitcase closer and rustlings of words—timetables, descriptions—flowed by. I glanced at the circulation desk.

Martin's sketchbooks and journals were silent. The words hadn't come from nearby new releases, either. Something was hidden in the case, something written. I poked around the empty suitcase's interior. Could papers be hidden in the lining?

Heart beating faster, I fumbled in the desk drawer for a paper knife. Gently, I widened the slit Rodney had started and slipped my hand beneath the lining. Inside were several sheets of lined notebook paper covered in black-inked notes. I eased them from the lining and spread half a dozen pages on the desk.

The papers were a log of someone's comings and goings, laid out in a meticulously drawn table. Dates spanning a month and a half ran down the pages. Across the top were columns labeled *location* and *notes*. Martin was tracking someone's movements in the summer of 1974. This part of the log appeared reconstructed, as if he had decided the dates would be valuable so had gone back to fill them in. At certain points, he attributed certain information. *According to the grocer*, was one such note. I scanned the pages before returning to the log's beginning. Nowhere did Martin list a name.

After half an hour's perusal, I saw a pattern emerge. Martin was keeping tabs on someone who lived on the Holloways' land—the same land Duke and Desmond now owned. Martin was especially interested in the stranger's forays out of town and on mysterious nighttime appointments. I closed my eyes and pictured the view from Helen Garlington's back stoop. Could Martin have seen the Holloway property from there? Certainly not now. Helen's house was a block away and the hedge was too tall. Of course, fifty years ago there may not have been a hedge.

After examining the log, I was certain the unnamed man was Lindy's ex-husband, Frank Holloway, the Empress's robber. The question was, Had this led to Martin fleeing town, and why? Naturally, my thoughts drifted to the bones Duke and Desmond had found. When did Frank Holloway go to prison? Somewhere here was a link. I was sure of it. But, what?

At my elbow, my cell phone rang and Sam's name flashed on its screen. I eagerly answered.

"I have some news for you about Larry Sutton," he said.

"Wait. You want to give me information about the case?"

He laughed and imagining the accompanying frown warmed me. "This time, yes. Brand new information, fresh from the medical examiner's office. You're the first to know."

"Just a moment. Don't go away," I told him. "I'm going to put you on hold for a second."

A mom trailing two kids came in with a stack of picture books. I checked them out as quickly as I could and waved goodbye with one hand while picking up the phone with the other.

"Sam?"

"I'm still here."

I clutched the phone closer. "Well, what is it? What news do you have?"

"It's about the cause of death. You remember how we couldn't find a murder weapon?"

Of course I remembered. "The medical examiner was going to do a toxicology screen to check for poison. Plus, the autopsy."

"Results are in. You'll never guess."

"You're toying with me," I said. "Tell me. What killed him?"

"Natural causes," he said.

I took a second to digest this. "I'm sorry, I didn't hear you. I thought you said natural causes."

"I did. Larry Sutton had a pulmonary embolism. We confirmed everything with his physician in California. He had high blood pressure and had just been diagnosed with a tumor on his kidney. Even the next morning, his blood alcohol was through the roof. All of this combined with the drive to Wilfred was too much for him."

Larry Sutton hadn't been murdered? This had nothing to do with Martin Garlington or Frank Holloway? The shock froze my tongue.

"Josie? I thought you'd be happy. There's no homicide. Helen Garlington is off the list of suspects."

"Then why was he at Duke and Desmond's property in the middle of the night?"

"Remember, he had a note in his coat pocket asking to meet there. Before you ask, it wasn't signed."

"I wonder why?" And did the person ever meet up with him?

"Who knows? Maybe he made a friend at the tavern. Maybe the note was old and had nothing to do with it at all, and he simply needed an out-of-the-way corner to relieve himself. In any case, it doesn't matter. He died naturally. Case closed. We're sending his body home."

Larry Sutton had gone to the churchyard in the middle of the night and collapsed on the symbolic grave of a stranger. He wasn't murdered—or so the sheriff's office had determined.

I didn't believe it.

Saturday afternoons Helen Garlington gave organ lessons. They were notably noisy hours at the library, so I scheduled children's story time for the same time. The parents who dropped off their kids didn't seem to mind the vibrato scales coming from upstairs. They passed the hour in the library's kitchen, drank coffee, and swapped tips about potty training.

Usually, I spent this time in my office with the door closed, going over paperwork. Sundays and Mondays were my days off, and I liked to make sure I was caught up as the week ended. Today, however, I was waiting in the music room when Helen arrived. Thanks to people stopping her on the way up to congratulate her on her new look, she arrived a few minutes late. Fortunately, her student was even later.

"Helen," I said as soon as she entered the music room. "Sam called. He said the sheriff has ruled out homicide. Larry Sutton died of natural causes, a pulmonary embolism. He wasn't killed at all. They're dropping the case."

"Oh my." Helen set down her purse—a new, lemon-yellow bag, but as capacious as her old one—and mechanically set out the morning's exercises. "Is he certain?"

"He is. But I'm not." I produced Martin's document case. "I found a secret compartment where Martin kept a log of comings and goings in Wilfred. I think he was tracking Frank Holloway."

Helen Garlington's former look of grief and befuddlement flashed across her face. Then her confidence returned. "You found something new of Martin's?"

I laid the papers on the organ's bench. "Just a few sheets of paper. I discovered them by accident. Rodney," I added, as if it would explain everything.

Helen held the pages and examined the tiny, precise handwriting. "They're Martin's, all right." She looked up at me. "What do they mean?"

I scooted forward on my chair. "From what I can tell, he was interested in someone staying at the old Holloway place. Duke and Desmond's."

"Where the bones were found."

"Exactly." I leaned back again. "My thought is he was tracking Frank Holloway. Could he have seen something he wasn't supposed to?"

She shook her head. "Frank was in jail. Besides, if he'd seen anything unlawful, Martin would have reported it to the police. That's how he was."

I was happy to note she used the past tense when she spoke of him. "What if the person Martin was keeping notes about threatened him or even threatened to hurt you? You said Martin wasn't known for his bravery. Maybe it scared him away."

The voices of children arriving drifted up from downstairs. Cherie, our volunteer for the day, would herd them into Old Man Thurston's office, now children's literature.

"He might not have been a superhero, but he had integrity. I tell you, if he'd seen something criminal, he would have told someone. He certainly wouldn't have left me in harm's way."

Helen may have finally moved on from Martin, but she lionized him all the same. "Fine. What about Lindy Everhardt and Frank Holloway? Can you tell me anything about them?"

"Oh, Lindy is a lovely woman. When Derwin was a baby, she and I used to share babysitting. Travis is just about Derwin's age."

"Her husband didn't come to the burial at Duke and Desmond's."

"He died not five years after they married. Lindy stayed in Wilfred a few months after Frank went to jail, but I think it was too hard for her to be here with the memories. She left town and returned soon after with a husband and Travis. Then her husband died." Helen looked away and shook her head. "Life. They're a close family, though. No, no."

"Helen, when exactly was Frank put away?" If Frank had been in prison while Lindy had given birth to Travis, well, even I could do that math.

"I know what you're thinking." Helen primly pressed her lips together. "As I said, Lindy quickly remarried. She had her choice of husbands. I don't see anything suspicious there."

Yet Martin had tracked someone's every move at the Holloway property. Helen's gaze drifted to a stack of sheet music, the top song being "Here Comes the Sun." Her thoughts appeared to be somewhere gloomier.

"What do you think?" I prompted. "The medical

examiner says Larry Sutton died of natural causes. Should we still investigate?"

Her attention snapped back to me. "Why, of course." She lifted pearl-varnished nails to tick off the reasons. "First, Bruno or Larry or whatever his name is wouldn't have come to Wilfred if not for me. Possibly, he would still be alive and happily preparing bodies in southern California. Second, it's not natural that he was wandering private property in the middle of the night. Something suspicious was going on, and his family has a right to know. Third, I understand he was found with a lot of cash on him. What was that about?" She dropped her hand. "Most importantly, it's what Martin would have wanted. I'm sure you can get to the bottom of it."

I raised an eyebrow. "Me? I thought we were in this together."

"I'd love to help, you know I would, but I can't."

"Why not?" I countered. "There's no murder case, so you're no longer a suspect. With both of us looking into it, we'll get answers sooner."

"Honey, I'm so busy right now. The painters and wallpaper people are at the house and I'm having the carpet pulled up. I'm considering a refresh on the kitchen, too. Between that and giving organ lessons, I just don't see how I can find the time." At my downcast face, she added, "I'm biased, anyway. You'll have a fresh perspective."

"It's your case, Helen."

Her student showed up, a sixth grade girl chewing a wad of gum. At Helen's stern glance, she spit the gum into her palm and dropped it in the wastepaper basket. Helen motioned to the organ bench and turned to me.

"If you don't want to follow up, I'll be disappointed, but I'll understand. Just let me know."

I could walk away now. I could accept that Larry Sutton had died from natural causes in an unnatural place and let it go. I could let Martin Garlington's disappearance recede into history where it had been submerged for decades, hurting no one.

Or I could scratch the investigative itch that was building in me and seek answers to these questions. The decision was easy. "I'm in."

CHAPTER 13

That night Sam worked an evening shift. Instead of something he might have cooked—a dinner of salmon and lentils lightly dressed with lemon and chervil, for instance, as he did the week before—I made a grilled cheese sandwich. I ate it, staring out my apartment's kitchen window, with Rodney curled at my side. The sky was a sea of darkening grays like a broken string of black pearls. A storm thickened and the wind rustled the cottonwoods along the Kirby River.

Had I made a mistake by agreeing to look into Larry Sutton's strange death? The sheriff's office had already dismissed it. Their investigators—with crime scene analysts, experienced interviewers, and a medical examiner's office behind them—had pulled up their yellow police tape and gone home. Alone, with the help of a few town gossips and old newspaper articles, I was going to crack the case?

From the floor, Rodney meowed and blinked his amber eyes. Yes, I had magic, something the sheriff's office was short on. But unless Larry had been battered to death by flying novels, I wasn't sure how it would help.

I pushed myself from the kitchen table and made for the stairway. A stroll through the library would ground me. Something about the flow of the books' energy through and around me was better than a hot shower for sloughing off gloom.

On the library's second floor, I visited each bedroom and walked through the stacks, letting my hands brush the books' spines. The books sighed and murmured as my fingers touched them. My mood was improving already. I straightened a lamp on one table and plumped the cushion in the armchair next to it.

In natural history, I stood in front of a floor-to-ceiling bookshelf while thunder grumbled in the distance. I raised my hands to play with the books. I pushed and pulled the air in front of me, and the books responded, forming patterns on their shelf as they popped their spines out and returned to their places, all while sounding off birdsong and lions' roars. This felt good. I'd needed to off-gas some magical energy. When I dropped my hands to my side, I saw the books had formed themselves into a question mark. Surprised, I inhaled sharply, and the books snapped into their places all at once, their spines now uniform on the shelf.

Yes, I needed to make a battle plan. From history across the atrium, Sun Tzu's *The Art of War* barked a military greeting. I saluted in return and made my way back upstairs to my apartment.

I lit a fire in the hearth and settled in on my sofa with a pad of paper. I did my best thinking with a pen in my hands. How should I go about investigating? As in response to my question, Rodney stretched on the hearth, belly toward the fire, and blinked slowly at me. A fir log crackled and popped in the fire.

Step one, I wrote. *Talk to the Everhardts.* Could I ask them straight-out about Frank Holloway, or would I need an excuse? It could be a tricky conversation. Travis and Kaydee hadn't even been born when Frank was incarcerated, but maybe they'd heard stories from their mother. I'd need to pin down the timing. Perhaps I could tell them I was looking for Martin Garlington and thought they could help me.

Step two. Trace Larry Sutton's steps. At the café that night, I'd paid more attention to Sam than to Larry Sutton. Darla and Orson would have a better idea of what Larry Sutton had done and who he'd talked to in his last hours.

This would get me started, but one step remained. I stood and Rodney stood, too, his tail straightening. He waited to see what I'd do.

I went to the hall outside my living room and looked down into the dark atrium. A flash of lightning threw splashes of jewel-toned color through the roof's stained glass cupola. The near-vanilla scent of old books infused the air, and from above the entrance to the foyer, Marilyn Wilfred's portrait seemed to watch me.

"Books," I said, "Tell me all you know about

Frank Holloway and his property. I'll meet you in Old Man Thurston's office."

I took the side stairs to the library's ground level. The rain had started now and thrummed against the windows. The night was so beautiful— so moody—that I didn't want to ruin it with electric lights. Besides, when I worked magic, lights tended to flicker and surge, and I always feared having to explain a circuit box freak-out to Lyndon.

As I crossed the atrium, barefoot on parquet floor, what looked like brochures flew by like paper airplanes toward Old Man Thurston's office. A bound volume I recognized as the *Wilfred Searchlight*, which had ceased production during the Great Depression, trundled past me at waist-height. Once in the office, I lit a candle and set it on the desk's corner, next to what appeared to be a land survey in a cardboard tube. I drew my chenille robe closer against the spring night's chill and got to work.

I unrolled the survey. It was dated at the turn of the twentieth century and showed the Holloway land platted with just about nothing around it. Wilfred's central drag, a rural highway smaller than many cities' main streets, ran through the middle of the document, and the Kirby River, at that time untamed by the dike and mill pond, curled around its edge. All the land to the west of river was marked *Wilfred plat*.

The Holloways went back a long way. Over the decades, their property had dwindled as they'd sold off portions to become Wilfred's residential area. The last remaining acreage had gone to

Duke and Desmond. How had Lindy felt about that? Besides the flowers she'd left for the dead stranger, she hadn't struck me as particularly sentimental.

I turned to the brochures that had fluttered to the desk's edge. They were church bulletins from Wilfred's heyday in the 1970s, when a congregation would have filled the church's pews. They must have come from an obscure shelf upstairs in local history. I picked up the bulletin on top. The schedule for the church service was laid out in blue ink from the church's ditto machine. On the left-hand side was the list of hymns and names of the Sunday school teachers. No Holloways here.

"Books," I said, "What do you want me to see?"

The church bulletins instantly flipped over. I picked up the nearest. *Words from the Rector*, it said.

> *You are all invited to a dime-a-dip dinner to support our dear organist Helen Garlington. Ruth and Pat Littlewood will host the dinner at the Grange Hall and request a potluck dish as the price of entry. Usable baby items will be accepted, and, as customary, dinner will cost ten cents for every item sampled. Thanks to the industry of the knitting circle, baby booties will not be required. Contact Ruth to see what type of dish is needed. (Please note, as the Littlewoods share their party line with the Tohlers, you may need to try repeatedly, or ask Annie to give up the line, as she will undoubtedly be chatting with her boyfriend.)*

I lifted my gaze from the bulletin for a moment to imagine Mrs. Littlewood and her long-dead hus-

band more than forty years ago. They would have
been so young—Ruth with a shag haircut and her
husband wearing sideburns, just starting to build
his fortune in his family's vegetable canning business. Ruth's take-charge attitude would have made
her the perfect host for a charity dinner.

Back to the bulletin.

> *As you have likely heard, Helen finds herself
> with child and will welcome this blessed event
> without the benefit of her husband Martin, who
> vanished two months ago. (Since we are not gos-
> sips, we will neither assign blame nor mention the
> possibility of other women, gambling debts, or other
> reasons a man would abandon his wife after giv-
> ing the tired excuse of having to work on the week-
> end. Without hinting of another errant
> Wilfredian, we are chagrined to note this has be-
> come a trend in our God-fearing town.)*

Who was this rector? Apparently the *BuzzFeed* of
Wilfred. And what did he mean about a "trend"? I
eagerly reached for the next church bulletin and
lowered myself into the desk chair.

With each bulletin, I ignored the service and
went straight to the rector's newsy message. According to the bulletins, the Thompsons' cattle
had tramped the Vittorios' vegetable garden, ruin-
ing a crop of green beans destined for market.
The rector tossed in the appropriate Bible verse
encouraging them to "love thy neighbour as thy-
self." Several Wilfredians had passed to meet their
maker—twice, the rector noted that Martin Garlington would not be able to aid in their transition

to their heavenly home, since he had still not returned. Helen's delivery of Derwin was noted with the mention of her mother traveling from Spokane to stay with her.

At last, the payload.

> *This week congregants were overjoyed to welcome the return of Lindy Everhardt (formerly Holloway née Renton) to Wilfred with her new husband Roy Everhardt and baby son, Travis Edward. To the relief of many Wilfredians, Lindy's former husband Frank Holloway has blessedly been confined to state prison for the past year, although I remind you of the Good Book's admonition, "Let he who is without sin cast the first stone." (Speaking of casting stones, some of you might wince to remember the spate of shattered shop windows when Frank was angry at being expelled from shop class.) We are pleased to learn Lindy has discovered true marital bliss in her recent union.*

I lifted my eyes from the bulletin and glanced at its date. As Helen had told me, Lindy had left town a few months after Frank went to jail and wasted no time remarrying and giving birth to Travis.

This information was fascinating, but it didn't form a complete picture. What was I missing? I needed a fresh perspective. I needed a sidekick. Hercule Poirot relied on Captain Hastings and even Nancy Drew had Bess and George. Helen wasn't going to be much help unless the situation called for a melodramatic sonnet. Roz was too tied up with sorting out her housing arrangements to turn sleuth. Lalena might make a good sounding board, if she had openings between clients, but I couldn't count on her for focus.

As I'd read, one by one the materials I'd requested from the stacks had floated back to their homes. Only one item remained on the desk.

"Not again," I said aloud.

Rodney jumped to the desk with a fluidity Baryshnikov would have admired, and he patted the book's cover. *The Complete Original Illustrated Sherlock Holmes.* If this book continued to trail me, I was going to have to send it somewhere on a library transfer.

"I'm becoming a detective, is that what you want to say?" I spoke the words into the darkness around me, and the books' varied voices jumbled into a quiet river of sound.

Just then, the candle flickered as if a window had been cracked, and the volume rolled to its spine and fell open. I leaned closer. The page revealed was a facsimile of *The Strand* magazine, featuring "The Adventure of the Musgrave Ritual." A black-and-white engraving of Sherlock Holmes and Dr. Watson filled the top half of the page. In the image, Sherlock crouched over an open trunk while Watson looked on. As I examined the story, puzzled—what could it have to do with Larry Sutton's death?—Sherlock Holmes turned his head and looked straight at me.

I gasped and grabbed the arms of my chair. Sherlock Holmes emerged from the page and became three-dimensional. Standing in front of me was the famous detective as a six-inch high, black-and-white figure.

"Josie Way, I presume?" he said.

When Arthur Conan Doyle published his first Sherlock Holmes story in the 1890s, readers had devoured them, picturing the heroes, the stories, and making them real in their minds. Since then, movies, radio and TV dramas, and pastiche had added to this energy until, combined with my ability to funnel their power, Sherlock Holmes could come to life.

Besides the fact that he wasn't in full color and the engraving had left slight hash marks where energy pulsed as it filtered through him, he was Sherlock, complete with a hint of pipe smoke and faraway snippets of violin music.

Sherlock appeared nearly as surprised as I felt. He stood on the pages and looked around the candlelit office. Finally, he raised an eyebrow and waited, perhaps for a polite greeting.

"Where's the deerstalker cap?" I cringed. Here was the great Sherlock Holmes, and all I could think to talk about was about his hat?

"You won't find one in the early original texts, certainly not in 'The Adventure of the Musgrave Ritual.' Nor a meerschaum pipe. That was all Hollywood."

His British accent, calm and cool, soothed me. "Wilfred, Oregon, isn't in those texts, either. Why are you here?"

"To help. I understand you require assistance with a probable murder case?"

Sometimes my magic just plain blew me away. "How did you know?"

"Didn't you ask for me? Weren't you thinking so earlier?"

Now that he brought it up, yes. "I did want a sidekick."

"Here I am. You could hardly ask for better than Sherlock Holmes. Master of disguise, keen observer, and student of human behavior. However, I am no sidekick. If you require my assistance, I must lead this investigation."

His hubris melted any awe I'd felt. "The only reason you're here is because of me."

"You are merely the tool for my genius."

Then I understood. Sherlock Holmes was Victorian, and Victorian men weren't known for revering a woman's intellect. "I get it. You don't respect women," I replied. "Watson mentioned it more than once. Was it because of Irene Adler? Were you so angry when she married in 'A Scandal in Bohemia' that you refused to have anything to do with us?"

Sherlock regarded me coolly. "It does you no credit to speak of things you know nothing about."

I'd been rude. But I was too peeved to acknowledge it. "Then let's say we're partners. After all, you wouldn't be here, working on a new case, if it weren't for me. Besides, I know the players."

"Very well." He eyed Rodney, who stared at him with a predatory fixation. "Please keep an eye on your feline. I'm better with dogs," Sherlock said. "Perhaps you read about Toby in *The Sign of Four*?"

"Rodney, back off. Sherlock Holmes is our guest," I told the cat. He jumped to the floor and ambled away as if he hadn't cared, anyway, but not without shooting a sullen glance over his shoulder.

"Thank you. Now, would you honor me by summarizing the case?"

"Yes." I pinched myself mentally. I still couldn't believe I was talking to the legendary Sherlock Holmes. "Of course."

A Victorian armchair complete with antimacassar materialized behind him just as he sat, and a pipe—a long, straight one, not the hooked meerschaum—appeared in one hand. "I'm listening."

I told him what I knew so far about Helen and Martin Garlington, Bruno Gates, and Larry Sutton, ending in Larry Sutton's death. Sherlock closed his eyes and nodded as he listened. From time to time a smoke ring rose and dissipated above him.

"What do you think?" I asked when I'd concluded the story.

"What are your next steps?"

"Talk to a longtime local, Patty, about Frank Holloway. Talk to Lindy and her children. See if I can find any link between them and Martin's disappearance. Trace Larry Sutton's last steps."

He opened his eyes. "I see." He stood and the pipe and chair vanished. "Do you still have Martin Garlington's notebooks?"

"No. I returned them to his wife this afternoon."

His expression told me how disappointed he was.

"What?" I said. "How was I supposed to know you'd come along?"

"Very well. We'll work through your list as well as visit the location where the unfortunate Mr. Sutton was found."

"Why? There's nothing there but a filled hole.

The place has been trampled and it's rained. You won't find anything."

"Perhaps you wouldn't. I am the celebrated Sherlock Holmes." He fastened me with a stare that, despite coming from a man smaller than a Ken doll, made its point.

It was a standoff. I folded my arms over my chest, prepared to tell him where he could get off. Then I let my arms drop. This time I'd let him set the agenda. "Okay."

Sherlock nodded and turned away to face the book. "I'll be here when you need me." Sherlock then flattened into the illustration. I pressed my palm to the page and felt its warmth draining away. Sherlock was now nothing but ink on paper.

I blew out the candle, then picked up the book and carried it upstairs. Too bad it was such a fat volume. If I wanted Sherlock's help, I was going to have to carry it with me everywhere.

I just hoped I wouldn't be tempted to chuck it off the bridge into the river.

CHAPTER 14

The next morning, I loaded the *Complete Adventures*, as I'd begun referring to the Sherlock Holmes compendium, into a tote bag. The book was heavy, but the flow of energy that washed between us made hauling it around a pleasure. After breakfast at the café, I crossed the street to Patty's This-N-That, where construction was in full swing. My plan was to talk with Patty, then revisit the outhouse's grave, as Sherlock had requested.

Duke and Desmond were at the front entrance, laying some sort of ramp over the three steps to the door. "A few inches closer," Duke said to Desmond. "There you go." Then, to me, "Howdy, Josie."

"Have you seen Patty?" I stepped around their construction and peered into the store, a mess of drop cloths, lumber, and dust. I waved at Babe Hamilton, the textiles dealer, who was taking photos of her space in the shop's corner. With its framed spaces, already the This-N-That was looking more like an antiques mall.

"Josie, is that you? Come in. There's someone I'd like you to meet," Patty said from inside the store. I found Patty bending over a floor plan unrolled on the checkout counter, the sole remaining structure in the gutted shop. For a moment, I had a flashback of last night's map of the Holloway land. Next to her was Gidget, a Wilfredian with whom I had a passing acquaintance due to her love of historical dramas, especially those set in medieval times.

"Gidget." She tendered a hand. Gidget's tawny brown hair, pulled into a ponytail, and jeans and T-shirt gave her a youthful look despite being comfortably in middle age.

As I shook her hand, the cover of Kate Mosse's *Labyrinth* popped into my head. Either Gidget was reading it or wanted to read it. At the same time, the volume of Sherlock Holmes stories in my bag let out a series of taps, as if Sherlock were knocking on its cover. *Not now*, I communicated silently.

"Nice to meet you," I said. "Patty, do you have a minute?"

"I'm just running out to the hardware store in Forest Grove. Can it wait?"

"Sure."

Time to move to plan B and hit up Duke and Desmond. However, fate was not ready to let me go yet. Behind Patty, steps rumbled down the stairs that led up to her apartment. Buffy and Thor, his cape trailing behind him, erupted from the stairwell.

"Here it is." Buffy reached up to slap papers on

the counter. "Roz and Lyndon's real estate proposal."

Thor eyed me. "To earn us a cool forty bucks."

"Each," Buffy added.

"Twenty each," I amended. "Forty total."

Buffy turned the page of her crayon-rendered booklet. "Option one. Duke's trailer is empty now. Move it next to Roz's trailer and build a hall between them. You know, hook up Duke's front door to Roz's back door."

Clever. I pictured the Habitrail-like dwelling this would make. "What about the garden space?"

"He still has all that garden up at the library," Buffy said.

"Try it now," came Desmond's voice from the front doorway.

While I was talking with Patty, Duke and Desmond had finished a ramp to the front door. Now, a wheelchair rolled up it, bumping over the threshold.

"It'll do," the man in the wheelchair said. He moved his arms freely and powered the wheelchair without a motor, but his legs were thin beneath his jeans. It wasn't his body that caught my attention as much as his wild black hair and beard, not to mention his stony expression.

"Josie," Patty said, "Meet Ian Penclosa. You two will get along great. Ian is the bookseller I was telling you about."

"Pleased to meet you," he said. Despite the word *pleased* his tone said, "I couldn't care less."

"It's nice to meet you, too." I barely paid attention to the words that were coming out of my mouth. Penclosa. Something about that was familiar, but how? From the book under my arm, Sherlock tapped again. I tightened my grip.

Ian Penclosa's attitude put me off, but an intriguing miasma of book energy clung to him. I'd only felt this sort of energy on a person once, from a retired librarian who'd stopped by Wilfred's library briefly this past winter after working sixty years in three libraries. Just then, Ian gave a lopsided smile, and I understood why he intrigued Lalena so much.

His wheelchair crunched over construction debris as he maneuvered to his corner of the antiques mall. I turned to the door. "Duke? Desmond? Could I talk with you a second?"

"Lunch break, Josie. We can talk, but we'll have to do it over sandwiches at our place."

At Duke and Desmond's, few traces remained of Lindy and her family's many years in residence. The ruffled curtains in the living and dining rooms were likely leftovers, as was the pale blue carpeting, but the rest was pure bachelor pad. That is, if the bachelors were mechanically minded neatniks.

"Home sweet home," Duke said as he passed me to walk through to the kitchen. Desmond, more the gentleman, stepped aside to let me enter before him.

"What'll it be, Josie?" Duke yelled from the kitchen. "Tuna or egg salad?"

"Nothing for me," I said, still taking in the room. A lit display cabinet showcased a collection of toy tractors, each parked at an angle. Above it hung a series of gold-rimmed commemorative plates featuring Shirley Temple movies.

"Please," Desmond said. "I made an especially good egg salad this morning."

"Thank you," I said, my gaze wandering to the dining room's built-in buffet. I bet when Lindy lived here, she'd filled its shelves with teacups and baby photos. Now it held engine parts, each resting on a crisp paper towel.

Duke wandered from the kitchen while Desmond took care of plating lunch. "Haven't been able to do much decorating yet. Just my commemorative plate collection. I have a few Western prints I'd love to get up, too."

They'd wasted no time stationing the television set. Two puffy recliners faced it.

I rested my canvas tote on a dining room chair, discreetly scrunching down its side to let Sherlock peek out, and I circled the table to the back window. "You can't really see where the outhouse was from here."

Duke joined me. "Nope. When we moved in, the stretch beyond the deck was overgrown vegetable beds. Lindy says it used to be their garden before her arthritis got in the way of gardening." He parted the top of my tote and lifted out the *Complete Adventures*. "Good grief, Josie. You bring reading everywhere you go?"

"I never know when I can squeeze in a few pages," I said. "You have a long strip of property. It's hard to imagine going that far to use an outhouse."

He shifted his gaze to the window and pointed to the garden. "Handy, really. And private. See that hedge between the house and the facilities? Some kind of flowering bush. We need to get Lyndon to let us know what's growing out there."

Behind us, the clunking of plates told me Desmond had readied lunch. "Probably why Lindy never saw fit to tear out the blackberry vines," he said. "You couldn't see them from the house."

Duke shook his head. "What a mountain they made. I figured it was the root cellar."

"I didn't know anyone had root cellars these days," I said.

"They don't, thanks to the refrigerator. I wouldn't be surprised if this one hadn't been used in a century."

The old Holloway plat had dwindled to two large lots set end to end. The house was separated from the street by a modest front yard. Behind the house stretched a deck, a neglected vegetable garden surrounded by a low fence, the hedge of mock orange bushes Duke had referred to, and finally the former outhouse, now raw earth. The churchyard with its falling-down wooden fence ran along the lot's right side.

From the churchyard, I'd seen the blackberry mound. Like everyone else, I'd had no idea an outhouse was tangled in them. In late summer, Wilfredians had harvested the bushes for pies and jam. The mound had simply been part of a neglected back lot and town shortcut we'd all taken for granted.

Duke and I stared toward the now-demolished outhouse as if it were still there.

"That would have been a good long walk for a

fellow needing the facilities quick-like," he pointed out.

"You're going to build your garage there, right?" I asked.

"I don't feel that great about it anymore," Desmond said from the kitchen.

"Two bodies. Bad karma," Duke added. "We've been talking about just building out the garage next to the house, the one that's already here."

"I still want to put a concrete slab over it. No one should have to look at the dirt where those two—Larry Sutton and Reginald—died."

I turned to the table. Desmond had laid out three plates with sandwiches, paper napkins, and a jar of pickles. These boys knew how to entertain.

"Did you see Larry Sutton the night he died? Maybe you stopped by the café?"

Duke and Desmond shot each other a glance that seemed to communicate volumes. Duke picked up the response. "Desi and I dropped in for a drink once we finished up at Patty's. We saw him all right."

"On his way to a real snootful," Desmond added. "Other than that, there was no hint he was hours from dying."

"What about later that night? Did you see or hear anything?"

Duke pulled out a chair and sat. Desmond waited for me to take my seat before he settled into his.

"Not a sound," Duke said. "My bedroom faces the back, too."

"I didn't hear anything, either," Desmond said.

"He might have come down your driveway, then gone around the house and walked through the garden," I said.

"Not necessarily." A Brylcreemed curl fell forward as Duke waved half his sandwich. "There's a break in the fence where the big cedar tree divides our property from the churchyard. You know it. It's practically a town thoroughfare. He could have come that way."

"Or from the back," Desmond added. "The lot is completely open. Probably the easiest way to get in. Lots of folks cut through the back of the lot on their way to the café."

Duke set down his sandwich. "I don't like the idea of people roaming the property at all hours. What do you say to postponing the garage until we get up a new fence?"

"After we lay the slab," Desmond said.

"When's that?" The egg salad was delicious. Plain and good with lots of mustard.

"Three, maybe four days. We'll be tied up at Patty's until then," Duke said.

I wiped my mouth. "What do you two think? Do you have any theories as to what happened back there the other night?"

"Sheriff says he died of natural causes. Maybe he was having some sort of attack and didn't know where he was going," Desmond said.

"So he wandered into a stranger's yard or found his way to the churchyard, then squeezed through an opening in the fence?" I said.

"That's the whole point of wandering aimlessly," Duke said. "You don't necessarily stick to major roads."

I glanced from man to man. Funny, they were beginning to look more alike in the months they'd spent together. They were both short and stocky and ran to engine grease under the fingernails. Desmond's eyes were a curious gray, though, like a silver teapot, and Duke's hair was a pomaded adaptation of something Elvis might have worn.

"Do you really think that's what happened?" I asked. "Not everyone knew he wasn't Martin Garlington."

Duke scoffed. "Martin? I was a kid when he left town, but I can't imagine anyone held a thing against him. He might have irritated someone. I see that. He was a little . . . what's the word, Desmond?"

"Pedantic," Desmond supplied, although I had no idea how he'd known either what Duke was thinking or what Martin Garlington was like.

"Right. Pedantic. That's what people said, anyway. He could go on and on about butterflies. But you don't go killing someone decades later because they annoy you."

"So, you saw nothing," I said. "No lights, no noise, no—"

"No curious cigarette ash or strange buttons," Duke finished. He pointed at my tote bag. "You've been reading too much of that fellow."

Desmond rose to clear the table. "We'd better get back to Patty's if we want to get the drywall up tomorrow."

I took that as my cue to leave. I gathered up Sherlock. "Thank you for lunch. Do you mind if I leave the back way?"

"Sure, have at it," Duke said.

I waved through the back door and picked my

way across the yard. The knee-high fence bordering the vegetable patch had fallen here and there, and the garden shed looked equally rickety, surely destined for Duke's tractor. The path through the hedge was overgrown enough that I had to part rain-heavy branches to pass through.

I arrived at the grave site. After making sure no one was watching, I slipped the *Complete Adventures* from the tote bag and laid the book on the soil where I'd found Larry Sutton. The book opened and Sherlock emerged. "Have at it," I told him.

He didn't even look around. In daylight, he was more transparent than usual. "You must be careful."

"Why? Don't you want to check out where Larry Sutton died? That's why we're here."

"At the shop, the one under construction, I felt something ominous."

I thought back to the This-N-That. The hollowed-out building had smelled of damp, ancient timbers. I'd seen Patty, of course. Said hello to Babe Hamilton and Gidget. And met Ian Penclosa. Remembering his intense manner and the white scar on his temple, my skin prickled.

"That's why you were bumping around in my bag," I said.

"My author, Arthur Conan Doyle, wrote *The Parasite*, a novella about someone named Penclosa. She had trouble with one of her legs and limped." He slowed his words to make sure I understood. "She was a would-be murderess."

I couldn't help but search around us—the cedar tree above with its branches that obscured the sky, the gravestones in the cemetery beyond the fence with its posts missing here and there, the fresh dirt in front of us. Were we being watched?

"What about her?" I asked.

"I'm not sure," Sherlock said. "She claimed to be psychic. I don't know how that affects you." He tipped his tiny head toward me. "You feel it too, don't you?"

"I do feel something. It feels more like a warning than a threat, but I can't put my finger on it."

"Your nemesis," Sherlock said. "All sleuths have their Moriarty and earlier today, I sensed yours."

From a tree branch above me, a crow cawed.

CHAPTER 15

As soon as I was safely in my apartment, I dumped my tote bag on my bed. The *Complete Adventures* tumbled out and opened to "The Adventure of the Beryl Coronet." Sherlock, in evening dress and still no bigger than the book's illustration, leapt from its pages. He stepped sideways to avoid slipping into the book's open spine.

"What do you mean, *nemesis?*" I said. "Who?"

"I was in the bag, Miss Way. I couldn't see anything. But I sensed it. My work has given me a strong instinct for danger. You have an enemy out there."

"Where?" I'd have shed my coat but was unwilling to leave the room to hang it up until I'd had an answer.

"At the shop. I couldn't see anything, but I felt it."

Chewing on this, I returned the coat to the closet. "I don't know who it could be. Besides Helen and now, I suppose, Patty, no one knows I'm interested in Larry Sutton's death."

Sherlock's hand came to his black-and-white photogravured chin, and he cocked his head. "Have you heard of my adventure in 'The Red-Headed League'? Perhaps your hair isn't quite so fiery, but you might have joined."

I preferred mysteries from the Golden Age, but I knew my Sherlock. "The League was only open to men, which is how you, a well known misogynist, would have liked it. Unless I were a certain internationally known contralto, that is."

"Ouch, my dear. No need to bring Irene Adler into this. Quite the redhead's fiery temper, as well."

Rodney had jumped to the bed and stared at Sherlock. He lowered himself to his haunches. Sherlock was still semi-sheer due to the illustration's hash marks and I was fairly certain he couldn't be injured, but I shot Rodney a warning glance, anyway.

"You think I have an enemy?"

"It was a sense I had. Watson makes me out to be pure logic, but my logic is usually sparked by an intuition." He reached out a hand and a pipe appeared in it. He lit it and drew in air until he exhaled a tiny puff of smoke. The smoke rose a few inches above his head and evaporated. Rodney watched in fascination.

"I'll keep that in mind." Clearly, Sherlock was being overdramatic. He'd been locked in the same mysteries for too long and was ready to invent one for the thrill alone.

"From now on, you'll have carry me, not put me in a sack. I need to be able to see. Without it, my keen powers of observation are limited to what I can hear."

Rodney's hindquarters twitched and he sprang on Sherlock. The great detective stepped neatly to the side, and Rodney skidded over the *Complete Adventures* and collided with a pillow. Rodney instantly raised a leg and began to groom it as if it were his plan all along.

"Get in the book," I said. "I've got to get ready."

Sherlock complied, eagerly melting into the illustration. "Where are we going?"

"You're staying here. I have a date." And it was no place for fictional detectives. Then I had an idea. "Have you heard of the internet?"

From the page, Sherlock raised an eyebrow. "Miss Way, don't you suppose people search for me online? Many, many e-readers contain my stories. My movies have streamed through millions of electronic devices. Yes, I know about computers and I'm certainly familiar with the internet."

Smart aleck. "All right, but have you ever used it?"

He reemerged from the illustration. "No."

"You're going to learn." I laid my smartphone on the *Complete Adventures*. At last, someone small enough to ace the phone's tiny keyboard. "This is how it works."

Five minutes later, Sherlock was seated at a wooden office chair he'd materialized, and he'd mastered a basic web search. The keyboard was still slightly too large for him, but he was a surprisingly speedy two-fisted typist.

"Sherlock," I said.

"Hmm." He didn't raise his gaze from the screen.

I couldn't help but think how different his adventures would have been had he and Watson had internet access.

"You'll spend some time researching the case?"

"Of course," he said, but I noticed he'd entered his own name in the search bar.

"Then I'll see you in the morning."

Sherlock had drained me. It wasn't so much the magical energy I'd expended—the readers had provided plenty of that—but the verbal sparring. My plan this afternoon was to forget all about murder. Instead, I'd do what I loved best: spend time with Sam.

Like most women in their late twenties, I'd dated my share. I'd been out with men who put me to sleep talking about video games, then, satisfied the outing had been a success, invited me to their place. No thanks. When I lived in Washington, DC, I'd gone out with countless Hill staffers who squired me to free buffets hosted by lobbyists and constantly glanced over my shoulder to make sure they didn't miss hobnobbing with someone important. A surprising number of adult men still lived with their parents. Mansplainers, leches, and the self-obsessed—I'd dated them all.

I'd been with only one man long-term—if two years qualifies as long-term. He was also a librarian, and our time together was mostly spent in solitary pursuits carried out in the same room. I read while he researched eighteenth-century painters, for example. We were comfortable together, but I didn't miss him while we were apart, except as one person alone misses the company of another person she gets along well with.

It wasn't his fault. At that time, my magic had been bound, and I'd lived as if encased in a murky shell, with my senses and enthusiasm dialed down. I wasn't capable of passion. The last I'd heard, my ex was living in suburban Virginia with his wife, a high school teacher. I wished him well.

Then I found my magic. And met Sam. Everything had changed.

For one, Sam was slightly older than I was and, unlike other men I'd dated, had lived a complex and interesting life. He'd been married, although for the last years unhappily, and his wife had died, leaving a baby. Over the year since, Sam had learned Nicky wasn't his biological son, but that didn't change his feelings. Nicky was still Thurston Wilfred, VI and as deeply loved as a boy could be. Before returning to Wilfred, Sam had worked for the FBI and had specialized in "ghosting," or tracking suspects. He was also slightly eccentric, as some people said I was, as well as warm and protective. In short, I was smitten.

No, it was more than that. I was unutterably, blindly in love.

Frowning happily, Sam met me at Big House's back door. "Ready? I thought we'd check out the opening day of the farmers market in Forest Grove. What do you think? Maybe pick up a few things for dinner?"

"I'd love it," I said. Truth was, he could have proposed an outing to the dump and I would have happily agreed. That's just how far gone I was. We left Nicky in the hands of one of the teenaged Tohler girls, where they were already building a fort of chairs and blankets in the living room.

As Sam's SUV passed the church, I could just make out Duke and Desmond's house down the street. No one would know that three days earlier a dead man had been found there. *No,* I told myself. That could wait. Today my plan was to relax.

Once we were in the hubbub of the farmers market, my wondering melted away, replaced by the smells and sounds of the crowd. The market couldn't have filled more than a city block, but it was practically a tiny world, with the clank of a tortilla machine here, the smells of locally made sausages on a grill there, and piles of spring produce everywhere.

Calm focus fell over Sam's face. I knew this look. It was the same expression he wore when he was on a case and his brain was fully engaged. Only this time he wasn't mulling over suspects, he was contemplating dinner.

"It's still early in the season, but I bet we can find what we need for a primavera risotto," he said. "Early asparagus, pea shoots, nettles, green garlic." Absorbed by a display of heaped greens, his voice trailed off. He wandered to a stall to talk with the farmer arranging jars of honey.

Watching him eye a dozen eggs the hues of a desert morning, my heart bubbled over. An hour later, when the basket was full, we bought paper plates of tacos and sat at a nearby picnic table.

Sam reached across the table and laid his hand over mine. "Isn't this nice?"

I smiled. I didn't need to speak for him to understand my feelings.

He withdrew his hand to clutch a taco. "I feel like I've come home."

"You have."

"I mean really come home. Home for the first time. Growing up in Wilfred was idyllic in some ways—fishing, playing in the woods." He stared toward the market but didn't seem to focus on anything in particular. "We were always the odd ones out."

I knew the story. Big House stood on the bluff, looking down at Wilfred. Similarly, his parents had looked down on the town's residents. Earlier generations, starting with Old Man Thurston, who'd built the mill, were part of Wilfred's fabric, taking part in Timber Days and smoothing Wilfred's transition from wilderness to thriving company town. Not so Sam's parents. His father had graduated from an Ivy League college and returned with a society wife and a different definition of success. That aspiration had ended with the mill burning down and a midnight escape.

All those years, Sam had simply wanted to be included. He'd wanted to play with the mill workers' kids without being shunned as the standoffish boss's son and next in line for the Wilfred dynasty. He'd tried for a better life with Fiona, an outgoing artist, but her extroversion was designed to draw people to her, not her to them.

Sam wanted a chance at the "normal" life. And I was to be that chance. Me, a witch. Magic made me far from normal, but, paradoxically, releasing my magic had given me the ability to truly love, too.

Without it, I wouldn't be here, now. As I saw it, I had two options and I didn't like either of them. I could continue with Sam and not tell him about my magic, or I could reveal I was a witch and risk losing it all. I was going to have to decide, and soon.

"Is that Travis Everhardt over there?" Sam gestured toward a stall with a pastry case flanked by bread. "We could use something for breakfast."

Travis, in a white apron with a hairnet strapped around his beard, restacked a pyramid of hand-shaped country loaves. Tacos finished, Sam and I wandered to Travis's stall, where he was giving a mother and child a broken snickerdoodle. "On the house. Now you run off and do your homework. I expect to see that story the next time you drop by." For such a big man, he had a heart as sweet as caramel. When they'd left, he turned to us. "Sam, Josie. What can I get for you?"

"A loaf of the spelt bread, please."

While Travis wrapped the loaf in brown paper, I edged to the table. I had an idea, a blind shot, but Travis was an Everhardt and had grown up on the Holloway property. "Isn't it terrible about Bruno Gates?" Sam shot me a look. He knew exactly what I was up to. "And then they find out he's someone else altogether."

Travis's expression turned sour. "Someone thought he was Martin Garlington and did him in. Lured him to the back of our old property and let him have it."

"Lured him," I repeated, watching Travis closely. "How?"

He looked from Sam to me and shrugged. "I

mean, that's my guess. It wasn't Helen. She's a sweet lady. Didn't deserve what she got with him."

This was a tricky conversation to lead. Sam watched with curiosity. "Sam says the sheriff's office has called off the investigation. The death was from natural causes."

Travis wrapped a loaf of bread in brown paper but didn't look up. Sam stood back. How would I proceed?

I looked Travis in the eyes. "That's what the medical examiner says, anyway."

Travis wiped his hands on the towel draped from his apron. Again, he looked at Sam, who stood immobile, his expression deceptively placid, then at me. "I don't know who this Bruno or Larry or whoever character is, but I'll tell you this: Martin Garlington didn't deserve to live."

Shocked at his outburst, I opened my mouth to press for details, when a couple with four kids trailing them pushed to the table. "Travis. We need three dozen cupcakes for Mariah's birthday."

Sam pulled me away before I could get in another question.

"He knew about the note in Larry Sutton's pocket," I said. "Don't you think that's suspicious?"

"You knew about the note, too," he pointed out. "Besides, he said 'lured,' not 'lured with a note.'"

"That he knew Larry Sutton planned to meet someone is suspicious enough."

"You don't give up, do you?"

Was Sam frustrated or amused? His mouth was set in neither a smile nor a frown. "That's what you like about me, right?"

He kissed my ear and his weekend-whiskery jaw rubbed my cheek. "You're right. Come on. We've got to get home. The babysitter has plans later on."

When we were out of Travis's earshot, I put a hand on Sam's arm. "Did the sheriff's office release the fact that a note was found on Larry Sutton's body asking to meet him?"

Sam shifted the basket to his other arm. "I see where you're going with this. We kept that information private, but it doesn't mean Travis couldn't have found out about the note from someone else—the person who planned to meet Larry Sutton, for instance."

I glanced back, trying to catch another glimpse of Travis, but dozens of people now stood between us. Follow-up would have to wait.

CHAPTER 16

By the next morning, rain had set in again. The earth in Western Oregon seemed a sponge with an endless thirst, turning water into moss-bound trees and thickets of ferns. The Kirby River swelled below the bluff, but thanks to the new dike, Wilfred would remain dry this year.

Sam had to go into work and I returned to my apartment, Rodney at my heels. I clicked lamps on to make pools of warm light against the dreariness. It was my day off and I had a lot to do.

"Good morning, books," I said, happy to be surrounded by their energy once again. When I'd first discovered my magic, the energy from the books had almost overwhelmed me. I'd accidentally burned more than a few slices of toast at Sam's after a blissful night. Slowly, I opened myself as a conduit for it, and now I felt like a longtime sea captain, happiest when in that curious place of both master and slave of the powerful ocean.

The books returned the greeting in a full range of voices, some in foreign languages, some bass, some whispering soprano, some nearly chanting.

I went to my living room upstairs and Sherlock was standing on the sofa's arm. Alert, Rodney sat on the sofa's back, staring at him.

"Rodney, settle down," I said. Rodney lowered himself and tucked his legs beneath him.

"I won't ask you about your night," Sherlock said.

He sounded irritated and I didn't know why. Unless it had to do with his attitude toward women. "Good," I said.

"Except to ask if you enjoyed your afternoon procuring fresh produce and the resulting spinach omelet this morning, accompanied by strong coffee with cream." His nostrils quivered. "Spinach and garlic omelet, that is."

I stopped cold. "How did you know that? About the produce and breakfast? Except the garlic," I added, vowing to brush my teeth.

"Elementary. I noted yesterday that you enjoy cream in your coffee, and minute particles of coffee grounds in your thumbnail indicate that you prepared it fresh this morning. You have a bit of spinach stuck on your top left incisor, and it's unlikely you were eating spinach by itself at breakfast. Therefore, I deduced the omelet." He folded his arms over his chest. "If you'd like further speculations about the night, I might add—"

"That's fine," I said quickly. "I get it." I moved the *Complete Adventures* to the end table. An armchair, just the size to fit the six-inch Sherlock, appeared on it, and Sherlock seated himself. A pipe materialized in his hand. "Well, then?"

"Well what?" he said.

"What did you learn last night on the internet?" I picked up my phone. Its battery was dead. Sherlock must have been at it for hours.

"Did you know there have been at least sixty-six films featuring versions of my character?"

It was beginning to dawn on me how'd he spent his evening. "Did you watch them all? My phone had a full charge when I left."

I may as well not have been speaking. "They take outrageous liberties. Always inserting Irene Adler, for instance."

"People are interested in your love affair."

He rolled his BB-sized eyes. "And the pastiche. One of the novels features me as a dog." He shook his head in horror. "In another, I'm a cowboy. *Holmes on the Range*," he said distastefully.

"I've heard that's a good one," I said. "But the question is, Were you able to tear yourself away from reading about yourself? For instance, did you learn anything about Martin Garlington, Larry Sutton, or Frank Holloway?"

From the look in Sherlock's eyes, I could tell he hadn't gotten far. "The phone died. This wasn't a problem on Baker Street when we used telegrams."

"You aren't very useful as a sidekick if you don't do any investigating," I said.

"I'm not your sidekick. We discussed this. Besides, I did learn one thing. Or, rather, I learned there's one thing it's not possible to find online."

"And that is?" Sherlock's night of watching movies seemed to have given him an irritating flair for the dramatic.

"Frank Holloway's obituary. According to the internet, he may not have died at all." Sherlock puffed his pipe in satisfaction. "Fascinating, is it not?"

"What do you mean?"

"I found no record of his death in the state's major newspapers for the past forty years."

I pondered this. "I'll ask around. He may be buried elsewhere. Or his family may not have wanted a fuss and buried him quietly in the churchyard. Then again—"

"Precisely, Miss Way. Then again he might still be alive, I believe you were about to say, although I couldn't find proof of that, either."

"Maybe he's living under an assumed identity." Sherlock and I exchanged knowing glances.

"We must still reconstruct the night Larry Sutton died, and we can't do that on the internet." He waved his pipe for emphasis.

"True," I said. "How do you feel about lunch at the café?"

At Darla's Café, I planted myself on a stool at the counter near the cash register. A spot here was my best hope at gathering information. Lunchtime always drew a crowd, and Darla would have to duck behind the counter to grab the coffeepot, post orders, and ring people out.

I flipped my coffee cup over to "yes, please," and Darla filled it, one eye on the door. "Take a seat anywhere," she said to someone over my shoulder.

It must have been a stranger. Wilfredians knew the first rule of the café: to grab whatever open table you found, and not to hog a four-top if there were only two of you. I swiveled on my stool to see Ian Penclosa, the rare books dealer. My breath caught short when I remembered his interest in books on the occult, and for comfort I rested my hand on the *Complete Adventures.* Ian wheeled to the table behind my stool, where a customer had made space for his chair. He pulled the menu from its holder.

I forced my attention back to Darla. "Any grits today?" I loved Darla's Pacific Northwestern take on grits, full of seafood, locally foraged mushrooms, and earthy herbs.

"Ran out. Montgomery's on his way to Garibaldi now to stock up on seafood. I'll bring you the waffle with plum compote."

This was the other rule of Darla's Café. At any time, she could decide your meal for you. I didn't complain, since I loved the spicy compote made from last summer's plums. Buffy and Thor had gathered them from trees in town to earn money for roller skates, and Darla had caramelized the fruit with cinnamon sticks, star fruit, and honey from the Tohlers' bees. Delicious.

I leaned forward and lowered my voice. "What exactly happened the night Bruno Gates came in?"

Darla raised her eyebrows and took the coffeepot to the floor. I didn't worry. She'd be back.

Moments later, she replaced the coffeepot and returned to the cash register. Although she wore leopard-patterned reading glasses on a chain, they were for show. Her dyslexia had trained her to use her memory to track the meals of every guest, and she rang up the ticket without a pause.

"I left after the dinner rush." Darla's fingers barely slowed as she spoke. "Bruno had the patty melt and left nary the stub of a fry on his plate. We could have put his platter back on the shelf, and no one would have been the wiser that it hadn't been run through the dishwasher."

I had guessed this much. "Any idea how much longer he was here?"

"Just a sec." She gave her attention to the couple at the cash register. I recognized the man from the library and his love of fantasy, especially Ursula Le Guin. "That's seventeen-forty-five."

Ian's order, also the waffle and plum compote, arrived with mine at the pass-through between the kitchen and front of the house. Darla placed one on the counter for me and the other on Ian's table. She lifted a finger to let me know she'd be back and disappeared again with the coffeepot. Getting information from Darla while she was working took patience.

When she returned, she said, "I didn't like him. Sure, he was a good eater, but he gave me the impression of being on the make. Couldn't rip his attention from women's bustlines. Didn't trust him." With that, Darla grabbed a platter of pancakes and vanished.

"Everyone comes here," Ian said from behind me.

I swiveled toward him. His voice was lower, grumblier than I'd remembered. He wasn't much older than I was—if at all—but there was something aged about him. His eyes looked like they'd seldom been surprised, no matter what they'd seen.

"There's nowhere else to go, except Gaston," I told him. Gaston's burger joint could never match Darla's offerings. You had to drive the hour to Portland for that. I glanced up to track Darla and found her occupied setting up a high chair for the family across the dining room. "How are you settling in?"

"I have a studio in Gaston, but it looks like I'll be taking Duke's old trailer at the Magnolia at the beginning of the month."

"That'll be convenient. It's accessible?" Lalena's front door was too narrow for his chair. I couldn't remember the front door at Duke's place.

Ian nodded. "Duke was thinking ahead. There's only one problem." He paused for drama. "He wired all the outlets to two-way switches. It's going to take me weeks just to figure out how to get the toaster to work."

Despite a mouthful of waffle, I laughed. Maybe this Ian guy wasn't as creepy as I'd thought. After I swallowed, I said, "I'm Wilfred's librarian. I don't know if we have anything in our collection you'd be interested in, but I'd be happy to show you around. There's a ramp to the front porch. Call from there and I'll let you in."

"Thank you. I'll take you up on that." He nodded to the *Complete Adventures*.

The book growled in response and I glanced at it in alarm. What was up with Sherlock?

"You like Arthur Conan Doyle?" Ian asked.

"He's a classic." Remembering Sherlock's comment, I added, "I understand there's another Penclosa. In his *The Parasite*."

Ian's smile tightened the scar on his temple. "Not many people catch that. Yes. I changed my name to match the heroine's. We both have disabled legs and a fascination with the unknown."

He offered no further explanation. "What brought you to Wilfred?" I asked. "Are you from around here?"

Wariness crept over his face. "Why shouldn't I have come to Wilfred?" Then, softening his expression, he added, "I'm from San Francisco, actually." He examined the blade of his dinner knife and pushed it away. "The rare book business happens mostly over the internet. Especially in my field. Rents are good here and Patty's giving me storage space in the basement. Duke made sure the shop's electrical system can stand up to a dehumidifier."

Darla reappeared and slid the now-empty carafe onto its burner. I swiveled to face her. She pressed a button and the coffee machine sputtered to life. "Orson says Bruno didn't leave the tavern until past midnight," she said.

"You two talked about it, then."

She tallied checks as she replied. "When there are odd situations at the tavern, he generally leaves me a note in the kitchen. He saw fit to leave a note that night."

"Is that unusual for him?"

"Very unusual. If you want more information, you'll have to ask him." She glanced at the black cat clock hanging above the counter. Its pendulum tail swung and eyeballs slid side to side in time. "He's probably up by now." She reached into the pie case for a cinnamon bun. "Take him one of these."

CHAPTER 17

Darla told me Orson lived in the old Empress theater. Not in the theater proper, but upstairs. She directed me to an outside staircase at the side of the building. As I crossed the street from the café, Sherlock in hand, Babe Hamilton, the textiles vendor, waved from inside Patty's This-N-That. I waved in return. The build-out was going quickly. The antiques mall would surely be open by summer, if not sooner.

Now that I knew the blocky building two down from Patty's had once been a movie theater, it seemed obvious. In my mind's eye, the lit Empress sign jutted from the building's front like the prow of a ship. If the decades-old plywood nailed over the Empress's front door were removed, the entrance to a lobby would surely be revealed, perhaps even with gothic chandeliers and a tiled ticket window.

This was where Orson lived. I climbed the theater's wooden external stairs and raised my fist to knock, when the door flew open. Orson, mug of coffee in hand, smiled broadly. "Come in. Darla called a minute ago and told me to make sure I had my pants on. Said you were coming my way."

I wiped my feet on his welcome mat and looked around. Jazz piano played from a turntable in the small apartment's main room. "Bill Evans, *Portrait in Jazz,* 1960," the liner notes whispered. Other than this sybaritic touch, the room could have belonged to any middle-aged bachelor not overly concerned with tidiness. A worn recliner sat in a corner. A table lamp illuminated the open newspaper on its seat. A small couch that looked as if it were never occupied faced the recliner.

Something about the apartment didn't feel quite right. What? Then I got it. It had no windows, except for a curtained area on an inside wall—a wall that would look down on the theater's seating area. Orson lived in the theater's former projector room.

"You moved into the Empress?" I asked. "I thought maybe there were apartments up here."

"Nope. No apartments. I inherited the theater, and no one was in the market for a movie palace in a town with a steadily shrinking population. Everyone goes to the multiplex at the mall."

"What about your family's house?"

"Mom kept it, and when she died it was easier to sell the house than the Empress. So I moved in. Have a seat." Orson gestured toward a door at the end of the galley kitchen. "My bedroom's through there, in the old storage room. Still smells like pop-corn."

"You weren't able to keep the theater open, then." I moved what I hoped was clean laundry and sat, placing the *Complete Adventures* next to me.

"Couldn't. Someone tried to burn the place down in the mid-seventies. The fire was put out before there was structural damage, but it was too late."

From the outside, the building looked to be sound. "There was nothing your family could do?"

Orson took his time responding, and when he did, it was in a matter-of-fact tone. "Firefighters found my father unconscious in the lobby. He died not long after."

"That's terrible. I'm so sorry." No wonder the family had never reopened the Empress. Theft, fire, and death—the place was full of bad memories.

Orson resumed his place in the armchair, which gave a squeak of springs when he sat. "Ancient history. It's a sweet old building, though. Someday you ought to stop by and look inside. Or give yourself a tour. I keep a key in a fake rock at the bottom of the stairs. Duke needs it sometimes for repairs."

"Thank you." The lamps lit here and there actually made the place cozy, not as claustrophobic as I would have imagined. With the quiet jazz piano, it almost felt like a classier version of the tavern.

"Darla says you have questions about Bruno Gates—or Larry Sutton, rather," Orson said.

"Yes. Helen feels responsible for his death. She doesn't feel up to asking a lot of questions right now."

"Helen thought he was her husband. That Martin is still out there somewhere." He shook his head. "Must have been a rude disappointment."

"You don't think Martin is alive? Helen says he sent her money for a while after he left."

Orson examined his coffee mug, then set it on the side table and shook his head again. "Darla should have told Helen the truth."

"What truth?" I asked. The record had ended and the turntable's arm noisily returned to its cradle.

"I've never said anything to anyone—it didn't seem right. But now might be the time."

I gave what I hoped was an encouraging look.

"One afternoon before the tavern opened— maybe ten years after Martin left—I arrived early to unpack the booze shipment—"

"You couldn't have been old enough to tend bar," I interjected.

He smiled. "You're right. I was a kid. But I did odd jobs around town. Darla had just taken over the café. She said she'd left the check for the deliveryman in her big checkbook behind the counter. My job was to unload boxes and pay the driver." His gaze returned to his coffee mug.

"And?"

"On the stub before the driver's check, I saw Helen's name for two hundred dollars. That was big money back then."

"Maybe Helen had done some kind of work for her, or Darla was simply helping her out."

"By taking organ lessons? Commissioning a commemorative poem for the café? I don't think so." He shifted in his seat. "Once the delivery truck left, I had another look at that checkbook.

Darla had written Helen a check every month since Martin left town." He let that sink in. "Every month. For ten years."

I could see this. Darla was generous and wouldn't have wanted Helen to suffer, especially with a child. Helen must have eventually been enough on her feet financially for Darla to have eased off the payments. Helen had no idea.

"She has a big heart, Darla does," I said.

"Indeed." A rapping on the kitchen window drew Orson's attention. "I'll be danged. That's never happened before."

I turned to see a crow hanging from the outside windowsill. He tapped his sharp yellow beak on the glass once more before flying off. I forced myself to breathe slowly. What was it about? I returned my attention to Orson.

"You think Martin Garlington is dead," I said.

He shrugged. "What else am I to think? I didn't want to tell Helen the man on the TV had to be someone else. One thing I've learned over my years as a bartender is sometimes you've got to let people figure things out on their own." He shook his head. "The night Bruno Gates or Larry Sutton or whatever his name is arrived, half the patrons thought they were talking to the fabled Martin Garlington. Of course, most weren't born when he left town. They never knew him, except through Helen's versifying."

This was more evidence that someone might have thought Martin was alive and well and back in Wilfred. "Who was at the tavern that night?"

"I was busy. I'm not sure I could recall many customers."

"Oh, come on, Orson." I smiled my sweetest smile.

"I don't want to get involved in the drama. 'Stay friendly, stay removed.' That's the bartender's code."

"I'm sure you remember who was there. You have an excellent memory. How else do you keep all those drinks straight?"

The armchair's vinyl upholstery sighed as he leaned back and popped up the footrest. "Put that way, I might be able to help. Let's see. Draft beer, cola—that'd be Duke and Desmond. They were in and out. Duke said they had a busy day at work coming up, needed their rest."

I nodded in encouragement. This matched their recollection.

"Two gin and tonics for the Weavers. I don't know why folks drink G and Ts in the winter. A gin martini when it snows? I get that. But, in general, gin should be saved for warmer months."

Get Orson opining on beverage choices and I could be there all day. Roz would be tapping her toes for me to return to the library as it was. "Who else?"

"Lalena had tea while she was taking readings. I keep a stash of lavender-chamomile tea bags behind the counter for her."

"Lalena was there?" She could be a good source of information.

"When business is slow, she sometimes sets up readings in the back booth. Not often, though. It's been months since I've seen her in the tavern, and I don't recall she had a lot of customers. A piña colada and an old-fashioned, I believe. Both ladies."

He shook his head again. "Cleaning that blender is a bear."

"None of the Everhardts came in?"

He drew his brows together. "Not that I recall. Travis works nights, remember. Kaydee has her family. As you can imagine, Lindy seldom comes in." Orson slipped back into a faraway look. "She doesn't get around much these days, but what a sweet lady. Lindy, that is. When I was a kid, I had a huge crush on her. We all did." He raised an eyebrow. "And Martin Garlington not the least, since we're speaking of him."

This was turning out to be a fruitful conversation. "Helen says Lindy was a real friend."

"Lindy didn't deserve Frank. At least his transgressions caught up with him early and gave her the chance for a new life. He was a drinker, too. According to the log, he was the rowdy type. Finally had to ban him from the tavern."

"You keep a log?" This was interesting. Maybe we should keep one in the library.

Orson nodded. "For problem drinkers. Lots of the regulars are maintenance drinkers. You know, get their regular beer or whiskey like they take coffee in the morning. The problem drinkers, they don't know how to stop, and they can get ugly."

"You wouldn't want that." I waited for an opening to steer the conversation back to Larry Sutton.

"Not in this state. Serve a minor or someone who's intoxicated, and you can lose your license. Whatever you do, never let a patron drive drunk." He shuddered, clearly imagining Darla's wrath if he threatened the tavern's ability to dole out boilermakers and vodka tonics.

"What about Bruno? You know, Larry Sutton? Did he talk to anyone?"

"Oh, yes. He wandered through the tavern like he was the host. Almost frenzied. At one point he said"—Orson leaned forward—"get this, he actually said, 'Let us eat and drink, for tomorrow we die.'" He rested back in his recliner again, earning a few squeaks from the seat springs. "All the ladies had a visit from him. Jody Rathback, now she gave him a piece of her mind."

I pictured Jody's muscular physique from her role as Gaston High's PE teacher. She'd perfected a laser glance of displeasure from corralling unruly students. Even so, annoyance wasn't a motive for murder.

"Oh," Orson added, "the new book vendor. The man in the wheelchair. I remember him because we had to get the door. He asked for a glass of milk. Isn't that something? Milk. Nice guy. I'm going to stash a carton of two percent in the mini-fridge for him."

I filed that away. "Did Larry Sutton talk to anyone in particular? Anyone he might have planned to meet later?"

"You mean the note they found in his pocket? The one asking him to meet where the old outhouse was?"

"You know about it," I said.

He tipped his mug into his mouth, then stared at the bottom of the apparently empty mug. "None of the patrons gave it to him."

Orson was performing. Another aspect of decades of bartending. I waited for the punch line.

"It was me. I gave him the note."

"You?"

He nodded and rose to head to the kitchen, a cramped area separated from the living room by an open counter. "Coffee?"

"No, thank you. Why did you want to meet up with Larry?"

"It wasn't me. It was a phone message. I simply delivered it." I opened my mouth to reply, but he cut in. "Before you ask, I have no idea who left the message. I can't even tell you if it was a man or a woman. The TV was going, people were talking, and I was busy. Thinking back, the caller might have even been disguising their voice. Can't say."

Larry Sutton had been summoned to the churchyard. Yet the sheriff's office was sure his death was from natural causes. "When the call came in, who was in the tavern?"

"I know what you're thinking. Whoever was there couldn't have called. That's not true, though. Not with cell phones."

"You're right." The caller might have come from anywhere. Untangling this wasn't going to be easy. "Do you remember anything else? Anything that might suggest why he went to Duke and Desmond's property?"

Orson made to shake his head, then seemed to think the better of it. "He'd had a lot to drink." He raised his gaze meaningfully. "A lot."

Thanks to the medical examiner's report, Larry Sutton's spectacular blood alcohol wasn't news. I rose and tucked Sherlock under an arm. "I see. Thank you for your hospitality. And information. It was super-helpful."

"You won't say anything to Darla about her checkbook?"

I mimicked zipping my lips closed. "I promise."

"You're good at keeping secrets," he said. "Almost as good as a bartender."

CHAPTER 18

I had to get back to the library. Roz might forgive my being a few minutes late, if I had a good reason, but I'd never hear the end of it if I left her alone to greet patrons. Her mood was rotten enough these days. I hurried up the hill and slipped in the kitchen door to find Roz at the table, staring into a cup of coffee. She didn't even seem to have noticed I'd left.

I stared at her a moment, then set the *Complete Adventures* on my desk and hung my coat. When I returned, Roz still hadn't moved. "Shouldn't we open?" I asked her.

"What does it matter?" she said. Her face throbbed red with a hot flash, but she didn't make the slightest move for her fan.

I glanced out the kitchen doorway, through the atrium toward the foyer. If we did have anyone at the front door, they could wait a moment longer.

Regulars would come through the kitchen entrance, anyway, for their cup of coffee and few minutes of pleasantries.

"What's wrong, Roz?" As I spoke, the title *Getting to Yes* flashed in my mind.

"It's the house. Or lack of house. This morning Lyndon and I had a big fight."

"Oh no. I'm sorry." I could certainly imagine Roz in a rage, but Lyndon? His method of fighting would probably be a stony expression and hasty exit to weed the tulip patch or turn the compost.

"We can't come to an agreement on where to live together. We're destined always to be apart. After all these years, too. I'd thought I'd found my soulmate, and now we can't even figure out how to live under the same roof."

"Maybe that's not so bad." I admit to comparing her situation to my relationship with Sam. It was too early to think about living together—not that I didn't have my fantasies—but how would I survive without the books' energy to greet me each morning?

She glared at me. "Of course it's bad. What do you mean, 'not so bad'? You want to find your true love, then still be forking through microwave meals for one at night? No? I didn't think so."

I backed away. Roz was going to have to burn this one off on her own. "I'll open the library."

By the time I'd unbolted the tall front door and taken in the returns, Roz had retreated from the kitchen to the conservatory to write—or pretend to. A few regulars had settled around the kitchen table. I left them to their discussion and settled in circulation, and I texted Lalena. From her booth at the back of the tavern, she would have had a better view of the night's action—that is, if she wasn't too wrapped up in readings.

I'll come up she texted back.

Fifteen minutes later she arrived at the library, her terrier mutt Sailor trailing her on the wide silk ribbon she'd fashioned into a leash. Rodney appeared from nowhere to headbutt Sailor's nose. Rodney settled into my recycling box and Sailor leapt in next to him. Lalena and I smiled at them with a mother's pride.

"I wanted to ask you about the night Larry Sutton, or as he was called then, Bruno Gates, died," I said.

She looked at the floor. "I didn't want to do it, you know."

"Do what?"

"See clients in the tavern. It's just that I needed the money since Mrs. Garlington dropped me. She said she didn't want to contact her husband anymore—she'd moved on. I counted on her for regular weekly income."

"You don't have to explain," I said.

"Orson is good about letting me take a booth for readings on slow nights." She raised her gaze to mine. "You won't tell Darla, will you?"

My guess was she already knew. "I promise. Were you there when Larry Sutton came in?"

She nodded. "He entered from the diner side when it closed for the night. He'd already had a few beers and was looking for more. He had the nerve to try to sit with me, but I told him it would cost him the premium fee for a reading." She leaned back. "He said he knew things the stars would never reveal, then he laughed."

A chill tickled the back of my neck. I leaned in. "What else?"

"I lost track of him until almost closing. He ordered one last drink and headed straight for the bar to pay, only stopping to hit on Kaydee."

"Kaydee?" Orson had specifically said none of the Everhardts had been in the tavern that night. Could he have forgotten in the hubbub of pulling beers and delivering curly fries? "Why was she there? I saw her when Sam and I were having dinner in the café. She was picking up a to-go order to take to her mom."

Lalena shrugged. "It was late. Near closing. She said something to Orson, glared at Larry Sutton, then left."

"What did Larry do?"

"At that point he was examining a note Orson had given him. He looked satisfied and tucked it into his inside pocket. He even winked at me," she added with disgust.

"You didn't see him earlier talking with anyone in particular?"

"I had readings to do. Marcia Stanton wanted to know whether she should go to beauty school."

I knew Marcia. I saved the new Heather Grahams for her. She would have had the piña colada and would have sat in rapt attention while Lalena dealt tarot cards and told her, no matter what cards came up, that the answer was inside her and that wealth was a matter of valuing what you have. The truth would be revealed. Etcetera.

"Lyndon dropped in, too," Lalena added.

"Really? I didn't even know he drank." Despite looking like the villain's silent sidekick in a Western-set film noir, Lyndon was vegan for ethical reasons. I guess I'd supposed he subsisted on carrot juice.

"I can't tell you what was in his glass, but he looked despondent. He spent a while talking with Orson."

Perhaps about his living situation with Roz. Orson hadn't mentioned this. Must be because of the bartender's code he liked to reference.

"Anything else?" Honestly, having Lalena there was almost as good as being there myself.

"Judy Wilkinson is trying to get pregnant. I pulled the Queen of Pentacles. She was over the moon." Lalena reached down to scratch Sailor between the ears. "It's public news. I'm not breaking psychic-client privilege."

Judy must have been the ginger ale.

"Oh." Lalena sat up straight. "I've saved the best for last. You know the guy who's going to sell rare books at Patty's? The brooding one with the sexy scar?"

"Yes?" I said warily. Lalena had a bad track record with men, and I could see where this was going.

"Ian Penclosa." She let the name roll over her tongue like a salted caramel bonbon. "He came in late. Rested just inside the door for a moment, like he was looking for someone. Judy had left, so I asked him to sit with me."

"And you didn't make him pay for a reading, unlike Larry Sutton, I bet."

She ignored me. "Did you know he's moving into Duke's old trailer?" When I didn't respond, she added, "We're practically professional colleagues, you know. I'm a psychic and he deals in books on the paranormal."

"Psychic, huh?"

She shrugged. "You know. We have a long tradition, back to the oracles. Anyway, I'm looking forward to seeing him again."

"You made a date?"

"Not yet." A dreamy look came over her. "We talked for a solid hour."

We could discuss all of this later, during one of Lalena's weekly bath and dinner nights. "Back to Larry Sutton. Were you there when he left?"

"I was talking to Ian." She clearly wasn't ready to end that conversation yet.

"Larry Sutton, Lalena."

She pursed her lips. "All right, yes. Ian and I left just before he did. It was late—past midnight. We were the last ones there besides Larry Sutton. Orson was getting ready to close the tavern, so we took the hint and left. Larry was a bit wobbly on his feet, but he looked pleased with himself. He didn't even wink on the way out."

"You didn't see where he was headed, did you? Larry, not Ian," I added quickly.

"Not with Ian and me. I can tell you that much."

CHAPTER 19

Thanks to a drug shakedown a few towns over, Sam had to work tonight. Normally I'd be bummed to miss an evening with him and would pass the hours reading on the sofa. I had a Ngaio Marsh novel started. But now, the library empty and my apartment a cozy cocoon against the gentle rain, I had a meeting with Sherlock Holmes.

My apartment was far from the bustle of Baker Street's turn-of-the-century London, with horses clip-clopping on the street, Mrs. Hudson busy in her kitchen below, and baronets arriving to beg for help recovering stolen jewels. While Watson and Sherlock Holmes had carried out their adventures on the other side of the globe, Old Man Thurston had been building his home—now the library—on the bluff overlooking Wilfred.

I brought a grilled cheese sandwich to the coffee table and opened the volume of the *Complete*

Adventures next to it. Sherlock stepped out of an illustration of a horse-drawn carriage, rising from the page to become three-dimensional. Rodney, perched on the sofa's back, watched a little too intently. I cast him a warning look.

Sherlock, dressed to weather a cold night, shed his overcoat and plucked a pipe from the air. "Thank you. Watson was being damned annoying, and I needed a break from tracking down the assailant in 'The Adventure of the Dancing Men.'" He surveyed me head to toe. "I can see you've been busy since we parted this afternoon."

I lowered my sandwich to the plate. "How can you tell?"

"From how quickly you're eating, I deduced you didn't have time for lunch."

I looked at my sandwich. "I'm sorry. Would you like a bite?"

He cocked his head. "Have you ever seen me eat? Even in a story? No, Miss Way. I take the occasional cup of tea or small glass of port, but that's all. All meals are quickly summarized by Watson. You never see me chew. I ingest nothing."

"Except cocaine."

"I'll ignore that. Now, let's summarize what we've learned." He tipped his pipe at me. "Please, you begin."

Sherlock was right. I had been hungry. I wiped my fingers on a napkin and pushed the now empty plate aside. "First, Bruno Gates, also known as Larry Sutton—"

"Let's call him by his legal name, Larry Sutton."

I nodded. "The night Larry Sutton died, he partied at the café, then the tavern, as if he knew it was his last. He threw money around, made advances on the women, and left around midnight after someone called the tavern and asked Orson to deliver a note to him." I laid my palms flat on the table. "Note that the caller didn't use Larry's cell phone number, nor did the caller ask to speak to him. Orson isn't sure of the person's gender, either. We can conclude the caller wasn't someone Orson or Larry knew well."

Sherlock slipped his pipe from his mouth. "Perhaps. I noticed that your telephonic device displays incoming numbers of people who call. We must consider the possibility that the caller didn't wish his or her number to be recorded."

Good point. Ignoring the feeling of being put to a test, I continued. "Soon after the call, Orson closed the tavern. We have conflicting stories here, as well. Orson says none of the Everhardts came to the tavern that night, but Lalena told me Lindy Everhardt's daughter Kaydee came in near closing. Orson might have forgotten her, or—"

"Or he was not truthful."

"A possibility. So, that night, we know at least Helen Garlington and Kaydee were out."

"As was Orson, remember." Little puffs of smoke rose from Sherlock's pipe, and his cheeks tightened and released as he smoked. His eyes may have been minuscule in his inch-high head, but his gaze was intense. He set the pipe on a plate that appeared from nowhere and hovered in the air.

Rodney watched Sherlock's hands move with a little too much interest. I rested a palm on his back until he relaxed from a crouch to cat loaf position. This was getting to be a problem.

"You don't think Orson had anything to do with this? What motive could he possibly have?" I asked.

"We're not examining motive right now, but opportunity. Consider the possibility that no one called the tavern."

"You mean Orson might have made the whole thing up and given Larry Sutton a fake note. But why?"

"Again, Miss Way. Opportunity." Sherlock leaned forward. "If we want to examine motive, let us ask ourselves who knew Larry Sutton's true identity that night. This is something for us to ponder."

"You mean, who knew that Bruno Gates was Larry Sutton, or that Bruno Gates wasn't Martin Garlington?"

"Presumably, no one knew Bruno Gates was Larry Sutton until the authorities obtained his wallet." Sherlock glanced at me to confirm this was true. I nodded. "To rephrase my question, Who knew Larry Sutton, masquerading as Bruno Gates, was not Martin Garlington?"

I considered this. "Besides Helen Garlington, I'm not sure anyone believed Bruno Gates was her husband. Helen"—it still felt a bit uncomfortable to use her first name—"was grieving and had been drinking when she saw Bruno Gates on TV. Plus, the TV has seen a lot of years at the tavern and its picture isn't very crisp." Orson was meticulous about mixing cocktails, but wiping the fry grease from the TV screen wasn't part of his daily procedure. "Most of us figured Helen simply needed to come to terms with the fact that her husband was dead and never returning to Wilfred. Remember,

Orson told me Martin had never sent Helen money at all, that it was Darla, the café's owner, who'd sent the money in Martin's name." I stopped for a breath. "On the other hand, Helen was convinced she'd seen her husband. She was so sure that she almost had me—and surely others— believing, too."

"Let me ask another way," Sherlock said. "Who might have feared Larry Sutton was Martin Garlington and not known the stranger was not Mr. Garlington? Mrs. Garlington met him at the library, no?"

"Correct. She saw him, shook his hand, and left. She couldn't have spent more than five minutes with him before leaving."

"And she went straight home."

"From all reports, yes." I imagined her, head down, joy crushed, marching toward her farmhouse. She might have raised a hand in greeting had she passed anyone, but she certainly wouldn't have stopped to chat. "Later she came by the café. She left as soon as she saw Larry Sutton." I winced recalling her stricken expression.

"Therefore, it's possible someone believed Larry Sutton truly was Martin Garlington. With his false hair and glasses, he certainly masqueraded as Mr. Garlington. That is, as Martin Garlington claiming to be Bruno Gates."

Pondering this, I poked the fire and added another log. "If the killer truly believed Martin Garlington had changed his name to Bruno Gates and returned to Wilfred, wouldn't they wonder why he was at the tavern and not with Helen? Wouldn't Helen and Bruno-slash-Larry have gone home together?" I returned to the couch and pulled up my legs. Perhaps this wasn't the pose the elegant Irene Adler would have made, but Sherlock would have to get with the times.

"I hardly consider myself an expert in the female persuasion's turn of mind, but a woman who was abandoned, furthermore with child, might not be of the disposition to invite her perfidious husband to dinner."

"She was so looking forward to seeing him. She'd had her hair done, wore her best pantsuit . . ." And had the hair redone and ditched the pantsuit when the years of grief and anger had finally boiled to the surface and released her to move on. I cocked my head. "You don't think she did it?"

He snorted. "Here? No, she would have told people she was visiting relations elsewhere, then traveled to Larry Sutton's home to dispose of him out of the public eye. No." He puffed furtively at his pipe. Thank goodness its smoke was as fictional as the detective. "We need more information."

"Like what?"

"Martin Garlington was tracking Frank Holloway for a reason. We need to talk with Lindy Everhardt and her children. Learn more about her ex-husband." He returned his pipe to his mouth for a moment and let a smoke ring rise. "Also, remember, we have no evidence that Frank Holloway is dead. I don't know yet what the link is to Larry Sutton's death, but we must keep this possibility in mind."

For a moment I was distracted by how real Sherlock looked. His body had almost filled out and had lost the illustrator's hash marks. So much reader energy must be burning off right now. "All right. Perhaps I can gain more information from the books."

"Hmm."

"Hmm, what?" I said.

"I've never knowingly encountered a witch. My author, Arthur Conan Doyle, was fascinated by the occult. Fairies and mediums, mostly. Not magic, as far as I know."

"It's a long way from the logic you're famous for," I said.

"As I told you, often my logic is born of an intuitive spark. But magic is beyond my understanding." Sometime during our discussion, his overcoat had morphed into a dressing gown. He leaned back in his tiny armchair and crossed his legs. "I deduce your power is fed by reader and author energy. You intentionally—or unintentionally, I observe—act as a lens for this energy, bringing it to life."

"That's about it." I pulled my collar aside to show my birthmark. "Everyone has some ability to funnel energy into hunches or to manifest certain things, but magic runs in my family, and women born with this mark have especially strong power." I let the sweater return to its original position. "Learning how to use this ability has been a work in progress. I have letters from my grandmother to help, but no mentor. I haven't met another witch."

"Let me correct you. You don't know if you've met one," Sherlock said. "Something otherworldly is afoot here."

"You've sensed it? That doesn't sound like you."

"I've seen it. The crows, for instance. That's not normal."

I wasn't sure how to reply. I'd sensed it, too, the feeling I was being watched. It didn't feel deadly—just creepy, as if I were on the edge of a canyon while clouds thickened and darkened on the opposite side, not knowing if the lightning beginning to spark was headed in my direction.

"Miss Way, I want you to listen to me. Carefully."

I leaned forward and Rodney chose that moment to leap from the side table, where he'd discreetly transferred himself when I was distracted by the discussion and made to grab Sherlock's shirt collar. His jaw went right through Sherlock.

"Rodney, naughty cat! Down. Right now."

Rodney gave me side-eye and dropped to the floor.

"To the bedroom."

He lazily stretched—just to show me he was doing things his way—and sauntered into the bedroom to jump to the bed.

"I'm so sorry, Mr. Holmes. He knows better than that."

Sherlock rolled his shoulders and dusted his dressing coat with his palms. "I much prefer a French bulldog."

"You were telling me something. Something important."

He glanced over his shoulder toward the bedroom before continuing. "Yes. If we are correct and Larry Sutton's death was intentional, a murderer is among us. You've been asking a lot of questions."

Sherlock was right. I hadn't hidden the fact that I was interested in Larry Sutton's whereabouts the night he was killed. "You're going to tell me to be careful."

"Take no risks. I can advise you, but outside the world of fiction, my skills at the Eastern martial arts are quite useless. Do you understand?"

I nodded. "I'll be careful."

"While your—ahem—suitor is occupied, you must open the door for no one. Watch your back."

"Definitely." In my opinion, he was overplaying the risk, but I'd keep the doors bolted.

He tossed me a salute. "Until tomorrow, then. We'll reassess and move forward."

The overcoat he'd been wearing when he'd emerged from the illustration had reappeared on his back, and his pipe vanished. He melted into the page.

That night, my dreams wove threads of the past few days into a crazy tapestry. A pint-sized Sherlock Holmes talked and gestured with his pipe, but I couldn't hear his words. Larry Sutton leered at me from the library's foyer. Helen Garlington stared down from the music room, her hair morphing from its former shellacked hairdo to a modern bob. I'd pulled my bedroom curtains closed, but somehow the moon thrust sharp slivers of light across the rag rugs and onto my quilt. And a cold wind blew.

Then someone was knocking on the kitchen door two floors below my bedroom window. I bolted upright, clutching the quilt to my chest. Wind rattled the windowpanes. Had I imagined the knocking? No, there it was again: urgent, furtive. My heart pounded as I remembered Sherlock's warnings about a murderer still being at large.

I closed my eyes and drew on the books' energy. I was in my safe place, I reminded myself. The books murmured and groaned as if they, too, had been awakened. A title slipped into my mind: *The Talented Mr. Ripley.* A novel about a murderer. And an imposter. Was I missing something?

I wrapped myself in my bathrobe and went to the window, attempting to see who might be downstairs, but whoever was at the door was obscured by my bedroom's bay window. I couldn't make out a thing but the rustling oak trees. Across the garden, Sam's house was dark.

Maybe the stranger would go away. As the thought entered my mind, the stranger rapped again. The crazy thought surfaced that it was Larry Sutton, risen from the dead.

Twelfth Night, the books whispered above the wind.

Really? A Shakespearean romance? No, the play was much more than that. And then I knew.

The wooden stairs were cold under my bare feet as I hurried down them and ran to the kitchen, not even stopping to flip on the lights. I unbolted the door and yanked it open.

I must have been a shock to the stranger, with my red curls wild around my head and pilled chenille robe knotted in haste. "Hello," I said, catching my breath.

The old man, thin with thick glasses and a shock of white hair, was too tired to manage a smile. "Hello. I'm Martin Garlington."

CHAPTER 20

We stared at each other a few moments while the oak trees groaned in the wind. "Come in," I finally told Martin Garlington.

If he was surprised at my willingness to welcome him, he didn't show it. He rolled his suitcase inside and swiveled his head, taking in the kitchen. "Looks the same in here."

Besides the new coffeepot, it probably did. "Follow me." I led him to my office, where it was warmer—that is, if Rodney wasn't lying on top of the heat register.

I removed a novel from the armchair—*Mistaken Identity* by Lisa Scottoline. Mr. Garlington lowered himself with the exhaustion of someone who has achieved his destination at last. It had taken only decades.

"You must be the librarian," he said. "The one

spite. I suppose it couldn't
...re."

...hundred and twenty
...ve," I said. With the real
...front of me, there was no
...s son Derwin shared his thick
...head, and slender build with ele-

...now who I am?"

...elen Garlington's husband. It really was you
...Tick Tock Cash, wasn't it?"

He relaxed into the armchair and let out a long sigh. "It was foolish of me to go on TV. I thought after nearly fifty years it would be all right. I should have known fate would draw Helen to the show."

Fate—or witchcraft. How the scenario had unrolled was clear to me at last, but I wanted to hear it firsthand. "Tell me what happened."

Rodney slinked in and leapt to Mr. Garlington's lap. He seemed to barely notice the cat's presence, although his fingers automatically went to Rodney's silky back. Rodney purred hypnotically, and Martin Garlington began to speak.

"When I left Wilfred in 1974"—he raised an eye to make sure I was listening, then let his focus drift—"I went to Pacific Grove, California. It was the first place that came to mind. The town is famous for its butterfly sanctuary. I found work and changed my name to Bruno Gates. It sounded tough, like something I wanted to be." He let out a sad laugh.

I nodded with encouragement.

Mr. Garlington's gaze rested on the window and the shapes of cottonwood trees rustling in the

night wind. "I thought about Helen ev
course, but I wouldn't let myself contact
for her own good."

"Why?"

He ignored me. His story had been penn
behind a dam of half a century, and it had to b
leased before he could respond to any of my qu
tions. "A thousand times I began a letter, the
crumpled it and threw it away. When the interne
came along, I was tempted to type her name into the
search bar, but I resisted. Over the years, it became
easier and easier to let Wilfred and my life here slip
away. It was better that Helen believe I was dead."

"Your driver's license identifies you as Bruno
Gates," I said, remembering that the sheriff's office had checked it.

"It wasn't so hard in those days to become someone else. Once you have a driver's license, you're
set." His fingers ceased caressing Rodney's back.
Martin patted his chest and he slipped his fingers
into the cat's silky fur once again. "When the receptionist at Eternal Respite told me you'd called,
it all came back."

"Helen asked me to help."

At the sound of Helen's name, Mr. Garlington's
eyes met mine for the first time since he'd taken
his seat. "Helen." He let his hand drift to the chair's
arm. "I wanted to protect her. I couldn't return to
Wilfred, but neither could I bear the thought she
might think I'm alive and had abandoned her."

"You did abandon her," I pointed out. "Did you
know she was pregnant?"

Martin's head jerked up so quickly that Rodney
leapt from his lap to mine. "You said what?"

"You have a son. Derwin."

His knuckles whitened as he clutched the chair's arms. He released his grip and his hands fell into his lap. "That was my father's name. Derwin. Oh, Helen, how could I do this to you?" He looked away. "She remarried, I suppose?"

He'd flat-out abandoned Helen. He didn't deserve information about her marital status. "You convinced your colleague Larry to pretend to be you and come to Wilfred in your place. You wanted Helen to think she'd been mistaken about you," I prompted.

"Yes," he said, his mind still clearly on his new-to-him son. "Yes. Larry liked to do things like this. He was a practical joker and always short on cash. Lately he'd been especially restless." Martin shook his head. "I didn't think he'd take me seriously, but he jumped at the opportunity. 'You only live once,' he told me. He bought a toupee and we counted on the television to mask the difference between us. I gave him money for gas and a hotel as well as something for his trouble."

"Cash?"

He nodded.

That explained the wad in the dead man's wallet. "He didn't know your real identity, did he?"

Again, Martin Garlington lowered his head and examined his hands. "No."

"Then Larry died."

"I had to come up, find out what happened to him. He'd stopped answering my calls, you see. Not that I was completely surprised. Larry had taken the whole week off. He was talking about stopping at a casino. Then he showed up at the

Eternal Respite. As a client." Martin caught his breath. "I had just been trying his number again when they rolled him in, a tag still looped on his big toe. I was, I was"—he searched for a word—"devastated. Devastated and confused. What had I done by asking him to go to Wilfred? I had to find out what happened."

Of course. Once the sheriff's office had determined there was no homicide to investigate, they'd sent his body home. As angry as I was at Martin Garlington for running out on Helen, it was awful imagining him seeing his friend laid out on a stainless steel gurney.

"The medical examiner determined he'd died of natural causes," I said. "An embolism."

"Brought on by kidney cancer, probably exacerbated by alcohol and hours behind the wheel of his car. I know."

"You're not convinced."

"A few things," he said. "Larry's right hand was clutched closed, as if he'd been holding something thin."

"He had a note. Someone planned to meet him the night he died."

"His right hand was clenched." Mr. Garlington slowed his words to emphasize his point. "Larry was left-handed."

"There was a note in his coat pocket, not his hand." Could someone have pulled it from his fingers to stash it somewhere safe—somewhere protected from the drizzle where investigators would be sure to find it? "What else?"

"There was a phone call."

I waited. I was learning that Martin Garlington's

approach was like climbing a steep hill. He needed regular pauses to catch his mental breath.

"Naturally, I'd been talking with him. He'd phoned when he'd arrived in Wilfred, but I hadn't heard from him since. I called every few hours. He wouldn't pick up." The thin moonlight through my office windows illuminated Martin Garlington's weariness. "I could have sworn I tossed and turned all night, not a second of shut-eye, but I must have slept at some point, because I found a message from him in the morning."

"What did it say?"

"It was brief. 'Martin,' he said. 'Met Helen. She didn't stick around, but Wilfred . . .'"

"But Wilfred what?"

"He trailed off. Just like that. He was laughing." Mr. Garlington shook his head. "Then he said, 'Well, hello' and hung up. My voicemail placed the call at twelve-twenty."

"About the time he died. He may have been greeting his murderer. Did it sound like he knew this person?"

"Larry knew everyone. He greeted complete strangers as if they were in the same bowling league." He pulled his phone from a pocket. "I saved the voicemail. Listen."

He put the phone on speaker. It was Larry Sutton, all right, and if I hadn't known he'd been drinking from the blood alcohol report, I'd have figured it out from his slurred words. His "Well, hello" sounded both welcoming and surprised.

I wished I'd brought Sherlock downstairs with me. We certainly would have some debriefing to do in the morning.

"Mr. Garlington, I understand why you came to Wilfred, but why the library?"

"I didn't know where else to go. I couldn't let anyone see me. Larry died because someone thought he was me. If anyone knew I was in town, I was a dead man."

"But the library?" I leaned forward and Rodney stepped up to the desk to watch us. "How do you know I'm trustworthy?"

He looked at me eagerly. "It was you who helped Helen look for me. That you helped her gave me the idea you were a kind person. Plus, the library was always a refuge for Wilfredians. Marilyn made sure of it. And then, well, Helen used to love playing the library's organ, so I had happy associations. It's still here?"

I nodded. "She gives lessons on it."

He glanced up, and warmth suffused his face for a moment before he became serious again. "Can I stay here?"

No. Absolutely not. I was deep enough in this drama as it was. "Why not drop in on Helen—she's still at your old house—and explain everything to her? That's who you should be telling this story to. She can help you. I'll call ahead so she has a moment to prepare."

"No," he said quickly. He rose and paced the three-step width of the office. "Don't you see? I can't."

"Why not?" The quick back-and-forths dizzied me. "Sit down, please. Surely you didn't expect you could knock on the library's door in the middle of the night and get a bed? Now that you're back in Wilfred, it's time to give Helen closure.

See her, meet your son"—I raised an eyebrow, intending this part about Derwin to be an added attraction—"and clear up the past."

He didn't sit, but at least he stopped pacing. He clutched the back of the armchair. "I told you, I can't. It's not just my life I'm worried about, it's Helen's."

"If you're so concerned about Helen's life, why did you run out on her?" This was my second big question and the most important one.

"I can't tell you."

Helen had said her husband was a coward. She hadn't mentioned what a stubborn coward he was. Martin had run off, then sent a stranger to Wilfred to continue the charade that he was dead. Helen was my friend and maybe even honorary family. She deserved better than this. "You aren't my responsibility." I stood and pointed to the door. "It's time for you to leave. You made this mess, you take care of it."

He collapsed into the chair and rested his face in his hands. His shoulders bobbed jerkily. He was crying.

Just like that, my anger turned to compassion. The poor man was obviously upset, and for good reason. But what was I supposed to do? I glanced at my desk clock. It was nearly two in the morning. Even if Martin did leave, the tavern was closed and there was nowhere to get a room. If Helen were smart, she wouldn't answer a knock—certainly not this time of the night, not since Larry Sutton's death—and she might have her phone shut off. I let out a long sigh, one Roz would have envied.

"All right," I said. "You can take the sofa in natural history. Just for tonight."

CHAPTER 21

When I woke, I had the overwhelming sense that something was off base, somehow wrong. Then I remembered: Martin Garlington was here. I tossed back the blankets. He'd answered a few questions last night, but not the most pressing—why he'd left Wilfred in the first place—and this time I didn't plan to let him off the hook so easily.

I slipped on my bathrobe and made for the door that connected my apartment to the library, but turned around before I'd opened the door. I needed backup. I tucked the *Complete Adventures* under an arm.

I found Mr. Garlington in the downstairs kitchen, opening and shutting cupboards. The kitchen light was bright in the overcast morning. "I thought you didn't want anyone to know you were here."

We both glanced toward Big House. Through the trees, its windows were still dark. Martin snapped off the lights.

"Lucky for you, the library is closed today," I said. "But that doesn't mean someone won't wander by anyway, or that you won't be spotted from Big House."

"Who's living there now?"

"Sam Wilfred. He's a sheriff's deputy." I rested the book on the counter and pulled the coffee and filters from a cupboard. "I assume you were looking for these?"

Martin nodded and kept looking toward Big House. "What happened to Jimbo and his wife?"

"Sam's parents? One night in the nineties, the mill burned down and they skipped town, taking Sam with them. With the mill gone, the town shrank. The post office is now a grocery store and most of the other shops shut down. Sam moved back about a year ago."

"A lot has changed here."

"Wilfred is nowhere as prosperous as it was when you left, but things are improving. We have a retreat center now." A camp for square dance callers was due to arrive in a few weeks. That should liven things up. "There's talk of a guest house opening, too."

Despite the comforting perk of the coffee maker, Martin Garlington look dazed.

"Watch out for Rodney's bowl, Mr. Garlington." Rodney liked to have food and water options both down here and up in my apartment.

"Call me Martin."

As the coffeepot worked its magic, I picked up

the *Complete Adventures* and felt its rising energy as I hugged it to my chest. "If we're going to get to the bottom of who killed Larry Sutton, I need to know why you left Wilfred."

Just as he had last night, he shut down. "I can't talk about it."

"You suspect someone killed Larry because they thought Larry was you, correct?" I could practically feel Sherlock in the book, struggling to crawl out and ask his own questions. I kept the volume clamped shut. Although Martin wouldn't be able to see him, Sherlock would be too much of a distraction for me.

"That's the only possible conclusion." Martin pointed at the book. "Why are you carrying that big book around?"

"I like to read. Don't change the subject." I took a step closer and dropped my bombshell. "Do the bones found on the old Holloway property have anything to do with why you left?"

Martin might have momentarily blanched, but before I could be sure, his features reorganized themselves into a stone wall. "I don't know what you're talking about."

"Human bones. Helen tested their DNA, in fact, to see if they might be yours."

This brought a softening. "She thinks I'm dead."

"Isn't that what you wanted?" When he didn't respond, I tried again. "Look, if you won't say why you left, how do expect to find the murderer? There are zero leads. The sheriff's office ruled Larry Sutton's death as from natural causes and closed the investigation. Isn't there anything you can tell me? Anything to help?"

He fidgeted with his coffee cup. He was on the brink of revealing something, I could tell. I held my breath as I waited to see what he'd say.

"Does Helen have organ lessons today?"

If I hadn't been holding the *Complete Adventures* for Sherlock's benefit, I would have been tempted to chuck it at him. "You've got to be kidding."

"I miss her. She'd play the sweetest songs on the piano at home while I was drawing my butterflies. 'Please release me—'" he sang in a warbly tenor.

"Stop. Martin, listen. If you want to reconnect with your wife, do it. Put on your coat and walk to your house and knock on the door. She might slam it in your face, but you're welcome to try." Maybe I was being too harsh, but he seriously irritated me. "If you want to find the person who killed your friend, you need to come clean. Otherwise, pack up your suitcase and go home. You're doing no good here."

"But, my son. Derwin." He smiled with a faraway look. "Derwin Garlington, my son."

"Helen will give you his address. Or, you can stop by the post office in Forest Grove. He should be packing his mailbag about now."

The *Complete Adventures* had heated in my arms, and I couldn't hold it any longer without resorting to oven mitts. I rested it on the table.

Martin turned to the coffeepot to pour a mug. The book flipped open and Sherlock stepped out, this time from an illustration in "The Adventure of the Naval Treaty." He wore a dressing gown and held a test tube in one hand.

Get back in the book, I silently urged Sherlock.

He ignored me and stood on the pages. The test

tube vanished and he folded his arms over his chest as he examined Martin.

"If you knew the details, you'd understand," Martin said when he faced me again. He glanced at the open book. Thankfully, Sherlock was invisible to him. "This is a strange time to read."

"Never mind that. If you want me to understand, I need details. Tell me."

His gaze met mine. He set the coffee mug on the table and straightened. "I'll tell you this, but only this. It has to do with the Empress."

"The Empress theater, the theater Frank Holloway robbed before you left town." An inexplicable chill ran up my arms.

Martin pushed his mug away. "That's all I'll say, and I probably shouldn't have even told you that."

"Then it does have to do with the bones found on the Holloway property."

His head snapped up. "I didn't say that."

"Then what? What are you saying?" I was ready to grab Martin by his thin shoulders and give them a good shake. "You can't just drop a hint and clam up."

"It's too dangerous to tell you. Forget I said anything."

I knew that stubborn look. Derwin had inherited it and had displayed the same firm frown and slightly raised eyebrows the time I questioned *American Libraries* magazine's torn cover after he'd delivered it. "Fine. You made it to Wilfred and you plan to track down Larry's killer. What are your next steps?" I kept my gaze on Martin, but I could feel Sherlock's doll-sized eyes bore into me.

Martin's shoulders relaxed and he adopted a

conspiratorial tone. "Funny you should mention that. I was thinking it over last night."

"Yes?" I knew where this was going.

"I said to myself, 'Marty, anyone finds out you're here, you're a dead man.' Then I thought, 'Say, here's an intelligent young librarian. Librarians are aces at research. I bet she could be your eyes and legs in town.'"

"You thought so, did you? You planned to send me out to scope a dangerous situation, but not tell me the facts?"

A forlorn look replaced the bonhomie. "What else am I supposed to do? I can't show my face. I can't tell you why I left. These are facts. But it's my fault Larry died. I owe it to him to find out who killed him."

Martin's voice quivered. I hoped he wasn't going to cry again. He had no idea his wife wanted me to track down the murderer, too, and Sherlock wasn't going to let it go. Truth was, I was already deep into this mystery and had no intention of quitting, either. I just didn't want Martin to know that. If only I could squeeze one little clue from him.

I made a show of indecisiveness. At last, I appeared to relent. "All right. I'll do some initial scouting, and you can combine what I learn with what you already know."

He visibly relaxed and slowly lowered himself onto a kitchen chair. "Thank you. I can't tell you how grateful I am."

"The library is closed today, so it should be easy to stay undiscovered. Just make sure you put your bedding out of sight in case Lyndon stops in."

"Who's Lyndon?"

"Lyndon Forster, the caretaker." That's right, Lyndon would have been a toddler when Martin left town.

Martin nodded, eager to show his gratitude.

"What are you going to do while I'm out?" I asked.

He looked around, not knowing the thousands of volumes of the library's books murmured seductively. For them, a day off was a day of waiting for a patron to touch a spine, or best, pull a book from the shelves with the intention of taking it home.

"I guess I'll read."

CHAPTER 22

I tucked the *Complete Adventures* under my arm
and made my way down the hill. Mist had settled over the valley, and the rising sun infused it
with a dusky pink. Pickup trucks were already
pulling into Darla's Café. I could almost smell the
coffee and yeasty waffles and hear the clinking of
forks on platters. I wasn't going to the café, though.
I was on my way to the Empress.

Sherlock had made it clear he would not be left
at home. "If, as you surmise, Mr. Garlington's escape from Wilfred is related to Larry Sutton's
death, this is our first solid clue. I must see it myself."

I was curious to see the inside of the Empress,
too, for a peek into Wilfred's history. "All right.
You can come along, but remember, the robbery
took place ages ago. According to Orson, the the-

ater has sat empty for decades. What do you expect to find?"

"I won't know until I see it."

"The police have already investigated. With more than a magnifying glass and an eye for boot tread. It's not like we're going to find bits of tobacco or anything else you've written monographs about."

"Your small-town police are not Sherlock Holmes, the greatest detective in history," Sherlock reminded me.

At last, we stood at the old theater's side entrance. Above us, Orson undoubtedly still slept. He would have worked past midnight.

As Orson had said, the door to the old theater was directly under the stairs to his apartment and the key was hidden in a false rock at the foot of the stairs. The door had swollen into the jamb, but with a push it was open. We were inside.

My eyes adjusted to the dark, and I once again pondered what a grand name the Empress was for such a dumpy little place. Once I could see well enough to find a light switch, I flipped it. A low-watt bulb barely illuminated the service hall, floored in an indoor-outdoor carpet whose musty odor indicated a leaky roof. To my right was a door with a dead bolt. I tried its handle. Locked. I went left, the only route open to me, toward the building's face.

The hall ended in two doors. I opened the narrow door on the left first and found myself in a box office barely larger than a coat closet. Its glass window looked into the now-boarded theater entrance, lined in framed posters of *Blazing Saddles*. I sneezed at the dust.

"Bless you," Sherlock said, his voice muffled by pages.

"Do you see anything useful to us?"

"Open up, please."

I laid the book in front of the slot where, decades earlier, so many Wilfredians had slid money for tickets.

A hunched shepherd stepped out from *The Hound of the Baskervilles*, rubbing his arms and legs as if to warm them. The shepherd shed his beard and battered hat—it was Sherlock in disguise. "It's chilly on the moors." Through the dust-smeared window he surveyed the Empress's former entrance, then materialized on my shoulder. "Continue on. There must be another door."

"In the hall."

This door connected to the theater's interior lobby. Although tiny compared to big-city movie palaces, the lobby's deco chandelier and dusty gilding hinted at a former grandeur. The light from the chandelier's two working bulbs was so dim that I couldn't make out whether the walls were green or blue, but a blackened streak ran up one wall, likely from the fire. The theater hadn't suffered major damage that I could see. Perhaps smoke inhalation had sent Orson's father to the hospital.

Ahead was a snack counter, unused for almost half a century. Behind it, to the far right, was another door that must connect to the locked room we'd passed when we entered. The office.

I touched the red velvet rope on a stanchion, and its brittle fabric crumbled under my fingers.

"What exactly are we looking for?" I asked, brushing my fingers on my coat.

"Stop here," Sherlock replied. "The thieves would have raided the box office, of course, and presumably the refreshment counter. The most effective way to do that would be to wait until the theater closed, then break into the office, where the evening's earnings would have been locked into a safe before being deposited at the bank the next morning. Am I correct in my assumptions? Let's try the door."

I sneezed and nodded. I was beginning to feel the book's weight. I was more like a bus driver than a sleuth. "Do you know about movie theaters?"

"I know about theaters, certainly. A popular form of entertainment in my world. I also know about films. Many, many films have been made of my exploits. Some are quite terrible, although I've developed a fondness for Basil Rathbone. Combine these concepts, and it doesn't take a genius to determine what a movie theater is."

"Elementary," I said, not missing the condescension in his voice.

I made my way behind the snack bar, navigating empty boxes and mouse droppings, to the office door. I tried the knob and to my surprise it opened. I flipped the light switch, but the bulb had long burned out. I tried the desk lamp and here had success.

We were in a small, windowless office with a desk, filing cabinets, and a low bookshelf. Two doors let onto the office—the one we'd just entered through the snack bar, and the door to the theater's side entrance, the first door we'd encountered when we'd entered the Empress. The locked door. I breathed through my mouth to avoid the musty smell.

"The safe," Sherlock said.

On the floor near the filing cabinets was a square safe about a foot-and-a-half high. Sherlock vanished from the book and appeared next to the safe. He plucked a magnifying glass from the air and examined the safe's dial. "Very interesting," he said. "Yes, interesting, indeed." The room was small enough that he could investigate it completely while still tied to my energy. "Miss Way, a lift, please. To the opposite door."

I lowered my hand so he could climb into my palm, and I brought him to the door to the side hall. He raised his magnifying glass to the door handle. This door was padlocked closed from the inside and Sherlock examined the hasps.

"Yes, quite illuminating." He turned to me, the magnifying glass vanishing. "To the viewing room, if you please."

We retraced our steps behind the snack bar and into the lobby. A gothic arch to the snack bar's left marked the way to the theater. My skin prickled. I halted at the heavy velvet curtain separating the lobby from the theater.

"Wait," I whispered.

"Hmm?" A pipe had materialized in Sherlock's mouth, and he contentedly puffed from his perch on the book.

I listened but heard nothing from the theater's

depths. "Something feels off. Do we really need to go in there?"

"You are basing your hunch on what?" Sherlock's pipe vanished and he stood. "Magic? Or perhaps bald fear? My dear girl, one must rely upon logic and the senses. Do you have any evidence of danger?"

I hesitated. "No. Do you?"

"I do not. We are simply in an abandoned building with poor illumination and, judging from how you clutch your coat, a draft. See the dust on the floor? I doubt anyone has set foot in here for years."

"True, but what does the viewing area have to do with the robbery?"

"We only assume Mr. Garlington's hint had to do with the robbery. We don't know for sure. Now, carry on."

"I have more than logic at my disposal, Sherlock. Remember, I'm a witch. You wouldn't be here if logic and the senses were all that mattered." For a moment, I imagined what another person—say, Sam—would see if he were here. He'd witness me carrying on a whispered one-sided conversation with a book.

Sherlock flared his tiny nostrils in frustration. "If you're frightened, you may place the book in the middle of the room and seat yourself near the wall. I want to examine the room's layout. It won't take long. Unless I'm mistaken, the locus of the crimes was elsewhere."

I didn't like it, but I complied with Sherlock's demand and pushed through the draperies into the theater's heart. Perhaps twenty rows of seats divided by a central aisle sloped to a two-story-high movie screen flanked by shredded brocade curtains. Plaster moldings ringed the ceiling depicting forests, woodsmen, and sharp-toothed handsaws. Directly above us, on the back wall, was Orson's apartment in the former projector room.

Heart racing, I hurried down the aisle and balanced the book on a seat before taking a place at the rear of the room.

Why was I so frightened? The box office and lobby were creepy, sure, but empty. Here I sensed something more. I steadied my breath and remembered Sherlock's words. No one had been here for years. As I began to calm, a thick chill settled over me, as if I'd been pushed into a walk-in freezer. My breath now clouded the air.

"Sherlock," I whispered in a panic. He didn't reply.

I straightened and searched the dark theater. Magic tied Sherlock to his *Complete Adventures* by five feet or so, and I barely made out his tiny outline scampering like a fairy among the seats. It was too dark to see anything else except the huge once-white screen now splotched with mildew at the opposite end of the room.

I wrapped my arms around my shivering body. I had to leave. My pounding pulse and burning birthmark told me something otherworldly was happening. Yet, I couldn't move. I was fastened to my seat by a force stronger than I was.

A motion on the movie screen caught my attention. Could it be? A woman's face materialized, in color, taking only a small portion of the screen. Her mouth moved, but no sound came out. The face was familiar, but this was long ago—the ringlets around her face placed her in the 1960s. My energy burned and tightened until I could breathe only in shallow bursts. The manifestation on the screen was drawing power from me, telling me something. The circle around the face widened, and I knew at once this was my grandmother. She was a young woman, and I saw my blue eyes in hers.

I tried to stand, but couldn't. I was pinned to the chair by a bone-chilling supernatural force— or was it simply fear, as Sherlock had suggested? Magic and blood pounded in my ears. On the screen, my grandmother was looking at someone with a fierce concentration, saying something, but although her lips formed words, all I heard was the pounding of blood in my ears. It was a spell— my grandmother was casting a spell. I only caught one word: "Begone."

With that, the image vanished and the energy binding me to my chair snapped. I rose so abruptly that I nearly fell forward. I tightened my fists against the tsunami of adrenaline saturating my system.

"Sherlock," I shouted, unafraid that Orson would hear me. I couldn't see Sherlock at all. I rushed to pick up the *Complete Adventures*, and it wasn't even lukewarm. The manifestation on the screen must have sapped the book's energy completely, taking Sherlock Holmes with it. "Sherlock," I said again, this time in a whisper. Nothing. He was gone, dead.

I'd sort it out later. I had to get out of there.

Book under my arm, I ran from the rows of theater seats, feeling eyes on my back. I hurried through the lobby, barely stopping to snap off the lights. In a few seconds, I was down the hall behind the box office and on the street, blissfully drinking in the moist spring air while my heartbeat slowly returned to normal.

From the roof, a crow cawed.

CHAPTER 23

When I reached the bridge over the Kirby River, I leaned against a stone parapet and caught my breath. What had just happened? My magic had never before materialized images on a screen. Books fed it, not films. Furthermore, I hadn't called on the energy. I hadn't asked it to tell me anything.

It was true that magic sometimes escaped my control. Lights might flash and books that I needed to read—whether I knew it or not—appeared on my nightstand. Then there were mini–freak-outs like the one the tavern's television set had when I'd entered to find Helen, the freak-out that had led me to where I was now. What had happened in the Empress was something else.

An unknown force was at work here. This force was bigger than Larry Sutton. Did it concern the bones on the Holloway property? I remembered the prickle I'd felt when meeting the rare books dealer. Perhaps it had to do with him?

I flattened my palm against the *Complete Adventures*. It was cold. The manifestation on the movie screen had sapped the energy Sherlock needed to appear. A shame—from what he'd said in the theater's office, he'd learned something.

Just as I planned to reshelve the book and say goodbye forever to Sherlock's help, he materialized, semi-sheer, on the back of my hand.

"I thought you were a goner," I said after looking around to make sure no one was within earshot. I'd missed the little guy.

"Fortunately, a book club in Dubuque is reading my adventures. They've kicked up some energy arguing about my relationship with Irene Adler."

"You admit you did have a relationship with her!" My voice was shaky with fear and relief he'd come back. "I knew it."

He folded his arms over his chest. "You believe you know." He dropped his arms. "The book club plus a film festival in Sydney has put me back in form. Speaking of films, please inform me about your experience at the Empress. One moment I was examining the movie house's setup, and the next I was back in the *Complete Adventures*."

I resumed my walk up the hill. Lights were on at Big House, but Sam was at work, so the lights would be for the babysitter and Nicky. She'd be too engrossed in keeping the baby out of trouble to spy on me talking to, seemingly, nobody.

"I'm not sure. The energy of the audiences must have been waiting for an outlet. It was so strange." I shook my head, remembering. "I saw my grandmother on the movie screen. From way before I was born."

"Did she have anything to say about the murder? Or maybe the thefts?"

"No. At least, I don't think so. She was warning someone away. Casting a spell, I think." I shook my head again, this time in bewilderment. "The air turned freezing. I was pinned to my chair and could only breathe—barely—and watch. It was horrible."

Sherlock's tiny brows knitted. For once, he didn't reply.

"Sherlock?"

At last, he spoke. "As I said, Moriarty. Your own, Miss Way."

"You think I have an enemy?"

"I've sensed it. Someone out there is powerful enough to understand your magic and use it against you. You'd best beware."

We'd reached the library's kitchen door. I couldn't wait to be in its warmth and safety, surrounded by books and their sweet energy. I unbolted the door and was momentarily surprised at the faint light spilling in from the atrium. That's right, Martin Garlington was here.

"Impossible," I told Sherlock. "I don't have any enemies."

"We'll delay our discussion of that incident for the moment. Remember, we have a murderer to find. My investigation of the theater proved quite fruitful."

Before I had the chance to reply, the organ moaned a bass note, launching up into a lugubrious rendition of "Release Me." Sherlock hastily reabsorbed into his *Complete Adventures*. The light I'd seen was not from Martin, but from Helen, conducting an organ lesson in the mansion's former dressing room—now music room—on the second floor. She thoughtfully kept the beginners, the students most likely to unsettle library patrons, for when the library was closed to the public.

Maybe Martin had decided to reveal himself to Helen after all. I ducked into my office and dropped the *Complete Adventures* on my desk before hurrying up the mansion's central staircase. I halted in front of pure science, where Martin gazed, mouth slightly ajar, at Helen's back. Had Helen turned, she couldn't have missed him.

Instead, Helen fussed with sheet music. A rapt eight-year-old girl with enormous glasses sat on the bench next to her. "Lily," Helen said, "Feel the passion in this song. The longing. Communicate it with your fingers."

I wasn't sure how much amorous history a fourth-grader could summon, or what enthusiasm she bore for Engelbert Humperdinck, but Lily nodded gamely. A sigh escaped Martin's lips.

"Josie, is that you?" Helen swiveled on the organ's bench and Martin leapt out of sight.

"Yes." I glanced into pure science. Martin hovered behind a bookshelf. "I came up to see how you're getting on."

Helen squinted. I didn't usually check in on her, especially on my day off. "Have you been napping in natural history? There's a blanket on the sofa. And a man's shoes tucked under it."

"Patrons." I shook my head. "You never know what they'll do next."

"Someone went home barefoot?"

"I'll put the shoes in lost and found. Thank you for pointing them out."

Helen turned to her student. "Lily, I believe you have to use the ladies' room right now."

"Yes, Mrs. Garlington." Lily slipped from her bench and obediently walked toward the restroom.

When she was out of earshot, Helen turned to me. "How has our investigation been proceeding?"

"There have been, um, unusual developments." Aware of Martin nearby, I added, "I visited the Empress this morning."

"The movie theater? What does that have to do with Larry Sutton?"

"It was a hunch. Frank Holloway robbed it. I thought seeing the theater might help us put the pieces together."

Helen pursed her lips. "I don't see how they're related. The Empress shut down decades ago. A shame. I remember the showing of Franco Zeffirelli's *Romeo and Juliet*." Her eyes took a faraway look. "Romance and tragedy. Just lovely." Her fingers absently reached for the organ's keyboard and the movie's theme, with added tremolo, rang through the library.

"Mrs. Garlington. I found this in the bathroom." Lily returned holding a shaving mug and razor.

Helen narrowed her eyes. "Josie, this is getting out of hand. The library is not a grooming parlor for patrons. Do I need to talk with the trustees about it?"

I took the shaving items from Lily. Fink. "I'll take care of it, thank you."

Helen cast me a stern glance and returned to her student. Music, with a bit more snappiness, rose from the keyboard.

I'd have to find somewhere out of the way for Martin—that is, if he insisted on staying and if I let him. This question was still up for debate.

I went downstairs to my office to open the pages of the *Complete Adventures* and learn what Sherlock had deduced from our trip to the Empress. Martin appeared, his thick white hair pointing in all directions from running his fingers through it.

"Helen," he said with more breath than voice. The organ music kept our conversation from reaching beyond my office.

I nodded. "Your bride. The woman you abandoned. When she was with child."

"I didn't know that." Anguish on his face, he dropped into the armchair. "I was doing what was best for her. I protected her."

"We've been over this." The only way through to him was to be blunt. I plunged ahead. "You were a coward. Surely whatever you ran from was less important than your marriage?"

He pulled off his glasses and rubbed the bridge of his nose. "She's still so lovely, so full of passion."

I couldn't respond. I felt awful for him, but I also felt it served him right.

"Did she remarry? I couldn't get close enough to see if she wore a ring."

He'd asked before. This time I answered. "No." I could have told him that although she thought he was dead, a part of her hoped he'd return, but I didn't want to give him the satisfaction. Besides, between Larry Sutton's death and discovering the bones in the outhouse weren't his, she'd moved on at last. It had been a hard-won step and I didn't want to endanger it. "Why, Martin? Why did you leave?"

At my elbow, Sherlock materialized on the open book. I hoped Martin would think my glance at him was merely me checking the time on my desk clock.

"Frank Holloway didn't rob the theater alone," Sherlock said in a voice only I could hear. I kept a straight face. "He couldn't have. The door to the hall was damaged to make it look like someone broke in, but the damage was on the inside of the lock, not the outside. Furthermore, the safe was unscratched. Someone let in the thief and provided the safe's combination."

"Mr. Garlington," I said. "You mentioned the Empress. What do you know about the thefts?"

He scrambled to his feet. "Nothing. I don't know anything about them. Why?"

"You didn't happen to leave Wilfred because you feared being arrested?"

He shook his head vigorously enough to knock his glasses down his nose. He pushed them up with a finger. "No. I'd never steal anything."

I'd struck a nerve, I saw. "You were keeping a log of someone's comings and goings. Frank Holloway's? He robbed the Empress. Is that what you were getting at?"

"You found my notes?"

I nodded. "Maybe you saw something, and you ran."

"No." He relaxed back into the chair. He clearly felt on safer ground here. "There was a complete investigation, remember? I had nothing to do with the robberies, and Frank was arrested. No, that's not it."

The music had stopped and steps creaked on the library's central staircase. I motioned for Martin to stay put and moved to the kitchen, shutting my office door behind me seconds before Helen and Lily appeared.

"You show a lot of promise, Lily," Helen said. "Remember, music is a more than a series of notes on paper. It's communication. Poetry for the ears. Stories for our souls."

Helen's appearance might have modernized, but her attitude was still firmly Edwardian, even if her taste in music occasionally ran to Vegas lounge singers.

"Yes, Mrs. Garlington," the girl said, clutching her sheet music.

"Unrelated question," I said. "Did Martin ever talk to you about anything unusual he saw at the Empress?"

"What does this have to do with Larry Sutton's death? As I said, I think you're getting far afield in the investigation." She slipped her purse on her arm. "It's ancient history."

"I thought you wanted me to find out who killed Larry Sutton."

"Of course I do." Helen pursed her lips. "I'll be in touch. Come on, Lily. I'll drive you home."

CHAPTER 24

So far, the robbery at the Empress was all I had to go on. That and a reconstructed timetable of the night Larry Sutton died. Mack Jubell—Orson's father and the Empress's owner—had passed on. There would be no interviewing him. I could, however, talk with Lindy Everhardt to see what she remembered about the robbery. Her husband had been prosecuted for the first break-in. She might have information linking it to why Martin had left town and who or what he had run from.

But first, as would do any good librarian, I planned to wring my available resources dry. Right now, these resources were Martin Garlington and back issues of the *Forest Grove News-Times*. Sadly, the *Wilfred Searchlight*, the town's dedicated newspaper, went out of business long ago. The Forest Grove paper was the next best option.

From the kitchen, I surveyed the atrium, then returned to my office. "The coast is clear."

Martin rose. "Good. I'll just—-"

"Not so fast." I held up a hand to stop him. "You want me to find out who killed Larry Sutton, right?"

He nodded and sank back into the chair.

"If I'm going to help you, I need your cooperation. You can't simply hang out here and mope about Helen while I wander town asking questions on your behalf."

"Why not? I bet you were at the café reading all morning." He stole a glance at the *Complete Adventures*.

I perched on the desk's edge. "Of course not. I went to the Empress. I took the book with me for . . . for inspiration."

"I heard you talking to Helen about Larry's death."

"That's right." I wasn't sure why I felt slightly defensive. "Once the medical examiner pronounced the death as from natural causes and the sheriff's office dropped the case, Helen asked me to help. She felt responsible for his being here and she— like you—suspected murder. Then you showed up and asked for my help." Not to mention room and board.

"Helen asked, too?" He pondered this for a moment. "You're so kind. I don't know what I'd do without you. I'm a burden, showing up unexpected, asking to be hidden. I realize that and I'm more grateful than you can know."

Looking at Martin's gentle eyes, bizarrely magnified through the lenses of his glasses, I was ashamed of being short with him. I couldn't tell him that my DNA as a truth teller was the flame to the tinder he and Helen had provided. "You're welcome. But I can only help if I have the complete information. If you're convinced someone killed Larry Sutton, then you must have an idea of why. Vague hints about the old theater aren't enough to go on." I placed my hands on my thighs and leaned forward. "Martin, why did you leave Wilfred? Can't you tell me more?"

He glanced toward the kitchen door through which Helen had just left, then at his hands, the hands that had prepared so many bodies for the beyond. He finally lifted his head. "Okay. I'll tell you this: I left Wilfred because if I hadn't, both Helen and my lives would've been in danger."

"And this was because . . . ?" As I spoke, I was aware of Sherlock puffing away at his pipe behind me.

"I saw something I wasn't supposed to see."

"At the Empress?"

"No." He fell to examining his hands again.

"Then what? Earlier, you said it had to do with the Empress." I had an easier time getting Rodney to wear his collar—and that was a chore requiring a full morning and a bag of treats—than I did prying information from Martin. "Does it have to do with the bones found at the Holloway property? Or the fact that you were"—I took a chance here—"tracking Frank Holloway's movements?"

"You've mentioned that before, but nowhere on those logs does it say I was following Frank."

"The logs always come back to the Holloway

place. Who else could it be? Lindy? I heard you were fascinated with her."

Fire charged Martin's expression. He said stiffly, "I was married to Helen."

This was all the proof I needed to know it was, indeed, Frank he tracked. Why?

A new thought occurred to me. Lindy's husband had been convicted of robbing the theater, among other crimes. Could Lindy have been involved? Perhaps she feared Martin would expose her. Even if he did, the statute of limitations for theft was surely long expired. Would Lindy Everhardt—a kind, now-frail woman—really murder someone to cover up her involvement in a forty-five-year-old theater heist? I had a hard time believing so.

"What did you see, Martin?"

He shook his head.

"Did you see Lindy Everhardt?"

"No," he quickly replied. "I did not see her."

I leaned back. "I give up. There's nothing to go on."

"Don't give up yet. Please. Just a few more days? Please? If not for me, for Helen?"

I hesitated. Naturally, I wanted justice done. I couldn't help it. But it wasn't fair of him to tie my hands like this.

"I'll give you a free embalming and I can get you a discount on a quality casket. You'd appreciate the solid construction and satin finish of the Merciful Hereafter line." At my horrified expression, he added, "Not that you'll need it anytime soon."

"You heard Helen. You're already about to get me in trouble with the library's trustees. Having you here is a liability."

"Josie." He spoke my name as a plea. "What I did was terrible. Horrible. But I had no choice and I've lived with the consequences ever since. Now, after all these years, my decision to leave has led to Larry's death. Please help me make it right. Maybe I can't make it up to Helen, but at least I can do right by Larry."

I couldn't say no to him and, I had to admit, I didn't want to. "All right. Two days. Two days from right now, this very hour, and you're on your own. After that, I refuse to hide you. You'll either have to leave Wilfred or reveal yourself."

"Thank you so much. I can't tell you how grateful I am."

"In the meantime, you have work to do. Bound copies of the *Forest Grove News-Times* are upstairs in local history. While I'm out, I need you to bookmark anything having to do with the Empress and the Everhardts. Or Frank Holloway." I stood and put on my sternest librarian voice. "I'll know if you're hiding something, so don't get any ideas." I really would know, too, thanks to how chatty the local rag could be.

He nodded vigorously. "I'll get to work right away."

"So will I." I picked up the *Complete Adventures*, and Sherlock and I prepared for another outing.

Kaydee's home was on the outskirts of Gaston—too far to walk. I loaded the *Complete Adventures* into my Corolla and found her home at the end of a paved road cut into the farm country separating

Wilfred from Gaston. A car idled in the driveway and its driver, no one I recognized, waved.

I returned the wave and turned toward the house. Living here must be a drastic change for Lindy. Instead of the listing wood floors, a second-floor bathroom, and drafty windows of her old home, this one was a modern split-level house built at angles with decks protruding here and there.

I walked past a few newly planted trees and up the steps to the front door. It opened before I could lift my hand to knock.

Kaydee's daughter Julia emerged, duffel bag in hand, and pushed past me. "Sorry! I'm late for practice." She hustled to the car waiting in the driveway. They pulled out seconds later.

The house's front door was ajar and I peered inside. "Lindy?"

The home's crisp interior matched its exterior but was comfortably cluttered with the by-products of a busy family—shoes piled by the door, a throw blanket crumpled on the couch, and a Labrador retriever wagging its tail at me. "Hello, boy." I stepped inside the front door. Someone was upstairs—I could hear them. "Lindy? It's Josie Way."

Laundry basket in hand, Kaydee came skipping down the stairs. She stopped short when she saw me. "Josie? I thought you were someone come to fetch Julia. Can I help you?"

"I was hoping to talk with your mother. Is she home?"

Kaydee dropped the laundry basket, bulging with sheets, on the off-white sofa. "Why do you want to talk with her?"

"It's about Martin Garlington. And Larry Sutton."

"I don't get it."

"Helen feels awful about his death since she'd invited him to Wilfred and, well, I'm helping her gather information."

Gaze still on me, Kaydee lowered herself to the couch next to the laundry basket. She pointed to the armchair. "Have a seat. I thought he died of natural causes. What does Mom have to do with it?"

The giant armchair nearly engulfed me. The black fur on the cushion told me it was the dog's favorite seat, and he wagged over to me now, tongue lolling. "I'm not sure. Helen feels responsible, since he was in Wilfred because she'd asked him to come. His death has really stirred up her grief. If I can gather information about when Martin Garlington disappeared, it will ease her mind." I bent the truth, but it was the only way I knew around Kaydee's obvious suspicion. "Lindy is one of the few people in Wilfred who knew Martin."

Kaydee relaxed into the cushions. "I can understand that and I'm sorry for being so confrontational. It's just . . . just that Mom isn't what she used to be. You understand? It's not simply her rheumatoid arthritis and hips, either. I'm not sure she can bear a lot of stress."

"Would it be hard for her to talk about old times?"

Kaydee played with the corner of a pillowcase dangling from the basket. "I suppose it's all right. She adored Martin Garlington and always had good things to say about him."

"She talks about him?" Somehow this surprised

me. I'd heard she and Helen were friends, both with sons about the same age, but Helen hadn't mentioned more than that.

"She said Martin was a real gentleman. Soft-hearted, but someone who cared about people."

"I wouldn't expect Helen would marry less."

"Helen is amazingly resilient. So's Mom. Of course, Helen was a single mother, and it was a lot harder in those days. Mom was always popular with men." She laughed. "You should hear her stories. She and Dad had a whirlwind romance. Two weeks between meeting and marriage."

"Once she'd heard Martin might be returning, was she looking forward to seeing him?"

Kaydee shrugged. "Like the rest of us, I suppose she wasn't sure if the stranger would be Martin or not. In any case, she didn't talk about it. Didn't make a point of crowding the café in hopes of a glance at him, like everyone else did."

"So, she was home that night."

"Of course she was." Kaydee drilled me with a stare. "Where else would she be? She was right here. Early to bed, early riser."

"Naturally," I said quickly. "I'd love to talk with her about Martin. Just for a few minutes. I'll report back to Helen whatever kind things she has to say." In all this time we'd been talking, I'd seen no hint of Lindy. "She lives here, right?"

Kaydee rose. "Yes. But not in the house. We had a mother-in-law apartment built off the side. I'll show you." She headed toward the front door, then stopped to face me. "You'll be careful, won't you? Remember, her health is fragile. The last thing we need is two deaths this week."

* * *

Kaydee walked me to the entrance to Lindy
Everhardt's apartment, past the front door with its
architect-inspired metal railings and halfway down
the driveway.

Kaydee knocked, then opened the door without
waiting for a reply. "Mom? Josie Way is here. She
wants to ask about Martin Garlington."

Lindy sat watching television in an armchair.
She clicked the remote and the sound muted. Remembering the events at the Empress, I quickly
turned away from the screen.

"Mrs. Everhardt." I offered my hand. "How do
you like it here?"

"I feel old enough being called Grandma all
day. Call me Lindy."

"I'll get back to the laundry." Kaydee's gaze
darted between me and her mother. Apparently
deciding I was all right, she left.

I hadn't seen much of Lindy since I'd come to
Wilfred. A cane leaned against her chair, and perhaps because of trouble with mobility she didn't
spend her free time lingering at the café or hanging out in the library's kitchen as did so many
other Wilfredians. She had a delicate frailty with
the beauty of a cut blossom that sweetened as it
faded in its vase.

She gestured to the couch and I took a seat.
Her own seat, which at first looked like a mid-
century–style armchair, revealed itself to be a
recliner when Lindy pushed back. She pulled a
colorful afghan of granny squares over her knees.
"It's so nice to have visitors. Since I moved, I've felt
a bit out of the loop."

Other than the modern chair and the couch where I now sat, the rest of her furniture must have been lifted from her prior house. It stood out of place in the modern setting. A dark wood buffet with spiral-turned legs and gothic trim held family photos, including those of her grandchildren, Kaydee's daughters. A mantel clock, deprived of a mantel, took the place of honor. Her coffee table, although polished, had clearly seen decades of board games and coffee mugs and it, too, was covered with framed family pictures.

My magic was always scanning the background for books. Here it picked up only a crossword dictionary and a few magazines.

"Reading?" Lindy nodded toward the *Complete Adventures* resting in my lap.

"Oh, that. The hazards of being a librarian." I was getting tired of the joke and forced a chuckle and slipped the book into my tote, letting the top of the book stick out so Sherlock could see. "Thank you for letting me drop in."

"You wanted to talk about Martin," Lindy prompted.

"Yes. Helen Garlington feels awful about the death on your property, and she asked me to look into it for her." When Lindy didn't respond, I added, "She blames herself for Larry Sutton being in Wilfred."

"Who's Larry Sutton?"

She hadn't heard? "The man who came to Wilfred."

"Larry Sutton," Lindy repeated. "Kaydee told me the game show contestant wasn't Martin, but I thought he was named something else. Bruno something."

Lindy must not have left the house for the past two days. Wilfred buzzed with the news. "Bruno Gates. You were right that he wasn't Martin, but here's where it gets strange: He wasn't Bruno Gates, either."

Lindy continued to look at me with puzzlement.

"Bruno Gates was really Larry Sutton. It was some sort of—some sort of joke, I guess. They were coworkers. Rather than come to Wilfred himself, Bruno Gates sent Larry in his place. Then Larry died. Helen's thought is that someone thought Larry truly was Martin Garlington and killed him."

Her eyebrows drew together more tightly. "How did he die?"

"Natural causes," I said, aware of my weakening case. "That's what the medical examiner says, anyway."

Lindy fidgeted with her armrest. "Helen blames herself for a stranger dying of natural causes? Is this what you're saying?"

"Yes."

Lindy continued to stare. Finally, she drew a long breath. "These days, I remember Bette Davis's quote a lot." At my puzzled glance, she supplied, "'Getting old is not for sissies.' I understand how she might want to try to close open loops, begin to put her affairs in order. I have."

"You have a nice situation here with your daughter."

She looked around her as if she'd never been in her own apartment. "Yes. I'm lucky to have such caring children. But it's not truly mine." She organized the afghan to better cover a hip. "Someday, providence willing you live a long, full life, you'll know what I mean."

"You miss your old home."

Lindy's hand fumbled for the TV remote control and clicked the television off. "My home was my own. It held my memories, good and bad. The measurements penciled on the doorway as the kids grew taller, the crack in the cupboard door where Travis hit his head when he was just a toddler. The patch of peonies I was sure would never come up but did. Every year."

"The mound the old outhouse made," I added, watching her.

She met my eyes and slowly nodded. "Thankfully, it was grown over enough not to tempt the children." She let her gaze wander to the color coordinated lamps and Berber carpeting. "Here I don't have anything to fix my life on."

Helen was younger than Lindy in years, but she seemed younger in other ways, too. Especially with her new hairstyle, I had to add. But it was her optimism and insistence on seeing the poetry in life that had kept Helen's outlook young.

"I'm not sure how it helps or what you're hoping to discover, but I'm happy to tell you what I know about Martin Garlington," Lindy said.

I nodded with encouragement and felt the *Complete Adventures* warm as Sherlock listened.

"Martin was a good man. A gentle heart. I always suspected he was sweet on me, the dear, although I'd never tell Helen so. His disappearance crushed the poor girl, especially being with child and all."

I noted she'd referred to Helen as a "girl," although Lindy was only a few years older. At least, chronologically. I nodded and began to speak, but Lindy was looking toward the window and had more to say. I waited.

"Our sons were schoolmates. Did you know that?"

"After your first husband went to prison." I held my breath, hoping the mention of "prison" wouldn't clam her up. I needn't have worried.

"Frank was a charmer. A charmer with a bad temper and the conviction that the world owed him a living. Martin understood that about him." Remembering, she made a small noise, like a kitten mewling. "I fell for Frank, all right. When he put his mind to making a woman feel desirable, there was no escaping him. And for a while it was good."

"Frank robbed the Empress," I said. "I understand that's what put him away."

"The shame of it was, I always had the feeling the robbery became more personal than about the money. The theater's owner had insulted him somehow. I never knew what it was about. Frank refused to let it die, but Mack Jubell, Orson's father"—she looked up to make sure I got the connection—"had the last word when he pressed charges." From the expressions crossing Lindy's face, she wasn't finished with her recollections.

I relaxed and let her talk, although I didn't forget Sherlock's theory that Frank Holloway and Orson's father were in it together.

"I can imagine Helen's pain." Lindy shook her

head and shifted her gaze to me. "But I really don't know how I can help you."

"It was a long shot," I said. "Since Larry's body was found where we buried the memorial to the remains Duke found on your property, I wondered if you might know of a connection?"

Lindy's confidence returned. "Why he was wandering Wilfred at night, I have no idea. Honestly, the sooner Duke and Desmond pour a slab over the outhouse, the better."

"You won't have to wait long," I told her. "It's scheduled for the day after tomorrow. It's just that since—"

"You've been involved in suspicious deaths before, haven't you?"

I saw where this was going. "That's why Helen asked me to help."

"It must be easy to see murder everywhere you go. No, I think you're confused. It was a coincidence." Exhaustion overtook her momentary flare of emotion and again she fell back into her chair, but this time closed her eyes. "If you don't mind . . ."

"Of course. I'll see myself out."

Before I could rise, the front door opened and Travis entered, a bakery bag in hand. Halfway through shrugging off his coat, he noticed me. His gaze shot to his mother, eyes closed, in her armchair. He dropped the bag on the counter and knelt at her side.

"Mother," he said gently. Then, to me. "What did you say to her?"

"Nothing. I asked a few questions, that's all."

He stood. "It was about the death the other night,

wasn't it?" He didn't wait for my reply. "We've been keeping quiet about it. Mom can't stand the stress. The whole point of moving her here was to make things easier for her."

I pulled on my coat. "I'm sorry. I don't know what happened. I was asking about the night Larry Sutton died and it was like flipping a switch. One moment she was . . . lively, and the next she'd had enough."

"That man's death had nothing to do with us. As I told the sheriff, I overheard him bragging about a date to meet someone at the cemetery."

"You were at the tavern?" No one had mentioned it. In fact, Orson had denied it, just as he'd denied seeing Kaydee. Had he really been so busy that night?

"No, I was on my way to work. I bake at night, remember? Sometimes I cut through the churchyard to carpool with a buddy. A habit I picked up from when we lived in the old place. Anyway, I heard Bruno or Larry or whoever he was talking on his phone. He was clearly waiting for someone, and I can guarantee it wasn't Mom. She's not well enough to go out alone. She was here all night. Ask Kaydee."

"Water, Travis," Lindy said weakly.

Glaring at me, Travis went to the kitchen.

I slung my tote over my shoulder. "Can I help?"

"Yes, by leaving," Travis said.

"Wait, Josie." Lindy pulled herself up. "You should know something."

I froze at the door. Travis hovered, too, water glass in hand. I saw him through the cutout to the kitchen.

"Frank isn't completely to blame for the robbery at the Empress. Ask Orson about his father."

"Does this have to do with Martin Garlington?" I asked.

Travis came around the counter and gently handed the water glass to his mother. "I won't have you talking about that man in this house."

I turned toward the door, then faced the room again. "Travis, why are you so upset about Martin Garlington?" Puzzled, I looked from son to mother. If anything, Lindy had seemed to enjoy talking about him, and Kaydee confirmed it. What was Travis's problem?

"Leave," he said. "And mind your own business."

CHAPTER 25

On the way home, I stopped for gas. As I waited for the attendant to fill the tank, I pulled the *Complete Adventures* from my tote bag on the passenger seat. The book opened to "The Adventure of Black Peter." Sherlock, wearing a newsboy's cap and a stern expression, rose from the pages where, if the illustration was any indication, he'd been questioning a rogue sailor.

"Did you get anything back there? The visit to Lindy didn't exactly go as planned," I said.

"In an investigation, there is no 'as planned.' The mind must remain observant and open, taking in whatever facts fall its way." As he pontificated, he raised a palm and his pipe materialized in it. "For instance, there was one fact I observed."

"What was that?" I asked. The attendant stared at me. I smiled at him and pretended to search my purse for a lipstick. Fortunately, his attention was diverted to a minivan that pulled up to the pump behind me.

"Did you notice the photographs on the buffet?" Sherlock asked.

"Sure. Family photos."

Tiny smoke rings rose from Sherlock's lips. "We may not have the complete picture, but the pieces begin to accumulate."

I tapped the steering wheel. "Could the bones be those of Orson's father? Maybe he partnered with Frank Holloway to rob the Empress, then ratted him out to the police so he could keep the money for himself. Frank got angry and killed him. Hid his bones in the outhouse." I shook my head. "No, can't be. Orson said his father died of injuries from the fire at the Empress. Besides that, Frank was in prison at the time."

Sherlock removed the pipe from his mouth. "Did you notice one additional piece of evidence?"

"What's that?" Now the driver of the minivan behind me was pointing at me and saying something to the man in the passenger seat. I didn't want to appear to be blabbering to myself, so I lowered my head, again faking a search through my purse.

"There were no photos of Lindy's first husband, Frank Holloway, but several of Martin Garlington."

I'd been occupied with Lindy and hadn't noticed. Judging from the flotilla of photos in her apartment, though, I wouldn't be surprised I'd missed a few.

Pondering his words, I turned the ignition key and Sherlock clutched the book cover's edge. He still wasn't used to motorized vehicles. "Let's go home. Maybe Martin found something in the archives."

The lights were off in the library when I returned, but, to my surprise, the kitchen door was unlocked. I clutched the *Complete Adventures* closer and stepped inside.

"Martin?" I said quietly. I crept through the rain-dimmed kitchen and pushed open my office door. He wasn't there. Who had left the door unbolted? I was sure I'd locked it when I left.

I stood in the atrium and scanned the floor above—at least, as far as I could see past the walkway circling the library's center and the open doorways letting onto it. All was quiet. The books whispered stories, providing a background murmur like a gentle stream, and I didn't pick up anything alarming. I poked my head into the conservatory. The tile stove gave out a gentle heat and the room smelled of damp earth from Lyndon's tropical plants. Otherwise, it was empty. Where was Martin?

Hurrying a bit now, I took the stairs two at a time. I'd left Martin with instructions to dig into back issues of the Forest Grove paper for information about the theater break-in. Maybe he was still in periodicals, absorbed by news of what had happened since he left town. Holding my breath, I turned into one of the mansion's former bedrooms and found him. However, he wasn't at the central table, but squirreled away behind a bookshelf in the corner, in an armchair, with bound vol-

umes of the newspaper around him and one open
on his lap.

"Did you go outside?" I asked.

"Hmm?" He turned a page of the yellowing newspaper.

"The kitchen door was unlocked. Did you
leave?" Maybe he was ready to go public at last.

He looked up, his weary features more deeply
etched than they had been even this morning. "Of
course not. It must have been the person I heard
rummaging around. I took my reading to the corner so I'd be out of the way. Keep your voice down,
by the way. I didn't hear anyone leave."

I inhaled sharply with surprise. "Who was it?"

"How should I know?" He placed a finger on
the page. "Did you see this? It's Derwin's birth an-
nouncement. I wish there was a photo."

I didn't dare tell him that Derwin would deliver
the mail tomorrow morning. "Wait here," I whispered and set Sherlock on the table. "If you hear
me shout, call the sheriff's office right away."

I made a circuit of the second floor. The old
master bedroom in the corner—now arts—was
quiet. No one in there. Same with the music room
and pure science. In natural science, I stopped
cold. From the doorway, I made out a pair of feet
on the couch—the same couch where Martin had
spent the night. I stilled myself to take in the
books' energy. They weren't alarmed. Whoever
was here on a day the library was closed to the public wasn't a threat. To them, at least.

Holding my breath, I crept forward. The fan on
the floor was the giveaway. Mouth open, dead to

the world, Roz gently snored on the sofa. As to why she was here, that mystery would have to wait. One thing was certain, though: She'd have to leave as soon as she woke. Either that, or Martin would need to come clean about being in Wilfred. There was no way Roz could keep that secret, and I couldn't house both of them here for the next two nights.

I returned to Martin. If we kept our voices low, we wouldn't be overheard. I found him deep in an article about one of the Tohler daughter's weddings. He had a lot to catch up on, but I didn't expect he'd care about that. Then I understood. "Did Helen play the piano at the ceremony?"

"I can just see her now." His gaze wandered toward the window. "She expresses herself musically with such feeling. The article says the bride chose Bette Midler's 'The Rose.' Just lovely, although I do prefer Helen's interpretations of Bach." He sighed. "And Engelbert Humperdinck."

Using the well-practiced technique librarians everywhere had honed for ejecting patrons at closing time, I smiled and slid the volume from his lap to lean it against his chair. "Did you find anything about the theater break-in?"

"Indeed I did. Three mentions." Peering around the corner to make sure no one saw him, Martin fetched two bound volumes and returned to his armchair. "Here's the first." He opened to a July 1973 issue and pointed to an article.

I pulled up a side chair and read.

Wilfred's residents awoke Monday morning to the shocking news that the Empress had been bur-

gled. *According to the Empress's owner, Mack
Jubell, he had locked the theater after the last show.
It was a Sunday night, and the office safe was full
from the weekend's ticket and snack bar sales.
When Jubell returned Monday morning to take the
proceeds to the bank, he found the theater's side
entrance bolt jimmied and the safe empty.*

*"The man who did this can't hide," Jubell said.
"Mark my words, he won't get away with it."*

*Sheriff Dolby asked for information from any-
one who might have seen someone near the theater
between midnight and seven a.m. Monday morning.*

"Also this." Martin flipped the thin issue to its
back page. Above an ad for a long-defunct phar-
macy was the *News-Times*'s editorial.

*The shocking break-in and theft at the Empress
this weekend is merely the culmination of an in-
crease in lawlessness. Until now, these infractions
have been limited to bullying, insults, and declara-
tions of hubris. The* News-Times*'s dedicated
reader will surely catch my drift. We cannot stand
for this type of behavior. Where will it end?*

The editorial then switched to a rueful account
of the chaos resulting from a tipsy dance caller at
the Grange Hall's square dance. I had to wonder if
the editor and church rector were related.

"The editor was definitely referring to someone
in particular," I said. "Frank Holloway?"

Martin leaned back. "No doubt about it. Until

then, no one could prove it, but we were all certain he was up to no good."

"You knew him. What was he like?" I kept my voice low and hoped Roz was still snoozing on the other side of the library.

"Handsome. Confident. Mean."

"He married Lindy young."

"Right out of high school. She was the prettiest girl in the county. The sweetest and kindest. When Frank set his cap on her, she couldn't resist. He could be the most charming man in the world. And the biggest bully. He was fine when he got what he wanted, but watch out if he didn't."

The gentle lilt of his description of Lindy reminded me that he'd had a crush on her. Nerdy Martin wouldn't have stood a chance. "That bad, huh?"

"Worse. If he couldn't have what he wanted, no one else could, either. He had his eye on a 1957 Chrysler Saratoga. Aqua with silver threads in the upholstery. He fiddle-faddled around with getting the money together, and the owner sold it to someone else. The next day, the car's windshield was shattered and tires slashed. All four of them."

Lindy had been playing with fire. No wonder she didn't keep his photo on her buffet. "Poor Lindy."

"Lindy was a fine woman, but she was no Helen. There is no one like Helen," he said.

"Helen is just down the hill, you know."

He hung his head. "After what I did, how I left her—she doesn't deserve me."

Reluctantly, I had to agree. "You said there were three articles. What is the third?"

He pulled another volume forward, this one from a year later. "Here. When Frank was convicted."

The article was to the point. Frank Holloway had been convicted of robbing the Empress, and the sentencing hearing scheduled the next month. "*As he was led away by the bailiff,*" I read aloud for Sherlock's benefit, "*He vowed vengeance on Mack Jubell.*" I set down the paper. "That's strange. Why would he threaten the man he robbed?"

"Because Mack pressed charges. Frank was incensed that anyone would dare to call him out for what he did."

"People were sure Frank was the culprit, right? He was in it alone?"

"Definitely," Martin said. "No doubt. If I remember right, they found his fingerprints on the safe."

"Did Orson's dad ever recover the money?"

"Nope. No one knows what happened to it. Lindy sure didn't get it, not if you look at how she lived."

Now it was coming together. If Sherlock was right and Mack Jubell and Frank Holloway conspired together to rob the Empress, Mack Jubell must have sold out Frank and taken his share. I still didn't understand why he'd rob his own business. Then the fire and Mack Jubell's death.

"There's one more thing." He looked back at me, his expression blank. "It was a long time ago."

"Yes?" I asked in my most encouraging voice.

"I'm an undertaker."

I nodded and barely breathed. I didn't want anything to stop Martin's confession.

"I cared for Wilfred's departed."

I tested a half-smile. "Yes?"

He paused, mouth open. The words were so close to coming out.

I whispered, "Including Frank Holloway?"

"No," he said quickly. "Mack Jubell."

Orson's father. Orson had said his father had been hurt in the fire and died because of his injuries. What did that have to do with anything? I hid my impatience. "And?"

"The fire didn't kill him. He'd been bashed in the back of the head."

"Whoa," I said. "He didn't die of complications from the fire—smoke inhalation or something like that?"

"Who are you talking to?" I whirled around to see Roz, hair mussed and waffle-weave blanket indentations on her cheek, standing in the doorway. Fortunately, Martin was out of sight behind a bookshelf.

I quickly rose and moved toward her. "Just chattering to myself. What are you doing here?"

"I'm going to sleep at the library for a few days."

"Here?" I managed to shepherd her into the hall. "Why?"

"I rented my trailer to Babe Hamilton, the lady selling textiles at the This-N-That. We'd decided to make Lyndon's cottage our home. I thought it would force a decision, lead him to realize we don't have enough room. Well, that didn't work."

By gently moving toward the staircase, I encouraged Roz to follow me downstairs to the conservatory, the furthest point in the library from Martin. "Why not?"

"He's too stuck in his ways. I can't set my coffee mug by the sink, because that's where he repots orchids. I can't squeeze my clothes into his closet because it's full of overalls. We moved my double bed to his bedroom, but now I can't even open the dresser drawers. The place is too damned small. As long as Lyndon has his garden, though, he doesn't care."

"What's it like in there, anyway? In Lyndon's cottage?"

"Who cares? All that matters is that it simply will not work for us. Until we come up with something else, I'm staying here. I'll sleep in natural history."

Arguing with Roz would be fruitless. With Martin also in residence, the library was turning into a motel. How would I keep him hidden? Now that Roz claimed the couch in natural history, Martin would need somewhere else to sleep.

Roz could take care of herself. I glanced toward the doorway. As for Martin, for tonight he could, too. I planned to take a break from Larry Sutton this evening and spend it with Sam.

CHAPTER 26

By the time I'd settled Roz in natural history and smuggled Martin to my apartment, where I gave him my bed and planned for a night on my living room couch, all I wanted was to laze in Sam's presence and talk with him about anything but murder. No Sherlock questioning my logic, no movie screen hijacking my ancestors, no Martin complaining about the choices he'd made in life but not having the guts to do anything about it.

Sam met me at Big House's back door. "I thought we'd eat in, maybe watch a movie. You don't mind?"

I walked up the few steps to the tiny porch off the kitchen and straight into Sam's arms. "I was hoping you'd suggest something like that." How was it he managed to smell like the ocean and the earth all at once? He was in stockinged feet and had changed from his sheriff uniform to jeans and button-up red wool over a T-shirt.

Rodney slinked in with me and sniffed around the kitchen's edges. Nicky cooed from his high chair, and the overture to *The Magic Flute* played quietly in the background. A pile of chopped parsley on the cutting board next to the stove told me dinner was underway.

Forget the harps and cherubs. This was heaven.

As Sam took my coat, he must have noted my lack of an overnight bag. "You're not staying?"

"I can't. Not tonight." I turned to him, unsure how to explain. I couldn't tell him a Wilfredian presumed dead was camping in my bedroom or that I needed to commune with Sherlock Holmes. "It's Roz," I said, suddenly grateful she'd shown up, but wincing at the half-truth. "She and Lyndon moved into Lyndon's cottage, and she's not happy about it. She's spending nights at the library until they work out a new situation. She's pretty upset."

Sam ran a finger down my cheek. "You're a good friend." He pulled a cast-iron skillet from near the stove. "Too bad. I'll miss you."

I watched his forearm flex as he lifted the skillet to the stovetop. Too bad indeed. To distract me from tumbling into a well of longing, I diverted my attention to Nicky. I lifted him from his high chair and set him on my hip. He grabbed a chunk of my hair in his sticky fist and put it in his mouth.

"Any further developments on Larry Sutton's death?" The words fell from my mouth, leaving me surprised. So much for my plan to take a break from the case.

"No. Why should there be? We sent his body home to California. Case closed." He turned toward me and leaned his elbows on the counter. "You still think it was murder, don't you?"

"There are too many open questions. I mean, why was Larry at Duke and Desmond's? In the middle of the night, no less?"

"According to the tavern's patrons, he'd been drinking. A lot. Maybe he was trying to walk it off before driving back to his hotel. I don't know and we can't ask him." Sam returned to making dinner and pulled a platter of chicken breasts from the refrigerator. "Whatever the reason, the combination of alcohol, the drive, and cancer led to a pulmonary embolism. That's it. End of story."

I replaced Nicky in his chair. He settled with a "gah" and slapped his palms on the chair's metal tray. "Sam, will you humor me? Let's play a game of 'what-if.' We'll start with 'what if Larry Sutton were murdered.' "

He frowned—amused—as he placed the chicken breasts in the skillet. "At your service. I didn't know I'd be working overtime today." His frown deepened.

"Then you won't mind if I ask you a few questions. Things you might have discovered before the medical examiner made her determination."

"All right. It can't hurt."

I circled an arm around his waist. "Where were Lindy and Travis at the time of the mur—death?"

My near-slip of the tongue hadn't fooled him. He raised an eyebrow. "According to Kaydee, Lindy was at home, presumably sleeping. Lindy's car never left the driveway—she made a point of telling us so. After picking up takeout, Kaydee was in all evening. Lindy stayed in the next day, too," Sam concluded. "Satisfied?"

"You only have Kaydee's word for it," I pointed out.

"Not quite. Remember, we were at Darla's Café that night and saw her."

I nodded. "Lalena saw her again that evening at the tavern."

"I'm not surprised." Sam whisked olive oil into a vinaigrette as he listened. He set the whisk in the sink and turned to me. "One thing I've learned over the years as an investigator is that, more often than not, people have something to hide that has nothing to do with the case. It's a pain, because it can confuse an investigation, but you always have to factor it in."

"You mean Kaydee might have had business at the tavern that she didn't want made public?" Kaydee, the nurse and mom. What would she have to hide?

"Her husband travels a lot for work."

"Really? You think she's up to something, with her mom living under the same roof?"

Sam shrugged. "I'm not saying I know anything, just not ruling it out."

"What about Travis?"

"We didn't have any reason to question him. I assume he was at work."

A movement caught my eye. "Rodney, off the table." He shot me a dirty look and jumped to the floor and wandered toward the living room.

"Although Travis did volunteer that when he was on his way to work, he saw Orson near the churchyard."

"Orson?" As I said his name, I remembered the Empress, and adrenaline shot through me as slick as an icepick. "You're not the first person to mention him. What was he doing there?" It wasn't on his way home.

"Can't say. Maybe he likes a little fresh air and took the long way home."

Orson. This bore following up. "Thank you for humoring me, Sam. Just one more question. Do you know anything about the robbery at the Empress?"

He turned to me. "The old movie theater? What does that have to do with anything?" His expression morphed from surprise to knowing. "Lindy's husband. I get it. You wonder if Frank Holloway has something to do with this. You're trying to tie Martin's disappearance and Larry Sutton's death to Frank Holloway." He returned to the stove. "Since we're playing the 'what-if' game, I'll bite. We know Holloway robbed the Empress. What if he was angry at Mack Jubell for testifying against him and killed him? We know there was a fire later and Jubell died."

I nodded with vigor. Sam was right on track.

He frowned in amusement and continued. "Martin was on a late-night butterfly hunt and saw Holloway emerge from the theater carrying rags and propane and looking gleeful. Holloway spotted Martin and threatened him with death not to say anything. Martin scarpered. Years passed and Holloway's sentence ended. He returned to Wilfred under an assumed identity. When he learned Martin Garlington was due back in town, he called the tavern and left a message luring the would-be Martin to the old Holloway place."

"Exactly," I said. "His old home base. It would have been natural to meet there."

"Holloway then killed the man he thought was Martin, using a method so ingenious that it fooled the medical examiner."

Sam was good. "How about the bones in the outhouse?" Might as well tie that in, too.

"Clearly another of Holloway's victims. What do you think?"

"No," Nicky said from his high chair. "No. No."

Sam turned off the burner and moved the skillet. "Nicky is right on this one. I'd have to doublecheck the date, but the theater closed sometime after Frank was put away. Therefore, he's clean."

"So much fits," I said. "Helen lent me her husband's journals and I found pages that had been hidden. It was a log of someone's comings and goings, and it centered on the Holloway property." I explained about the slit in the lining.

"That's interesting, I admit." Sam snapped a bib around Nicky's neck. "Remember, people often have other motives, and if you assume everything they do has to do with the crime you're investigating, you'll end up with a lot of confusing data." He shook his head. "I appreciate the creative thinking, but evidence doesn't bear it out." He reached to the cupboard for dinner plates. "Maybe Martin kept the log because he was tracking an elusive butterfly. Or maybe he had a thing for Lindy."

"Also, I did some digging around, and there's

no obituary for Frank Holloway. He's not still in the state's prison system—"

"He wouldn't be, not after all these years, not for robbery."

"—And I can't find any record that he died."

"You think he's been lurking in the woods around Wilfred, waiting for Martin Garlington to return?"

I leaned against the counter and folded my arms over my chest. "Okay, Mr. Pro Detective. Remember our 'what-if.' If we assume Larry Sutton's death wasn't an accident, and it wasn't Frank Holloway, what would you think happened?"

"First, let me go on record as saying that despite circumstantial oddities like the log you mentioned and the fact that Larry Sutton died where bones were found, he was not murdered. There was no murder weapon and no sign of being killed—no wounds, no strangulation, no poison."

"The game, Sam. What would you say?"

"It could be just about anyone, besides the mysterious Frank Holloway, hiding among us with murderous intent." He frowned in amusement and I tried to hide my smile. "From what you say, when Larry Sutton died, both Kaydee and Orson were near the churchyard—in other words, a few steps from where Larry was found—and not copping to it. If this were an open investigation, I'd follow up on that. Plus, Travis seems to bear an illogical dislike of Martin Garlington, a man who left town before he was born. If he thought Larry Sutton was Martin, we can add Travis to the list of suspects. He works nights and on his way to the bakery may have passed where Larry Sutton died.

Then there's Helen, who admits to wandering town the night of the so-called murder."

"Yeah," I said, deflated. "That's where I ended up, too. One more question, then I swear I'll quit. What happens to the bones now?"

"Until they're identified, the state police will hang onto them. Remember the DNA sample Helen Garlington asked for? By now forensic genealogists are on the case, looking for links to family members. Once they determine who the bones are, they'll go to the family for burial."

As I was setting forks and napkins on the kitchen table, Sam said, "What's that?"

I looked up from my chore. "What's what?"

"The light. A tree's in the way, but I think it's coming from your bedroom." He was on sheriff alert mode now, muscles tensed, gaze keen.

A month later and oak leaves would have obscured the view. I turned him toward me, away from the window. "Must be Roz. Getting something." These words came too easily.

"Right." He visibly relaxed. "Although I did hear Mrs. Littlewood complaining about finding a pair of dirty men's socks in the library."

"Roz and her big feet." Actually, Roz's feet were remarkably dainty. "You didn't think I was harboring someone in my bedroom, did you? Ha ha." Lying to Sam wasn't easy, but I'd promised Martin. I'd tell Sam the truth as soon as I could. Hopefully within a few days. His now-dead wife hadn't been faithful to him, and it occurred to me that he might still be on edge about it. I buried my face in the side of his neck. "Why would I when I have you?"

"I'm sorry I'm so jumpy." He pulled me close, chest to chest, and kissed me. Too bad I wasn't staying. "A bad habit you're putting to rest. It's so nice to have a normal life now. You, me, and Nicky, cooking dinner at home." His hand moved over my back. "The best things are the little things, you know? No drama. We haven't known each other that long—"

"A year and a half," I said.

"But this feeling, this peaceful, rich, utterly normal feeling. I want that for a long, long time."

With a witch, I added silently and the warm puddle of emotion my heart had now chilled. How would he feel about that? At the moment, I didn't have the courage to find out.

CHAPTER 27

When I returned to the library that night, instead of the dark, quiet space I usually found at night—the books slumbering, dreaming of worlds from the moon to ancient Persia—two people were awake, each in separate parts of the old mansion.

First, I checked on Roz. She'd dragged a side table and lamp next to the sofa in natural history and sat, propped by pillows, with her reading glasses perched on her nose and a copy of *The Good Divorce* open on her flannel-covered chest.

"Roz," I said. "You can't be thinking of ending your marriage. You love Lyndon."

She narrowed her eyes at me over her glasses. "What do you know about it? You, so lovey-dovey after an evening with Sam." The book slid to the side as she folded her arms. "What does it matter how you feel about someone if you can't live with him? There's more to a marriage than emotions. There's practicality."

"I'm sure you can find a solution."

"I've given up the trailer—my home of thirty years—for what? A lumpy sofa and uncertain future. And cat hair. I had to lint roll it off the blanket. Plus, I found a toothbrush in the cushions. What are the library's patrons doing up here, anyway?"

I sat on the sofa's edge. "You can't be the first person who's run into this problem. We'll figure it out. You and Lyndon are meant to be together."

Roz's face reddened, but she didn't reach for her fan. Both her book and eyeglasses slid to the floor and she burst into tears. "Oh, Josie. I don't know what to do. For so long all I wanted was to be with Lyndon. Now we're married, and we can't make it work." She pitched herself forward into my arms.

I patted her back. "Logistics. That's all you're talking about."

Roz's reply was muffled by my coat.

"We'll find you somewhere you can live together, even if we have to build you a place."

She lifted her head, her cheeks wet. "He doesn't want to leave his cottage."

"It's late now," I whispered to myself as much as to Roz. "Things will look better in the morning. You'll see. Now, do what you can to sleep."

Upstairs, Martin was also in a distraught state of mind. Thankfully, he hadn't gone to bed yet—I wasn't prepared to see a stranger in my bed—but was lounging in an armchair next to the cold hearth. I hung my coat on the coat-tree and closed the door to the landing so Roz wouldn't overhear us.

"Hello, Martin. Did you have a good evening?" I needn't have asked. His expression told me everything I needed to know.

"I'm a failure."

Once again, I was destined to become library therapist tonight. I bet this was how Orson felt on his shifts at the tavern. I stacked a few pieces of kindling in the grate. I had a hunch I wasn't going to bed anytime soon.

"Tell me about it," I said.

"I'm a damned good mortician." He straightened in his armchair and set the book he'd been reading—*Profiles in Courage,* I noted, wondering if the book had selected itself for him. "But I can't seem to get my personal life right. I had a wonderful wife and now, as it turns out, a son, but I blew it. I ran away."

"You returned. You're here. It's a chance for redemption."

"What about it? All I'm doing is hiding out and encouraging the town librarian to do my work for me. I don't have the guts to face up to my past. Worse, I've been making excuses, saying what I did was okay because I protected Helen. The plain fact is that I'm a coward."

In the half-light of the table lamp on one side and fire on the other, Martin looked every one of his seventy-plus years, and the mere two days in Wilfred had only deepened the lines on his forehead and worry in his eyes.

"Do you wish it were otherwise?" I asked.

"I'm so ashamed of myself. I would give anything to be brave."

I edged forward on the sofa. "Do you really mean that? If you were to awake tomorrow determined to face Helen and explain your actions, you'd be happy?"

He dropped his head and nodded. "I'd give all I have to be that person. Coming home has been like looking in a mirror, and what I see is a man too scared to do anything but hide."

This was the response I needed. Now that he wasn't making excuses for his cowardice, there was hope. "It's late," I said, keeping my voice gentle. "I'll be up for a while longer . . . taking care of things, but you should get to bed."

He slowly rose from the armchair and let himself into my bedroom. The door's latch clicked into place when he closed it behind him.

With Martin in the room next door and Roz snoozing on the second floor, I'd have to be quiet. In stockinged feet, I let myself out to the landing and closed the living room door behind me. I placed my hands on the polished wood railing and gazed down into the quiet library, the night so dark that the moon barely illuminated the stained glass in the cupola above the atrium. Yet Marilyn Wilfred's portrait over the entrance seemed to glow. Was it a trick of the light, or did she smile?

"Books," I whispered. Rodney rubbed against my calf.

The books awoke one by one, with a rising murmur that rose and swirled like a swarm of bees. Their energy flowed over me and within me, coursing through my blood. The birthmark on my shoulder tingled. This was magic.

"Books," I repeated. "Bring me courage."

Without Martin's explicit permission, I couldn't use magic to help him. But when he told me—and truly meant it—that he wanted to be more courageous, I could step up. I glanced toward my apartment to make sure he wasn't watching. The door remained closed.

I raised my arms and the books' energy buzzed and fizzed and snapped with power. A volume rose from the atrium and slipped into my grasp, warm and sure. It was a children's book, *Hercules—The Complete Myths of a Legendary Hero*. I set it on the floor next to me. *The Iliad* followed, then *The Red Badge of Courage*, *Captain America*, and *Crockett's Devil*, the cover of which featured Davy Crocket dodging a knife. The stack next to me nearly reached my knees. Plenty of literary courage. I lowered my hands and sat in the open hall, surrounded by these volumes.

The stack of books shimmered with power, prickling my palms. Not just the authors, but centuries of readers had imbued these tales with energy—all surrounding courage. Rodney purred and closed his eyes.

Using my hands like I was pulling wool, I gathered the strands of energy together one by one into a hot ball and suspended it between my fingers. The magic was strong enough that I had to steel my trembling fingers to continue the spell. Slowly, eyes fixed on the glowing mass, I returned to my apartment. Rodney bumped the door open ahead of me. The courage was so powerful that it burned between my palms.

Still holding the scalding ball of energy, I knelt in front of my bedroom door and lowered my hands to the floor. Drawing a deep breath, I visualized the energy flattening under the door to swirl around Martin in his sleep.

This was a new technique for me, but it appeared to be working. The red-hot courage turned green, like flame on copper, and flowed beneath the bedroom door. I harnessed all my power to push it, to ease it toward him, and the ball of courage diminished as it flowed. Finally, the last of the energy had disappeared under the door. I rubbed my palms together to dispel any lingering magic and sat back, depleted.

The rest would depend on Martin.

CHAPTER 28

I woke early the next morning, my back aching from the lumpy sofa. Rodney lay curled in a warm spot he'd carved out between my feet and the sofa's padded back. From the French horn–like wail of Martin's snores, he slept well in my bedroom. Downstairs, Roz probably tossed and turned, too. After a night on the sofa in natural history, I bet she'd go running back to Lyndon's cottage.

My clothes were in my bedroom with Martin, so I scooped Sherlock's book under my arm and went down the hall to my little kitchen to make coffee. I opened the volume on the table and Sherlock emerged from "The Adventure of the Beryl Coronet" dressed, noted the illustration, "as a common loafer."

"Cute hat," I told him. "You don't often see a beret with a tassel."

"We don't have time for sartorial commentary, Miss Way. Martin Garlington could awake any time, and I wouldn't put it past the melancholic assistant librarian—"

"Roz," I supplied.

"—to interrupt us." He looped his thumbs in his vest and sat, an armchair appearing under him as usual just when needed. "Last night while you were amusing yourself with the sheriff, I had the opportunity to observe Martin Garlington."

Coffee now underway, I pulled up a kitchen chair. "What did you see?"

"He spent quite a while perusing back issues of the town's chronicle."

"The Forest Grove paper. Probably looking for anything to do with his wife or son," I said. Helen would be noted regularly for playing at weddings and funerals. For a while, she ran an ad bordered in musical notes offering *lessons in piano and organ by the 1969 Forest Grove invitational gold medal winner Helen P. Garlington.*

"Yes, yes, of course. But he also spent quite a while reviewing obituaries. Not just idly perusing them, but searching for a particular name."

"Frank Holloway's," I said, suddenly certain.

"Undoubtedly." Sherlock now smoked his pipe, the long-stemmed one with the small bowl, not the crook-necked pipe that so often appeared in movies. Again, I marveled at how the smoke rose and dissipated.

"He didn't find it," I said.

"No."

I put forward the theory from Sam's and my game. "Is it possible Frank Holloway did return—

under another name? After all, Martin changed his identity. Maybe Frank knew that Martin had witnessed him murdering Orson's father, Mack Jubell."

"It would have been a foolish move. The town's residents feared or loathed him and would have recognized him."

"True. Yet . . ." I just couldn't shake the idea that he was alive and among us. It would tie up the murder so neatly.

"In my experience, Miss Way, men like that must have some situation where they can wield control over others. I hardly think Mr. Holloway would wait patiently for decades for his opportunity for revenge, especially in so hopeless a situation."

"Maybe he has been getting his revenge," I said. "We still don't know whose body was in the out-house."

"Josie?" Martin called from down the landing. Good, he was awake at last. The library opened in an hour and I had to get dressed. Plus, I was eager to see if the courage spell had taken hold.

"Josie, are you up?" came Roz's voice from downstairs.

Good grief. I should put out a sign: BOOK A ROOM AT WILFRED'S LIBRARY. SPEND THE NEXT CHAP-TER OF YOUR LIFE AMONG THE STACKS. I was a librar-ian, not an innkeeper. Or a detective, I supposed. At least, most of the time.

Roz's singing accompanied my morning rounds of the library. I pulled curtains open and flipped on lights to a robust if off-key version of "Oh, What

a Beautiful Mornin'." By the time I reached the
conservatory, Roz had built a fire in the tile stove
and was having coffee with Lyndon. A plate with
an egg and half-eaten slice of toast was next to her.

"Did you sleep well?" I braced myself for a barrage of complaints.

"Amazingly well!" Roz reached a palm over the
side table and Lyndon placed his hand over hers.
"Who knew the couch was so comfortable? The
cushions must be down filled." She gave a satisfied
sigh. "We may have found the answer at last."

"So convenient," Lyndon added. "Steps from
my cottage."

"Now, look," I said. "You're not moving in here
permanently. There's room for one person here,
and that person is me."

"This is a huge old mansion. We could put a bed
in your living room. Besides, I bet you spend lots
of time at Sam's. I'd only need somewhere to sleep
and work, that's all. Maybe store my clothes and
take showers. Sometimes use the kitchen—Lyndon's
is so small. You'll never know I was here."

Roz? Not know she was there? "Impossible. Absolutely not. You two need to find your own solution. Get used to living in small quarters or buy a
house together."

Roz appeared unperturbed. "I told you, there's
nothing available in Wilfred. Nothing habitable,
that is. It might take months for something to
open up. In the meantime, I'm plenty comfortable
here. I can't believe I haven't taken advantage of
the tub yet. Lyndon, have you tried it? It's long
enough even for you."

Lyndon, a man of few words, merely nodded.

Oh, boy. This would not be easy. "I'll lock my apartment and be down in ten minutes to open for business."

Roz rose, her hand slipping from under Lyndon's. "No worries. I'll take care of things. You'll find it's extra-convenient to have me around more often."

I plodded upstairs, where Martin was dressed and carrying out what looked like calisthenics in my living room. He stopped mid–jumping jack when I entered.

"There's coffee for you in my kitchen," I said. "But make sure to stay near the wall so none of the patrons see you."

"Thank you. Does Helen have lessons today?"

"Not until tomorrow afternoon." I studied his face. Besides the faint flush of exertion from his exercises, I didn't see anything that looked like courage. No burst of bold promises, no gallant posture. I tried a question. Maybe he'd be brave enough to finally answer it. "Did Frank Holloway have anything to do with why you left Wilfred?"

Martin blanched. Definitely not the face of courage. "You keep asking."

"Martin, I'm at a dead end. If you won't tell me anything, there's nothing left to go by. We'll have to assume Larry died of natural causes, as the medical examiner says, and let it go. There's nothing left for me to follow up." I stepped closer. "Helen will never know you're alive. You'll never shake hands with your own son. You'll go home and nothing will have changed. Unless you tell me, I can't help you."

He slumped to the sofa. He teetered on the

brink of revealing something, I knew it. "I need to protect Helen."

I'd heard him say this before, but this time there was less conviction. If I played it right, he might reveal his secret at last. "Tell me," I said softly. "Is Frank Holloway after you?"

He was just about to reveal something. I knew it. His mouth opened to speak.

"Josie!" came the yell from up the atrium. "We're open!"

CHAPTER 29

Martin's face hardened and mouth clamped shut. If he were going to tell me more, the interruption had changed his mind. The courage spell had been a bust.

"Josie!" Roz yelled again.

"Stay hidden," I told Martin. "I'll be back when I can."

Downstairs, Babe Hamilton, the new textiles vendor from the This-N-That, stood with Roz in the atrium. "I could never deprive you of your home. I haven't even fully moved in. Why don't I get a room in Forest Grove and give you back your place at the Magnolia Rolling Estates?"

Yes, I thought with gratitude, why don't you?

"I couldn't do that," Roz said. "A promise is a promise. I rented you the trailer and that's the end of it. Besides, it's quite comfortable here and right next door to Lyndon. I don't know why I didn't think of it sooner."

My spirits sagged. Roz looked rested and happy. Who knew how long she'd stay at the library? Martin wouldn't be here forever, but Roz might. I could say goodbye to practicing magic. Not to mention peace and quiet.

"If you're sure—"

"Positive," Roz said. "That part of my life is over. Enjoy my old home, and Lyndon will stop by soon to fix the drip in the kitchen faucet." With that, Roz, humming "Our House," returned to the conservatory to work on her romance novel.

The textiles vendor stood alone a moment in the atrium, looking from doorway to doorway.

I stepped forward. "Can I help you, Mrs. Hamilton?"

"Yes, in fact." She drew a lace tablecloth from her tote bag. "I wondered if you have anything about lace patterns? I can't figure out what technique was used here. Feel this."

The tablecloth was loosely crafted in a spider-web-like pattern. I let my fingers run over its surface. A tingle akin to magic rose from it, likely the residue of the hundreds of hours a woman had spent working and dreaming over it. "Is that linen thread?"

"I believe it is." She raised her gaze to mine. "You appreciate texture, don't you?"

I did now. Since my magic had opened up a year and a half earlier, my senses had opened, too. Colors were richer, scents deeper and more complex, and suddenly my old acrylic-blend sweaters and scratchy blankets were not good enough.

Something else caught Mrs. Hamilton's eye. I turned to see she was staring at the full-length oil portrait hanging over the entrance to the foyer.

"That's Marilyn Wilfred," I said. "The library's founder and daughter of the man who built the mansion."

"Classic flapper gown," Babe Hamilton said. "Beaded silk organza, I bet. So beautiful, but a nightmare to restore. The threads are so old they tend to dissolve. Is that a cat at her feet?"

As if on cue, Rodney sauntered in and rubbed against my ankles. I reached down to scratch his ears and he backed away, his hackles rising. "Rodney, what are you doing?"

"Could be the same cat," Babe Hamilton said.

"He's a classic. You'll find textiles upstairs in applied arts. Take a left at the top of the staircase."

After she left, I crossed the atrium to the conservatory to see what had gotten into Rodney. After I checked on him, I'd go upstairs and see if I could persuade Martin to tell me the truth about Frank Holloway. He'd been just about to tell me something important. In the conservatory, I found Rodney curled up in the kindling box next to the tile stove, as if nothing had frightened him. I also found Buffy and Thor seated next to Roz, who had closed her laptop.

Buffy pointed to a crayon drawing of a house with a curl of smoke rising from its chimney and flowers out front as tall as the front door. "Here we have a fine home for you and Lyndon."

Roz pulled the drawing closer. "I don't recognize it."

"It's the old Satterfield place," Thor said, adjusting his eye patch.

"Ha," Roz said. "That house doesn't even have a roof over the kitchen. We can't move there."

"Lyndon is handy," Buffy said.

"Show me a house with a roof," Roz replied.

Buffy pulled out another drawing, this one an interior view. All I could make out was that it was dark.

"Where's that?" I asked.

"Grandma's," Buffy said. "Conveniently located in downtown Wilfred."

"This is Patty's basement, isn't it?" Roz said. "No way. We're not moving into the This-N-That's basement."

"Roz," I said. "I need to go upstairs for a second. Could you keep an eye on the desk?"

"Fine. It's not like I'm getting a lot of writing done, anyway."

Maybe the courage spell was simply slow-acting, and Martin was getting ready to fill me in on the complete story. It had to be about Frank Holloway. He was out of prison, perhaps living under a different name, and he knew Martin suspected him of killing Orson's father. Once I'd confirmed these suspicions, the next step would be to link Frank to Larry's murder.

My other hope was that I wouldn't be interrupted by a patron while I was trying to get upstairs. But when I heard my name from across the atrium, I turned with a wide, genuine smile. There was Sam, frowning back. Happy. I moved toward him like he was a magnet and I was a pile of iron filings.

"Good morning," I said, my worries falling away. It never ceased to amaze me how I could feel this wave of emotion over and over, and every time as fresh as the first. This wasn't the place to fall into his arms—it wasn't professional. But I was tempted.

"I thought I'd stop by."

"Oh. Great." I sounded like an idiot. A happy idiot.

"I have two pieces of news for you."

"About Frank Holloway's jail time?" I was on work time, but I indulged myself by grabbing Sam's hands in mine.

He nodded. "Big news. Frank Holloway was out on bail between his conviction and sentencing, the same time someone set fire to the Empress. Not only that, he jumped bail. Never returned to serve his sentence."

I nearly gasped. I was not at a dead end. Frank Holloway had not been in jail when Orson's father died. I wished Sherlock were nearby to hear this. "You're sure?"

"Absolutely."

"Then it's true. Sam, we guessed it. Frank Holloway is the missing piece." My brain whirled. "The next step is to find him."

"There's more."

I dropped Sam's hands. "More?"

"It's about the bones. Remember how I told you we had a forensic genealogist looking at the DNA test Helen Garlington ran?"

I nodded.

"We have a match. The bones belong to Frank Holloway."

* * *

Sam's information took a moment to soak in. Frank Holloway. The bones were Frank Holloway's. Frank Holloway couldn't be after Martin and hadn't killed Larry Sutton. He'd been dead for decades.

"You're certain?" I asked Sam.

"Forensic genealogy is astonishingly accurate," he said. "We're sending a deputy to Frank Holloway's brother for a DNA sample to be sure. And, Josie?" He stepped forward and slipped an arm around my back. "Keep it on the down-low for an hour or so, will you? Someone is notifying Lindy Everhardt as we speak." He kissed the side of my head and pulled away. "I've got to go. Are you around tonight?"

I nodded, my brain churning. Sam waved and left through the front door.

I glanced toward my apartment. What would Martin have to say about this?

CHAPTER 30

I ducked into circulation, where Roz was still perusing Buffy and Thor's presentation.

"I'm going upstairs to grab some lunch," I told
her.

"Already? We just opened." Then, looking at
Buffy with a crayon-scrawled house in hand, "You
really think I could create something with Lyndon
from scratch?"

"See you in an hour."

I crossed the atrium and took the side stairs two
at a time. At the top landing, I opened the door
and made a hard right to my living room door. I
burst in and Martin cowered in the armchair by
the fireplace, raising a book to cover his face. The
courage spell had been a bust. It had felt so powerful while I was casting it, but clearly it had met its
match in Martin.

He slowly lowered the book. The *Complete Adven-*

tures, I noted. Sherlock would be loving that. "We discovered the identity of the bones in the out-house." I waited for a reaction that didn't come. Sam had asked me not to reveal who they belonged to, but I felt safe telling Martin. "They're Frank Holloway's. You knew that, didn't you?"

Despite Martin's efforts to appear unmoved, at last his expression crumbled. His already pale face blanched further.

"Anything you'd care to tell me?" I asked.

He shook his head in a ticktock motion.

Exasperated, I dropped to the sofa. "Martin, you've got to come clean with me." I sat up and leaned toward him. "How do I know you didn't kill Frank Holloway yourself?"

"No," he croaked.

I knew he hadn't. The thought of Martin rushing the town bully was too ludicrous to be believed. "How am I supposed to help you if you won't tell me why you left and who might be after you?"

"I can't."

I adjusted my approach. "How about this? I ask you questions and you respond with a yes or no. That's it. Simple. You're not telling me anything, simply confirming or denying. Okay?"

He stared at me, eyes wide, then nodded once.

"All right." We might get somewhere. "Did your leaving Wilfred have anything to do with Frank Holloway?"

Nothing. Honestly, Martin might have turned to stone. The only hint he'd given me, at all, was that it had to do with the Empress—the theft and Mack Jubell's murder. Frank Holloway had been arrested for robbing the Empress, and Martin had tracked his movements. Frank may have killed Orson's father. Orson was only a boy then, but could he know something? If so, he hadn't enlightened me. Kaydee and Travis were both spotted out the night Larry died, yet they denied it and even seemed to lie to cover for each other.

"Do you have anything to say about how Frank Holloway ended up dead in the outhouse?"

"That's not a yes-or-no question," he observed.

"You know, if anyone discovers you're still alive, you'll be the top suspect."

From Martin's expression—or lack of it—he might have been one of the bodies he'd spent decades preparing for the grave.

This was going nowhere. I stood. "I'll give you until the end of the day to tell me the truth. If you won't give me anything to go on, I'll have to let this go. Larry Sutton's death will go down as from natural causes. You'll return to Pacific Grove to ponder the life you could have had—the one fate dealt you a second chance on. Think it over. But don't think long."

Roz would be watching the clock for my return, but I had more tasks to accomplish before I could get back to work, and it would take me out of the library. I'd threatened Martin that I'd give up the investigation, but I couldn't rightfully do so until I'd talked with Helen. After all, I'd promised to help her. She was reasonable. Once she understood I wasn't making any headway in Larry Sutton's death, she'd release me.

I grabbed my coat and eyed the *Complete Adventures*. Should I take Sherlock? I decided to leave the book so Sherlock could observe Martin. Not that Martin could do much confined to my apartment. Unless Martin's fear could somehow trigger the courage spell. Remembering the look on his face, I doubted it.

Down the hill, across from the café, I took a right into the few square blocks of homes that made up Wilfred's residential district. Helen's farmhouse sat tidily back from the street, the crab apple tree in front just beginning to show tight pink and cream buds. I pulled open the screen door and knocked. In fifteen minutes, this could be over. I could go back to my normal life. Truth told, I wasn't sure how I felt about it.

"Josie, it's so nice to see you." With her new bob and lilac wool tunic, Helen looked fresh and rested. Behind her, a man on a stepladder rolled paint onto the walls. "Come in. Step right over the drop cloths. Don't you think it looks brighter in here?"

It did. The dark furniture and boxes that had filled the living room, leaving only a trail to the dining room, were gone. The dark brocade curtains were gone, too, and midday light flooded the room. Only the piano remained, now covered with a canvas cloth. A new cream couch shrouded in a plastic drop cloth had been pushed to the room's center. My gaze shot to the buffet. Martin's photo was gone.

Helen watched me. "That's right. I put Martin's photo away. I finally admitted it's time to move on."

"If, say, he were still alive, and if he came to Wilfred, and if he wanted to see you—"

"That's a lot of 'ifs,' isn't it?" she said serenely. "I've spent decades waiting to hear from him. The events over the past few days have made me understand that, in fact, he had given me a message decades ago. A clear one. By leaving without a word, he'd told me everything I needed to know."

I should have been happy that Helen was now free of her grief over Martin, but I felt strangely melancholic. I wanted so much to tell her Martin was still alive and from all appearances still in love with her, but it wasn't up to me.

"Now, how can I help you?" She led the way to the kitchen, where we each took a chair at her linoleum table. "Coffee?"

Martin had missed out on a wonderful life. "No, thank you. I've got to get back to the library. I wanted to check in with you about Larry Sutton's death."

"Any leads?"

"Not really. That's why I'm here. I've talked with everyone who might have seen him the night he died."

"Nothing came up? Nothing unusual?"

"Lots of pieces, but I can't see how they fit together. Orson and the Empress came up, and I've even heard the suggestion Mack Jubell was murdered—"

"Oh, my." Helen clapped a pink-tipped hand to her mouth.

"—but I can't connect them to Larry's death. Or to Martin. Did Martin have anything to do with the Empress? Or, by chance, did he say anything about Mack Jubell's death?"

"No. We didn't socialize much with the Jubells."

Then there was Frank Holloway. "Helen, would you want me to keep digging around if it revealed something . . . something that cast a different light on your husband?" I was convinced Martin hadn't killed him, but Wilfred's public opinion might differ once word got out.

She placed her palms on the table. "Honey, Martin left me, pregnant, well over forty years ago. The light cast on him now isn't exactly a heavenly glow."

"What if it were something darker?" I ventured.

"I loved that man. I knew him better than I knew myself, and I'll tell you this: Martin was not capable of doing anything more egregious than running away. Why are you asking me?"

She had a good point. Imagining Martin facing down a mouse was hard enough, let alone killing a man. Sam had asked me to keep the bones' identity under wraps. I could be circumspect. "What if the bones in the outhouse were Frank Holloway's?"

Helen raised an eyebrow. "Do you know something, Josie?"

"Just, what if?"

She shrugged. "Frank was in prison. I suppose he was released at some point, but I certainly never saw him in Wilfred. You're not suggesting Martin killed him, are you?"

I didn't point out that it was unlikely Frank would take organ lessons. "Suppose Frank was out on bail earlier and returned to Wilfred without anyone knowing."

"What does this have to do with someone wanting Martin dead? I don't see a link."

"I'm not sure there is one. I simply don't know." I let all the air out of my lungs. "I'm at a dead end."

Behind Helen, the man rolling paint had paused to listen in. Helen gestured toward him to continue his work. "I can see you've exhausted your leads, Josie. Why don't we let this go?"

I felt both relief and frustration. Relief because I was released from an obligation I couldn't fulfill. Frustration because I hated leaving loose ends. A murderer—maybe two—were still out there. I stood. "Thank you. I—"

"After you do one more thing. Check in with Orson. You say he denies being near the churchyard that night?"

I nodded. "He says he left the tavern after midnight, as he always does. He cleaned up, locked the doors, and went home. He saw nothing."

Helen tapped a finger on the tabletop. "That's what he says, does he? Tell him I saw him with Larry Sutton."

CHAPTER 31

"Helen! You saw Orson? Why didn't you say anything?"

"Oh, Josie."

"Please." I retook my chair. "Tell me what happened. All of it this time."

She dropped her gaze. "Everyone was so concerned about me. I'd expected Martin to arrive, then it was this other man. Larry Sutton." Her voice sharpened to a tone I recognized from overhearing organ lessons with recalcitrant students. "And he wasn't very nice."

I couldn't deny any of this. "You had trouble sleeping that night."

"I had some hard thinking to do. Several decades of it. I went for a walk. I told you about it. I didn't want to go into the forest and wandering along the highway seemed foolish, so I circled town. Once the tavern closed, Wilfred was completely silent. Dark. The Siggersons were up with the baby, but that was it."

"When did you see Orson?"

"At closing time. I wasn't surprised when he came out of the tavern, but I'd expected he'd head home. Instead, he stopped for a minute in the parking lot, then kept walking. Right to the churchyard."

"Did you see Larry Sutton?"

Helen shuddered. "No, just Orson. But he was on his way to Larry Sutton, I'm sure of it now. He was walking with purpose. Kind of looked around furtively. I didn't think anything of it at the time. After serving everyone at the bar, he might have wanted to make good with his God."

"In the cemetery?"

"It wasn't for me to question. Until I heard about the death. I was going to tell you, but I didn't see the use of implicating myself further. Derwin didn't need to carry the burden of having his mother suspected of murder." At my flabbergasted expression, she added, "Of course, Orson is innocent. Why would I get him in trouble?"

She hadn't told me. I couldn't believe it. Orson hadn't said anything, either. "You're sure it was Orson?"

"Absolutely. As I told you, I saw him leave the tavern and lock it up." She twisted her tunic's hem in her fingers.

I turned and looked through the dining room toward the living room, where the painter had again halted work and baldly stared our way. I raised an eyebrow and he turned to the wall with his roller, but it was obvious he still listened. I calculated ten minutes until a newsy lunch break at the café and half an hour, tops, before everyone in town know about Helen's midnight perambulations.

I had to see Orson and see him now.

It was near noon now. Surely Orson would be awake. I hurried toward the old movie theater, but slowed as I approached. A chill gripped the back of my neck and it wasn't the early spring breeze. I wouldn't be going into the theater, I reminded myself. Just to Orson's apartment. As for Orson himself, there was no way he was a killer. Or was he?

I slowed my steps. What motive could Orson have for killing Larry Sutton? I didn't see it.

I mounted the stairs up the outside of the Empress. As before, Orson opened the door before I reached it. "Heard you coming up the stairs. Can I help you?"

"It's about the body at Duke and Desmond's."

"Again? Come in."

He held the door open. This time, instead of taking in the galley kitchen and Naugahyde sofa, my gaze went straight to the window that looked into the theater. Thankfully, the curtains were drawn.

"I need the help of your bartender's brain," I told him.

His back to me, he took a moment longer than needed to retrieve his coffee mug from the counter separating the kitchen from his main room. Finally, he settled into his recliner. "Lay it on me."

"Here are the puzzle pieces." I wouldn't put it past Wilfred's laser-fast grapevine to have some-

how already delivered the news of the bones' identity. I raised my hand to tick off my fingers. "First,
we have a man coming to town, supposedly Martin
Garlington. He turns out to be someone else.
Next, he's found dead on a freshly dug grave."

"A grave containing an outhouse."

"Nevertheless." Should I tell him? I decided to
do it, especially since it might concern his father.
"An outhouse that had once contained bones.
Sam's getting confirmation, but it's ninety-nine
percent certain they're Frank Holloway's."

Orson slid to the front of his recliner. "No kidding?"

I nodded and watched him carefully. "This is
where I need your help. What's the link?"

He relaxed back into his chair. "How am I supposed to know? Frank Holloway, huh?"

"The man who robbed your father's business,
the Empress." As I spoke, I could feel the theater
calling me in low, slow words, as if Orson's phono-
graph was spinning albums far below their required speed. I refused to look toward the window.

"I was a boy then," Orson said. "Barely twelve.
You don't expect me to remember anything about
that?"

No, I told the entity in the theater. *I resist you. No.*
Magic welled in me and the theater's voices sub-
sided. I caught my breath. "Frank Holloway," I told
Orson. "And your father."

He reached for his mug, but it was clearly a ges-
ture from habit, not desire. As quickly as he'd extended his hand, he pulled it away and jolted from
his chair. He strode the two steps to the kitchen,
then across the room and pulled back the curtain

to the theater. I grasped the sofa's arm to anchor myself.

He dropped the curtain and turned to me. "You think there was a link between Frank Holloway and my father."

A statement, not a question. I watched him without responding.

"You're right."

Sherlock had called it. "The night of the robbery, your father let Frank in, with the understanding that they'd split the proceeds. Then your father double-crossed Frank Holloway and sent him to jail."

Orson slowly returned to his recliner and sat. "One night I was cleaning the popcorn machine and overheard Frank and my dad talking about the break-in. Dad gave him the combination to the safe."

"How did your father profit from robbing his own theater?" This was the angle I hadn't figured out.

"He didn't own the theater outright. He paid a portion of the earnings to a business partner, and he was having a hard time getting by." Orson toyed with his coffee cup. "That's why I sold the house after my mother died. To pay off the note. It's why I live here."

"Your father died not long after the robbery, right?"

He looked up, hope in his eyes. "Because of the fire."

"Did you suspect your father's death was murder?"

"You mean, did Frank kill him for revenge?"

Orson shook his head. "Couldn't have. Frank was in prison."

We'd come to that later. One issue at a time. "Orson." I clasped my hands in my lap. "Helen Garlington saw you in the churchyard the night Larry Sutton died. You can't deny it this time. What were you doing there? Did you lie to me about the telephone message?"

At first, he didn't reply. He let his arms fall to the chair's sides. "No, that was the truth. He did get a message."

"You followed him."

"All right, yes." He fidgeted in his chair. "I did. He'd had a lot to drink. I was afraid he'd try to drive." Orson's voice rose in pitch. "You know what the laws are like for bartenders who overserve? I could have lost my job. Worse, cost the tavern its liquor license." He shook his head. "I had to close up the bar, so I didn't leave right when he did. Since I'd taken the phone message, I knew he'd be at the back of Duke and Desmond's yard, so I wasn't worried. Plus, his car was still in the lot. I figured I'd intercept him, take him to my place until he sobered up."

"And when you arrived?" I knew what he'd say, what he'd found, but I wanted to hear it from him.

"It was completely quiet. No one was there except Larry Sutton." Orson hugged his middle. "He was lying on the grave. I lifted his arm and checked his pulse, but it was too late. He was dead."

"Orson, why didn't you tell anyone?"

He turned away. "He died of natural causes, right?"

Orson hadn't wanted to be called out for over-serving Larry Sutton. I understood that. "What time did you find him?"

"He left the tavern just after midnight. I kicked out Lalena and her friend and closed the tavern. I found Larry Sutton about ten minutes later. He was talking to someone—at least, I thought he was. I heard his voice from the churchyard. By the time I got to him, to try to convince him not to drive, he was dead."

"You heard him talking, but you didn't see anyone?"

"No. The person might have heard me and hid. In the root cellar, for instance. Or behind the hedge."

"Are you sure he wasn't on his phone, that no one was there at all?" Larry could have been leaving Martin the voicemail message I'd heard.

"It was definitely another person. I heard the other person shout. As I said, by the time I got to Larry, whoever it was had gone."

"What did the person say?"

"It sounded like, 'How dare you.'" He shook his head. "That's all I know. Honestly."

Someone had been with Larry Sutton when he died. Larry Sutton had indeed been murdered. Helen didn't know it, but she might be lucky to be alive. I glanced at Orson and read fear, but most of all relief, on his features. "You know you need to tell Sam."

He nodded. A few minutes later I left him, pensive, in his recliner.

CHAPTER 32

"Where have you been?" Roz said, batting her fan at her neck. Whether it was anger or a hot flash that reddened her face, I didn't know. "You're more than an hour late."

"Any emergencies here?" I asked.

She snapped the fan shut and tossed it on the circulation desk. "No."

"Good. I need more time." Before she could respond, I hurried up the stairs to my apartment and found Martin sitting stiffly with his jacket folded over his lap next to a packed suitcase. I stepped back in shock. "What are you doing?"

"Waiting until the library closes. When the coast is clear, I'm going home. Besides, you gave me two days, and they're nearly up."

Stunned, I lowered myself to the sofa. "Leave? Why?" Although I'd warned him he'd have to leave, I was strangely reluctant to see him go.

"I was foolish to come. Larry was never in the greatest of health—I've laid out bodies in better shape than his—and I should have been satisfied with the medical examiner's determination."

"Yet you came anyway," I said.

He looked at his lap. "Part of me wanted to see Helen, see the life I missed."

"Helen is still here."

I gave this statement a moment to sink in but saw no change in Martin's demeanor. As far as I could tell, my energy casting the courage spell could have been better spent doing something practical, like ironing. Despite Martin's stony expression, a hand worried at his jacket's fabric.

I tried again. "You're leaving. Fine. Before you go, what can you tell me about Frank Holloway? He had something to do with why you left, didn't he? I know he did. Please, Martin."

Martin's body didn't move, but his gaze darted from my bedroom to the living room door to the sofa.

"You say Larry's death was from natural causes, but I know you're suspicious. You told me about it. You had years to check on Helen, and you chose to come back to Wilfred now." I scooted to the sofa's edge. "This is your chance to come clean. How did Frank's body come to be in the outhouse?"

He looked up at me, then yanked out his phone and tapped at its screen. I'd gone too far. He was ordering a cab. "I'll take my chances with library visitors," he said. "If I use the side entrance, no one will see me leave, anyway."

"This is your chance to show courage," I urged. "For Helen. For Lindy."

His hands shook as he pocketed his phone, his task finished. "We've been over it. I'm going home."

"There's nothing I can say to make you stay?"

He shook his head and looked away. Half an hour later, a cab pulled up to the library. I abandoned the circulation desk to follow Martin into the chilly afternoon. The cabbie put his suitcase into the trunk. "It's not too late to change your mind."

"Thank you for your hospitality," he replied. He situated his gaunt frame in the back seat and the cab pulled away.

I stood for a moment looking down the drive, thinking he'd change his mind and the cab would come bumping back up the road. It didn't.

Roz had left to spend the evening with Lyndon, although she informed me she planned to return later to her bed on the couch in natural history. For the first time in two days, I was alone. I changed my sheets and put my bedroom in order, returning my hairbrush to where Martin's shaving kit had been, and repositioning the chair he'd used to hold his suitcase. It was almost eerily quiet.

I picked up the *Complete Adventures*. "Well, Sherlock, I guess it's time to put you back in your shelf."

The volume warmed and vibrated. I set it on the table and let it fall open. Sherlock, dressed at last in a deerstalker cap, stepped out from an illustration in "The Adventure of the Solitary Cyclist" where he'd been examining a bicycle tire.

"Giving up on the case so soon?" he said.

"Officially, there is no longer a case. What am I supposed to do? I'm at a dead end."

I sat on the edge of my bed. Sherlock took a seat on the nightstand, letting his legs dangle off its edge.

"Maybe Martin did it," I said. "At the funeral home he discovered that Mack Jubell had been knocked in the head. Maybe he knew Frank Holloway was out on bail and concluded that's who murdered him. Martin then killed Frank, stuffed him in the outhouse, and ran off before he could bring shame on Helen."

Sherlock was smoking again and staring into the distance. "You don't really think so, do you?"

"Martin is used to death. It doesn't faze him." Rodney leapt up next to me, his tail switching. I rested a hand on his back to make sure he didn't take a swat at Sherlock. "That said, you're right. No, I don't think he killed Frank. He had no reason to kill him. Besides, why would he tell me Mack Jubell had been murdered if he himself was his murderer?"

"In addition, we have evidence that contradicts it," Sherlock said. At my inquiring glance, he added, "Martin Garlington was tracking Mr. Holloway's actions before Mr. Jubell was killed."

I nodded slowly. Sherlock was right.

"Could he be covering for someone else?" Sherlock asked.

"The only person I can think he'd cover for would be Helen, and I don't see her killing either Orson's father or Frank Holloway. No, he kept saying he left Wilfred to protect Helen."

"Let's be logical."

I wasn't sure what Sherlock thought I had been if not logical, but I humored him. "Yes, let's." Rodney twitched under my hand and I scooped him to me.

"Frank Holloway ended up in Wilfred. Permanently. We know that much now that his bones have been identified."

"Yes, but why did he come? And why didn't anyone say anything? Lindy, for instance? Why didn't she tell us her husband had returned?"

Sherlock pulled his pipe from his mouth. "Maybe she didn't know. Or maybe she killed him. We can hypothesize he was in Wilfred about the time Mr. Garlington left and not long after the Empress suffered its fire, and not only because he was out on bail."

"Why is that?"

"Travis Holloway is about the same age as Mr. Garlington's son, is he not?"

Realization dawned. Yes, he was. Helen had said Derwin and Travis were schoolmates. I scooped the *Complete Adventures* under my arm and ran down the stairs to periodicals. I clicked on a table lamp and scanned the bound volumes of the *Forest Grove News-Times*. After ten minutes of flipping through newspapers, I found the one about the fire at the Empress. July 28, 1974. Martin had left Wilfred in August.

"It matches," I said. "Frank returned to Wilfred and Lindy hid him." I closed the volume. "It all fits." I reshelved the volume and turned to Sherlock.

"Frank Holloway had returned to seek vengeance against the owner of the Empress. He attempted to burn down the theater and succeeded in ending Mr. Jubell's life." A few puffs of smoke rose and vanished above Sherlock's head. "Mr. Holloway was quarrelsome. Someone killed him in return."

"Lindy . . ." Lindy might have killed him. They may have reconciled long enough to conceive Travis. Then, something happened and she killed him. Maybe he abused her. Or maybe she knew what he'd done at the Empress and had exacted her own vengeance. It all sounded so unlike Lindy. I had to remind myself that the Lindy of today wasn't the woman of forty-plus years ago with a farmwife's strong hands. Did Martin witness the murder and she threatened to kill him, too?

I continued. "Assuming that Martin's departure and Frank Holloway's death are linked and that Lindy killed her husband, it would have had to have been Lindy who killed Larry Sutton. But we know that wasn't so. She was home. She doesn't even have a driver's license any longer."

"However, her son and daughter were not home. They could have acted on the part of their mother. Furthermore, Lindy Everhardt still believed Larry Sutton was Martin Garlington."

My head hurt. With all these false identities and cross-motivations, who could ever figure it out? "I don't know if we'll ever discover who killed Larry Sutton." Remembering the medical examiner's determination, I added, "If he was actually killed." I shook my head. "I give up. I'm stumped."

"I'd like to visit the grave site again."

"Why? Tomorrow they're pouring cement."

"Then we'll have to go tonight."

The wind blew rain against my bedroom window like shrapnel on a battlefield. "Tonight? You've got to be kidding. There's nothing new to see."

"It's not what we'll see, it's who."

Who was I to argue with the great Sherlock Holmes? That said, the rain was really picking up. "Are you sure?" I asked Sherlock. "It can't wait?"

"Miss Way, it's tonight or never. The identity of the bones has been revealed. In this town, that news has almost certainly spread from farmhouse to trailer. Tomorrow, Frank Holloway's crypt of decades will be sealed under a concrete slab. If anything is going to happen, it will happen tonight. Of this I feel certain."

"Why would anything happen at all?"

He stared at me as if daring me to defy his wishes.

I gave up. "All right. I'll get my coat. You want to go out to the grave site? We'll go."

Sherlock posed himself on the open book, ready to be reabsorbed. "Yes, the grave site. But more importantly, the root cellar."

CHAPTER 33

The rain pattered in the darkness around us. Sherlock and I had taken the bumpy, muddy route to the grave site, picking our way through the back of Duke and Desmond's lot so not to disturb them. Now I stood in the partial shelter of the ancient cedar tree straddling the border between the churchyard and the old Holloway property.

I pulled the *Complete Adventures* from my knapsack. Sherlock leapt out, clothed in a warm mackintosh.

"Do you want to go back in the book?" I whispered. "It's drier in there."

"No. Set it closer to the grave, will you? I want to look around."

"It will get wet."

He looked up at me with a Victorian version of "no duh."

"The book is library property, you know."

He cocked a tiny eyebrow. He was expert in non-verbal communication. I felt sympathy for Watson.

"Oh, all right." I glanced toward Duke and Desmond's house, but a hedge, just beginning to leaf out, obscured the view. I inched forward and set the book on the mud.

Sherlock, a tiny magnifying glass materializing in his hand, roamed first the fresh earth of the outhouse's grave, then wandered into the grass and weeds surrounding it. The tractor tread was deep enough for him to have to lift his feet to step over it. My eyes had adjusted to the night, despite the thick cloud cover, but I couldn't imagine Sherlock could see much. Maybe fictional characters had fictional night vision.

At last, he crawled onto the book and motioned for me to retrieve him. Back under the cedar tree, he wiped his hands and the magnifying glass vanished.

"Besides the tractor, we had a memorial service," I said. "Then Larry Sutton died and EMTs and the sheriff's office were all over it. Not to mention Orson, Kaydee, and Travis. As far as I know, none of them were smokers, either. So much for your famous monograph on cigarette ash."

"Are you finished, Miss Way?"

"For the moment. Did you find anything?"

"No. Nothing useful, that is," he admitted. He tilted his head, a sort of firefly-like hologram in the night. "The crows are here."

I followed his gaze and saw three crows, big as ravens, perched silently above us. My breath stuck in throat as I remembered Sherlock's warning about my own Moriarty. Whatever evil this was extended far beyond Frank Holloway and Larry Sutton.

"What next?"

"The root cellar," Sherlock said.

My heart sank. A grown-over root cellar? In the middle of a rainy night? "Let's wait until morning. Maybe the rain will let up." I didn't care how early I'd have to get out of bed. "Say, first light? Duke and Desmond won't have started by then."

"We can't take any chances. Orson Jubell saw Larry Sutton moments after he died, did he not? Mr. Sutton was speaking with someone."

"Yes." I was starting to see where this was going.

"Travis Everhardt admits to being in the area at that approximate time, and his sister and Helen weren't far away."

"How is it they didn't see each other—or won't admit to it? That's what we want to know, right?" I rubbed my arms. The moisture in the night air drew cold straight into my bones. Where we were going was colder than this. "The root cellar. When the murderer heard someone coming, he had to hide, and the root cellar was the best close place. However"—I raised a finger in the air—"there are other places. Behind this tree, for instance." I patted the cedar tree's rough bark.

"Anyone coming from the tavern, through the churchyard, would pass this tree and would have been seen. No, the murderer hid elsewhere." A raindrop had found its way through the thick canopy and fell through the hologram of Sherlock.

With dread, I looked at the vine-covered mound that was the root cellar. "Are you sure?"

"Carry on, Miss Way."

I slogged the few yards past the torn-up soil of Frank Holloway's grave to root cellar's door just beyond it. Overgrown grass covered the ground, so it wasn't muddy. Just cold and wet. I set the *Complete Adventures* on the ground and gingerly pulled blackberry vines away from the sodden wooden door. The vines were broken, as if they'd been recently ripped apart.

"You're the one with the magnifying glass. Do you want to examine the door?" I asked Sherlock. "It looks like it's been used."

Sherlock emerged from my pocket and strolled over the door's wet wood. "Hmm. Used very recently, I'd say."

I gripped the cold handle. I really did not want to go down there.

"Make haste, Miss Way."

I pulled the handle. The hatch lifted with a creak, revealing a steep staircase into a black pit smelling of the earth. I pulled up my phone's flashlight function and shined it into the cellar. The beam of light found the first two steps, then was absorbed by a dark so thick it clung to the air like shoe black.

"Do we have to go?" I asked.

"This is our best chance of identifying the murderer. The root cellar is protected from the rain, so footprints will show. In the murderer's haste, he may have left other clues. The sooner we do this, the sooner we return home."

All of the "we" and "us" got on my nerves. I was the one staring down the cellar. I didn't give Sherlock the satisfaction of a response. I held my breath and took the plunge.

Without a handrail to grip, I hitched slowly down the wooden steps. My phone's flashlight was a joke against the cellar's dead black. At last, I was on firm ground, but I hesitated to move beyond the base of the steps. Down here, the air was choked with mildew and the smell of rodent droppings. I might have been in a mud-bound crypt. The cellar's entrance was merely a paler shade of night above me.

"Now we'll explore," Sherlock said.

"Are you comfortable enough in my pocket?" I set the *Complete Adventures* on a step.

"Sarcasm doesn't become you," Sherlock replied. "Aim your torch around, please."

I held up my phone and slowly shone it through the cellar, which couldn't have been larger than eight square feet. The flashlight's beam showed rotting shelves where garlic had once been laid and two deep barrels that once might have held onions and potatoes. I gasped and nearly dropped the phone when a rat's beady red gaze stared back at me.

"I want out of here," I told Sherlock.

"Down there," he said. "To the right of the stairs. Do you see something?"

I pointed my phone toward the foot of the stairs. Sherlock was right. A footprint marked the earthen floor. It was long, from a man's boot. Next to it was another boot print, this one scuffed.

"It's his. It belongs to the murderer," I said.

"You're right," came a gentle voice above us. It was Lindy Everhardt, leaning on a cane. Dull moonlight illuminated her thin frame, but her features, facing us, were too dark to read. "I'm so sorry to do this, Josie, but I have no choice."

The door slammed above us.

CHAPTER 34

No!" I scrambled up the steps, slipping on them and righting myself before pushing forward. I worked by feel. I thrust my body against the door. It gave an inch but didn't open. "I should have known from all the detective novels I've read," I said. "Rule number one: Never, *ever* go into an abandoned root cellar in the dead of night when a murderer is on the loose."

Gasping, I retreated a step. Lindy must have threaded her cane in the door's handles. Duke and Desmond planned to pour concrete tomorrow morning. Would they be able to hear me shout under the roar of the tractor engine?

Turbulent spikes of emotion flared my magic, and my phone burst one last shot of light before dying. I punched at its screen, but it was dead. "We're sunk," I groaned.

"Josie?" came a voice from the black soup directly below me. I shrieked and grasped the wooden stairs.

"Don't shout. It's me, Martin." From the squeak of his suitcase wheels, he'd moved into the cellar's center. "Who are you talking to?"

"What the—" I nearly collapsed with shock on the splintery stairs. "Martin? You left. Why aren't you at the airport?"

"I can't really say. I mean, I can, but I don't understand it."

The courage spell. It had worked. I took a few measured breaths to center my energy. "Tell me more."

"I was on my way home." In the dark he couldn't see me nod, but he paused all the same. "I left the cab at the airport and was crossing the terminal to the ticket counter when I heard a woman yell. She'd been pickpocketed and the thief was running my way. Before I had time to register what was happening, I grabbed his arm and wrestled him to the ground." Martin's voice sounded as surprised telling the story as I felt hearing it. "Security hauled him off and the purse was returned to its owner."

"You showed . . . real courage," I said softly.

"That's not all. I went to the restroom to splash water on my face, and a boy—he couldn't have been older than nine or ten—was crying near the sink. Normally, I would have alerted the attendant."

"Not this time," I said, pressing my hands against my forehead. It was damp with the sweat of fear.

"I talked to him. Directly." Martin seemed shocked at his own actions. "Turns out he'd become separated from his parents. I didn't have long before my flight, but I stayed with him until he was reunited with his family."

"So brave." For Martin, that is. "And then? You decided to stay?"

"No. I bought my ticket for Pacific Grove. At the station next to me, a young woman was trying to buy a ticket home, but her credit card was declined. She said her father was sick and she needed to be there."

"So you cashed in your ticket and gave her the credit."

"Didn't even hesitate. I knew what I had to do. I rented a car and drove back to Wilfred. Larry's death still isn't worked out. More importantly, I need to see Helen and explain why I left her all those years ago. I won't ask for forgiveness. What I did was unforgiveable. But she deserves an explanation."

"Bravo," I said. "Martin, I admire your courage and your desire to do the hard thing. However, Helen doesn't hang out in abandoned root cellars. What are you doing here?"

"This is where the murderer hid, right?"

I knew Martin had to be staring at me with the slightly goggle-eyed look his glasses gave him, but the air between us might have been a wall of coal. Even if I'd held my hand an inch from my face, I wouldn't be able to see that, either. "We've got to get out of here. Duke and Desmond are leveling this place in the morning and sealing it in with concrete."

A creak told me Martin was likely settling on his suitcase. "Yep. We're toast. Us and a family of rats."

"Where's your courage?" I said, stepping higher on the stairs. The rats could stay on their shelf. "Maybe between the two of us we can push the door open."

"Not with my back," Martin said. "Why don't you give it another try?"

"The *Complete Adventures*," Sherlock whispered. "Use it. I'll help."

Of course. The birthmark on my shoulder burned. I gave thanks for every one of Sherlock's millions of readers over the past century—their imaginations, their energy would make this possible.

"Okay," I managed to say.

I reached for the fat volume of Sherlock's adventures. It nearly flew to my hands. I was tempted to hold its warmth close for a moment to loosen my cold-thickened fingers, but the book quickly heated enough to pulse flares of orange only visible to me. I climbed as close as I could to the door—the door that had resisted the thrusts of my shoulders—and heaved the book against it. *Bam!* It was as if the book were powered by an engine. All my hands did were to direct its force.

Bam! Bam! The door cracked and then splintered. The energy throbbing through my system nearly blinded me. Behind me, Martin shouted, whether through shock or fear, I didn't know. Another sound joined the book's thunder—a cat's yowling. Rodney. I teetered on the brink of mad laughter and jags of tears as the door fell away.

Never had midnight felt so light and free.

I'd been right. Lindy's aluminum cane had secured the root cellar's door. It was bent now and slick with rain, but I grabbed it and held it as a weapon. Rodney rubbed against my calf.

I hadn't needed to defend myself. Lindy leaned against the cedar tree like a fallen rag doll, tiny and helpless. No walker here. I held her cane. Her hands covered her face. She was crying.

Martin scrambled from the root cellar behind me and rushed to Lindy. "Are you all right?" He shrugged out of his coat and laid it on the cedar boughs covering the ground. His voice was as gentle as if he were talking to a child. "Here. Sit here." He eased Lindy to the ground, where she continued to sob quietly.

I placed a hand on Rodney's back. *You know what to do,* I told him. He looked me in the eyes and flicked his tail before scampering away.

We weren't alone for long.

"Mother!" Kaydee ran from the back of the property, with the sure steps of someone who knew its potholes well. She halted, panting, by Lindy's side. "You're upset. What are you doing here? I heard the car pull out. You know you aren't allowed to drive." Her voice morphed from urgent to gentle. "You shouldn't be out in the rain in the middle of the night. Come home."

Lindy shook off her hand. "Frank died here."

Kaydee looked at Martin, clearly a stranger to her, then at me. She spoke for our benefit. "Mother, I want to talk to you about wandering town at night. You can't keep this up. Dementia. You aren't responsible for your actions."

Kaydee had emphasized the last part. She knew. She was laying the groundwork for a future day in court. Sherlock materialized on my shoulder to better take in the show.

Lindy raised her head. "What are you talking about? My mind is as clear as ever."

Kaydee nodded at Martin. "We haven't met."

"This is Martin Garlington," Lindy said. "Martin, meet my daughter Kaydee by my second husband."

"Martin Garlington?" came yet another voice, a man's. Travis Everhardt appeared from my right. He must have slipped down Duke and Desmond's driveway and made his way past the overgrown vegetable garden. "Or should I call you Dad?" The sharp fury in his voice could have sliced steel.

The final puzzle piece snapped into place. As the whole picture came together, I caught movement at the field's edge to my right. Good grief. Someone else? Yes, Helen Garlington, prudently dressed in a rain slicker and carrying an umbrella.

Martin looked stoically at Travis, neither confirming nor denying that he was Travis's father, then tended to Lindy. My gaze shot again to Helen, who was now near enough to hear everything.

"You . . . you." Travis drew back a meaty baker's arm as he found his words. "You, a married man, knocked up my mother, then left town for her to survive on her own. You coward. You thoughtless, immoral coward."

Now I understood why Travis detested Martin Garlington. Under the tree, arms at his sides, Martin kept his silence.

Travis swung. I jumped to intercede but arrived

too late. The punch landed in Martin's face, knocking him to the ground.

"Stop!" Lindy said. "He's not your father. Frank was. Martin defended me. And he kept his silence to protect us."

To protect his own skin, as well, I amended silently, but no matter. He'd indeed showed courage by returning. I knelt over Martin, who was out cold in the mud. Then Helen was there, cradling Martin's head in her lap. Martin's eyes fluttered open and his lips mouthed words with no sound. Travis retreated behind Lindy.

"What are you doing here, Travis?" Lindy asked.

Travis and Kaydee exchanged glances. "I asked him to come," Kaydee said. "To help me get you home."

Martin would be all right. I turned to Lindy. "Tell us the rest."

"I'm sorry, Josie," she said to me. "So sorry. There's no excuse for what I did to you just now."

"I'm fine." I'd have a few bruises, but I was alive, and what threat I'd felt had drained away with the magic I'd raised, leaving me trembling and tired. But not yet finished here. "Tell us what happened."

Lindy laid a hand on Travis's arm at the same time Kaydee said, "Mother," in warning.

"No, honey," Lindy said. "It's all right. I'm tired. It's time for the truth to come out—as it will, anyway."

The rain had lightened to a night-thickening mist. Above me, the cedar tree rustled and the crows took flight.

"It happened like this. When I married Frank, I

was just a girl. He was passionate, charismatic, and slightly dangerous, and I was beautiful, if I do say so. He was also a bully. He loved me. I know he did."

Martin let out a low moan. Helen smoothed his white hair from his brow.

"Late at the tavern one night, he hatched a plan to rob the Empress theater with the help of the theater's owner, Mack Jubell. Martin will remember him." She nodded toward Martin Garlington, still prone, his head still in Helen's lap. "Mack double-crossed Frank, turning him in to the sheriff and keeping the money. Frank was outraged."

"Mom, you don't have to tell them," Kaydee said.

"Let's go home," Travis urged.

"I'm not finished," Lindy said. Now I knew where Kaydee got her authoritative voice. "Frank was convicted of robbery, but his sentencing hearing wasn't for another month. He was let out on bail. I didn't tell anyone, but he came home." She turned to Travis, who stood behind her. "You were conceived." She returned to her audience. "He vowed revenge on the theater owner."

"Martin saw him," I said.

"I was hunting butterflies," said Martin, weakly. He raised himself to sitting, but let Helen continue to mop his brow. "I had no idea Frank was home."

Lindy was in another world now, hearing nothing but her own story. "One night, Frank broke into the Empress and started a fire. He killed Mack Jubell and planned for the fire to hide the evidence, but he'd miscalculated. The volunteer fire department arrived right away, and there was little lasting damage to the building, but they couldn't save Mack." She took a shallow, shuddering breath. "Frank was gleeful when they attributed Mack's death to smoke inhalation."

Kaydee knelt near her mother and placed an arm around her thin shoulders. Travis was mesmerized by his mother's confession.

Lindy continued. She'd been waiting a long time to tell this story. "Frank had a temper. It had been a relief to me when he was arrested. Then when he came home . . . He saw Martin and accused me of having an affair with him. I was in the vegetable garden, weeding the row of tomatoes, and he grabbed me by the hair and threatened to kill me. His time in prison had done him no favors." She stopped to gulp a breath. "I stabbed him with the dandelion fork."

"He threatened me and I ran off, but I was worried for Lindy," Martin said. "When I returned, Frank was dead in the zucchinis. I suspected Mack Jubell had been killed, see. Knocked with something on the back of the head. I knew it when I embalmed him."

"You didn't tell the sheriff?" I asked.

"No. If they hadn't declared it murder, why should I make waves?" He squeezed his eyes shut and opened them. "I'm ashamed I hesitated. It was wrong."

All around us, Wilfredians were sleeping and dreaming of their days to come. Besides the good things—summer mornings, children playing, good dinners with friends—woven through life were jealousy, greed, and rage. Every once in a while they sparked murder.

Martin swallowed and continued. "I was shocked to see Frank. I'd thought he was in prison. When I found his body, no one else was around. I yelled Lindy's name, but she didn't answer, and I didn't know what to do. I ran home."

"Poor darling," Helen said.

"Why did you come here?" I whispered to Helen.

"Insomnia. Again," she whispered in return. "Then I heard your voices."

"After I saw Frank dead, I couldn't sleep." Martin's voice cracked. "I had to tell the sheriff. I decided to call from the funeral home. I wanted to keep Helen out of it. However, when I arrived for work I found a note saying that if I told anyone what I saw, they'd kill Helen."

Lindy sat straighter, shrugging off her daughter's arm. "I'd seen Martin. I dragged Frank to the outhouse. It hadn't been used in years. I let the blackberries take it over, figuring the lime would dissolve his bones in time. It was me who left the note at the funeral home. I'm sorry, Martin. I didn't know what else to do."

"As for me," Martin said. "I left town. Changed my name to Bruno Gates." He turned to Helen. "Will you ever forgive me?"

Helen had inched from him. Now that her initial instinct to protect him had faded, she appeared to have second thoughts. She studied his face. Martin was going to have one heck of a shiner.

"We'll talk," she said finally.

Sherlock whispered in my ear and I nodded.

"We still have one mystery to clear up. Larry Sutton's death. Larry came to town, pretending to be Martin. Well, pretending to be Bruno Gates, actually." I pointed at Lindy. "You found him dead that night, didn't you?"

She dropped her head. "I thought he was Martin. I wanted to . . . to thank him for covering for me all those years ago." She glanced at her daughter. "Just because I'm not supposed to drive doesn't mean I don't know how to."

Kaydee put her hand on Lindy's arm. "Mom—"

"Hush, Kaydee. I thought you were all asleep. I rolled the car, lights off, down the driveway before I started the engine. I had no idea you'd heard me." The strain of the night wore on her, and she slowed her words. "Helen had been so sure it was Martin who was due to show up. I believed her. Kaydee had mentioned she'd seen Bruno Gates at the café. All evening I toyed with the idea of seeing him, then dismissed it, then took it up again. Finally, late, I made a deal with myself. If Bruno Gates was still there, I'd see if I could get in a word with him. I'd know right away if he was Martin. I called the café and they patched me through to the tavern. I had Orson pass along the note."

Helen spoke at last. "You asked to meet here? In the middle of the night?"

"It's quiet here. It seemed fitting—my old home. Where I'd last seen him."

It all spooled through my mind now, as if it were a movie. "When you arrived, it wasn't Martin at all, but some stranger with a toupee. And he was dead. You knew Travis passed through here on work nights, and you feared he'd killed him because he

thought Bruno Gates—actually Larry Sutton—was
Martin and that Martin was his father." I then
pointed at Kaydee. "Coming after your mother,
you found Larry Sutton dead, too. As you did
tonight, you heard the car pull away and followed
your mother. When you saw Larry, you thought
your mother had killed him. You didn't catch up
with her, but you saw Larry Sutton. Being a nurse,
you knew right away he was dead. Meanwhile,
Travis hid in the root cellar, a place he knew well
from when he was a kid. Later, you two conspired
to protect your mother."

Kaydee didn't speak, but she looked at me as if I
should start my own psychic hotline. Four people
had seen Larry Sutton dead, and all of them had
run away, not telling anyone. Lindy, Travis, Kaydee,
and Orson.

Travis looked ashamed. "For years, I'd thought—"

"I'm sorry, Travis," Lindy said. "I led you on
about Martin. When you found my marriage cer-
tificate with Roy and figured out he wasn't your father, I had to tell you something. I was trying to
spare you the truth."

Helen rose to her feet. "The question is, who
did kill Larry Sutton?"

I looked at the crowd under the cedar tree. Martin was still prone, his head propped on Helen's
sweater. Lindy rested against the tree with Kaydee
supporting her. Travis stood a bit apart, his arms
folded over his chest. Helen, although near me,
kept stealing glances at Martin.

"Let me give this a try," I said. "No one killed
Larry Sutton. He died of natural causes. Just as the
medical examiner said." No one responded, but

they darted glances between each other. "He'd been diagnosed with cancer and knew his days were numbered. That's why he was so willing to come to Wilfred and why he was so manic while he was here. He'd hinted as much that night."

Lindy wearily extricated herself from Kaydee's grasp. "Come on. Let's call the sheriff and get this over with."

We didn't need to call. Flashlight beam bouncing as he walked, Sam came up the drive, Rodney leading the way.

CHAPTER 35

The next evening, I stood still in the library's empty atrium and listened. Listened to exactly nothing.

Martin had disappeared with Helen, and they were likely still examining the past and hashing out the future—if they were to have one together. I hoped they would. Word on the street was that Helen had invited Derwin for dinner and a formal introduction to his father. A stock boy at the PO Grocery had seen Helen leave with a pot roast and a pint of pistachio ice cream.

Roz had packed her overnight bag and left, too. This afternoon Buffy and Thor had presented her with further options for homes, including a travel trailer and a yurt. They left with crisp twenty-dollar bills when Roz saw Buffy's moonscape-like drawing of a patch of naked land—the land where the old outhouse and root cellar had stood. Roz liked the idea of building a custom home, and Lyndon was eager to get the old Holloway vegetable patch producing artichokes and carrots again. Duke and Desmond were more than happy to build their new garage closer to the house. I wouldn't be surprised if they replaced the house with the garage and moved straight into that.

At last, I was alone.

The kitchen door opened and Sam came through to the atrium. There were even better things than being alone, I reminded myself and kissed him hello.

"You hid Martin here for three nights," he said.

"I hated keeping it from you, but he made me promise not to tell. He was afraid he'd end up like Larry." I leaned into his chest. "Did you really think I had a man in here?"

He laughed and I knew if I looked up, I'd see he was frowning. "You did have a man in here."

"You know what I mean."

He ran a hand over my back. "I trust you."

After a moment, I linked my hands in his and pulled back. "What will happen with Lindy?"

"Lindy has confessed to killing her first husband. Given her age and decades of living a law-abiding life, plus a plea of self-defense, it's likely she'll be let off lightly. She seems relieved. If anyone's suffering, it's Travis. He feels betrayed."

"To discover your mother killed your father, and that your father was himself a murderer—well, that can't be easy."

"He wasn't entirely innocent himself." Sam shook his head. "Four people saw Larry Sutton dead, and none of them did anything about it. One of them was a nurse, even."

"Decades ago, Martin saw Frank Holloway dead and ran."

"Courage is something easy to talk about, but less easy to put into practice." Sam tilted my chin toward him. "I've missed you. Will you come for dinner? I'm making *pasta e fagioli*."

"Absolutely." Behind him on the table in the center of the atrium was *The Complete Original Illustrated Sherlock Holmes*. "I'll be over in a moment. There's something I need to do first."

"Don't be long." Sam frowned with happiness. I almost frowned, too—Sam's habit was catching— but my emotion spread into a wide smile.

After the kitchen door closed, I opened the *Complete Adventures*. Sherlock rose from an illustration of Watson and him smoking pipes by the fire.

"Finally," Sherlock said. "I don't know if I could have listened to more of that romantic parlay."

"You're just sore because Irene Adler married someone else."

"Always going on about Irene Adler," he said.

Movies portrayed Sherlock Holmes as a caustic intellectual, but the stories showed his kindness, kindness I'd certainly experienced. How he felt about me, I didn't know, but I'd miss him. I bet he'd miss my smartphone.

"We've had a successful case. I must congratulate you," he said. "Too bad Watson isn't here to record it."

I shrugged. "You never know." I reluctantly pulled the book toward me. "I guess it's time to return you to your shelf."

Sherlock showed no sign of moving. "It's been

stimulating to have a new case to investigate. I was getting weary of *The Sign of Four.*"

"I've enjoyed it, too. We won't be able to work together again, will we?" I asked. Sherlock carried a nearly unprecedented amount of energy from readers, not to mention endless spin-offs in movies and television. I'd siphoned off more than my fair share of that energy. It needed time to rebuild, and what magic remained should be used to inspire more and richer interpretations of Arthur Conan Doyle's work.

I moved to close the book, but Sherlock held up a hand.

"Miss Way? Remember what I said about watching for your own Moriarty? I was serious. Something is going on out there. It concerns you and it's not of this world. You must be careful."

Sherlock's warning caused me to turn and examine my surroundings. Red and blue light poured through the cupola's stained glass and over the wood floor. The library's three floors were peaceful. The books' chatter was calm, even in the building's darkest corners. I felt entirely secure.

"I will," I told him. "Thank you. I'll be careful."

"One more thing."

"Yes?"

"About Irene Adler."

"What about her?" I asked.

Sherlock gave one of his rare smiles. As he melted back into the Sidney Paget illustration, he said, "It never was romantic, you know. She reminded me of my mother."